A Winter's Mercy

The Blood Scouts
Book 3

PHIL WILLIAMS

MMXXV

ISBN-13: 978-1-913468-30-9

Cover art by Stefan Koidl
Cover design by P. Williams

Published by Rumian Publishing

Visit **www.phil-williams.co.uk** online for more information and
regular news regarding the writing of Phil Williams.
Join the newsletter to be the first to hear about new projects.

Map of Boldarow, c. 720

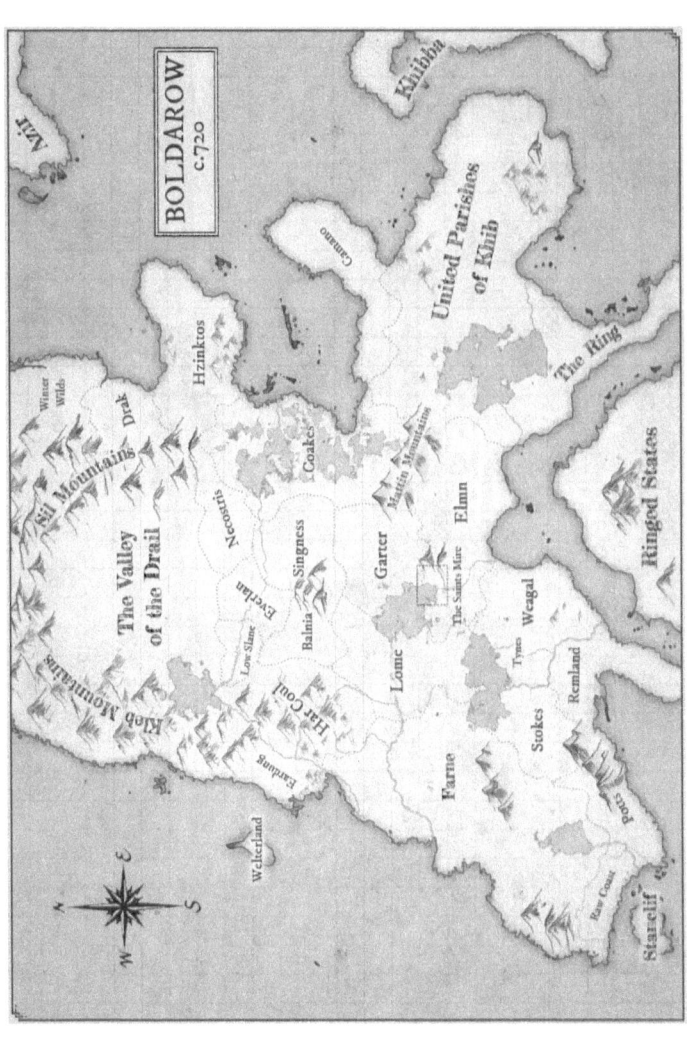

Map of The Harmonial Woods, c. 720

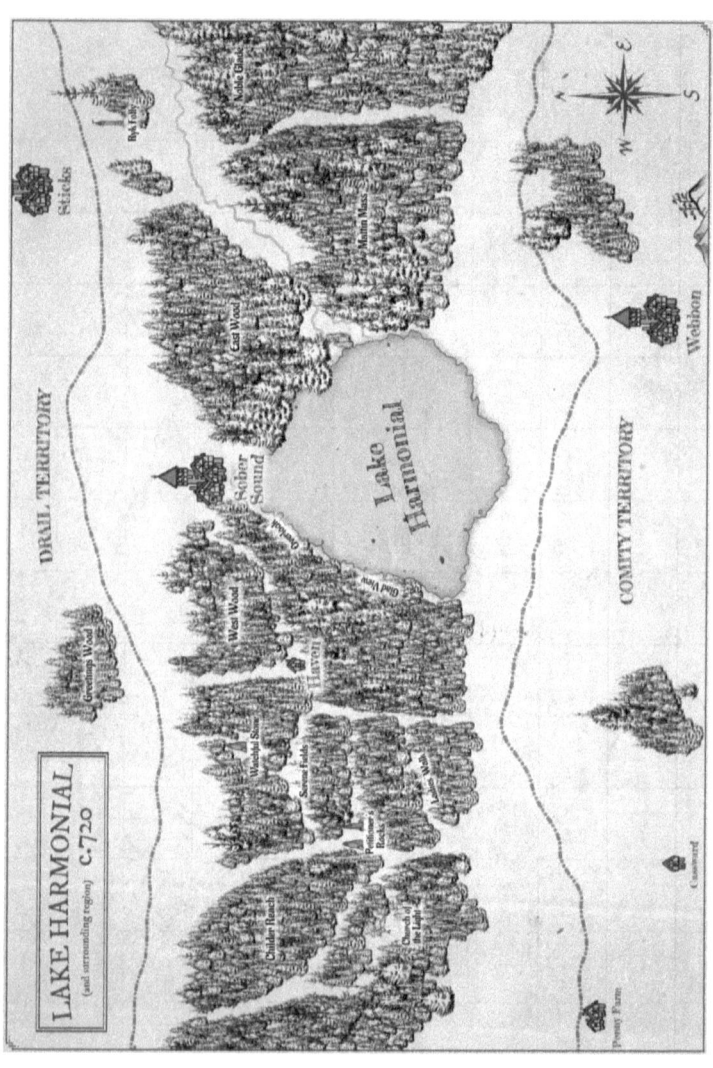

Languid's Recap

Abridged from "Languid's Recap", *Languid's Everyman Guide to Gross Tragedies of The One War (Issue 21: Sober Sound)***, pp. vii-x**

Now, if you want to delve into exactly what went down at Sober Sound during the One War, and the whole Harmonial affair, it's pretty important to first understand where our main player in it all was at: that old Languid favourite, "Wild Wish" Evans. Captain, at this point, in charge of a new Blood Scouts platoon.

Why new? Well, we're going into the winter of 720 here, with the One War hostilities that gripped the entire continent of Boldarow getting into full swing. We have the Comity of Stanclif and Khibba fighting together against the Drail Empire, three major powers polarising every nation in the world, and our Wild Wish was reeling from two major operations that cost her an awful lot of friends. Firstly, she'd gone way up north, behind enemy lines, on a tip from adventurer Captain Rikard Brade that the Drail Empire were preparing a doomsday bomb in Low Slane. Under Captain Tate, the Blood Scouts left behind the terrific Battle of Green Rise, where Wish mowed down her fair share of men, and trekked through Har Coul and Eardung, over Heaven's Eye Lake and through the Devil Woods, to reach a Dread Corps enclave. Half of Wish's mates were killed along the way, and the survivors were left behind when she dashed back to the front line to explode a massive train and dent the Drail from behind. Phew!

But with the old Blood Scouts scattered to the wind and Tate gone, Wish wasn't long in recuperating before Command found a new job for her. Charged with a couple of ogres, some veteran Rebel Raw Boys and a bunch of green scouts, Wish set out to investigate a disturbance in the reclusive Saints Mire. That was religious territory, mostly untouched by the war. Until, that is, Colonel Atmoor went in with a Drail expeditionary force to check Kin Kasidee's rogue irregulars.

Wish and her chums took a boat through the marsh, past the ominous priory of Drown Deep, and off into the Midwood, where pretty much her only friend left, the mindless mage Emi, got shot and needed rescuing from the Drail. Sneaking her way around a small army of goblin soldiers, Wish somehow got into the priory of Carlwen and chatted with, rather than killed, Atmoor, realising there was something strange going on in the Mire. And that strangeness, it turned out, was Kasidee's people on a raiding mission, stealing relics from the priories to unlock a forbidden magic, guided by their unstable librarian general, Havikare Eens.

Ah, but we gotta take a step back there, because Wish met Havikare, and had kind of fallen for her, which seemed welcome after her former infatuation, fellow scout Newk, was last seen with a broken head up in Low Slane. They had a funny connection, Havik and Wish, both fanciful dreamers – only it turned out Havik was dreaming of absolute chaos. Unfortunately for all, Wish didn't rally her troops and Atmoor's quite quick enough to stop Havik getting her final puzzle piece in Drown Deep. Havik put together some horrendous device that called up the native grescind – monstrous creatures that tore everyone apart. Wish fought with her, also kissed her, and lost her in the battle that saw pretty much everyone out there dead. Except, that is, for the newly formed hardened core of Blood Scouts, then left to Wild Wish's care.

We find her here, a little after these dual disasters, on the march again with a loyal little platoon of Blood Scouts, including two of the originals – Emi and Scraper, a quiet but rather dangerous lady. Wish still had her contingent of Rebel Rawboys and one surviving ogre, Ohno, to give her a little stability in what was becoming an increasingly unsettling war. She was only young, right, and already she's killed more men than most people are likely to meet in a lifetime, as well as having fallen for a blatantly disastrous stranger in the far reaches of an absolutely horrible land.

All this while hoping to get back home and settle in the

countryside with her friends. But as you'll know, this war had a hell of a long way to go, and things were mostly gonna keep getting worse for everyone involved . . .

Languid's Glossary

Abridged from **"Languid's Glossary"**, *Languid's Everyman Guide to Gross Tragedies of The One War (Issue 21: Sober Sound)*, p. ii

Hey. Want a who's who and general discourse on places and things you might need to know during this little leg of the One War? My friend, I can help.

Though the main concern we've got around Lake Harmonial and the disaster of winter 720 relates to Stanclif's 12th/5th Imperial Artillery, you'll also wanna know about the mysterious Blood Scouts who supported them and both the town of Sober Sound and its supposed defenders. You don't have to study up on all this in detail; it's just here if you need it, right? Some do, some don't – I'm looking out for the everyman, as always. Now – here's the skinny:

Lay of the World

The Rocc: *the stone we stand on; everything, this whole world. You know this.*

Boldarrow: *the biggest and baddest central continent of the Rocc.*

The One War: *global conflict where empires clashed, 719-728.*

The Drail Empire (people: Drail / the Drail (collective), adj: Drail): *an empire comprising (dominating) seven nations in the Valley of the Drail, headed by Drail itself and bolstered by Low Slane, Har Coul and that lot; proponents of "Purification".*

The Comity: *countries unified in taking down the Drail, led by Stanclif and Khibba.*

Imperial Stanclif (people: Cliffer(s) / Stain(s) (derogatory), adj: Stanish): *an empire with a seat of power in the small southwestern isle of Stanclif. These lads promoted the "Civilisation" movement.*

Khibba (people: Khib(s), adj: Khib): *a monstrously big empire*

way off in the Eastern Continent, with old-fashioned religious values and a big melting pot of inhuman races.

Azir (people: Azirian(s), adj: Azrian): large, broadly isolated empire far north of Khibba, variously got in on the action on both sides.

The Raw Coast (people: Rawboys / Rawgirls, adj. Raw / Rae): long-contested coastal region near Stanclif; part of the Empire at the start of the One War.

Lome (people: Lomen, adj. Lomian): large central nation subject to heavy fighting during the One War, previously a seat of high culture.

Har Coul, Necostria, Balnia and Low Slane: countries within and around the Drail Valley.

The Saints Mire: holy borderland between Garter and Elmn.

Lake Harmonial: mid-sized body of water in eastern Lome, adjoined by the dense Harmonial Woods, mostly given over to recreational space for rich nobs.

The Emerging Isles (collective people: Islers, flogs (derogatory): way distant bunch of islands far south of Khibba, colonised late, including Tarrland (people: Tarries, adj. Tarrish), Gonland and Carper.

Other Places of Interest

Vasseer: capital of Stanclif.
Sober Sound: resort town on Harmonial Lake.
Haven: village in Harmonial Woods.
Wick: walled city on the border of Farne and Har Coul.
Rock Stable: Stanclif training ground in Lome.
Swelig: a small village in Stanclif.

Institutions

The Church of the Venerate Flesh: once dominant religion that followed prophet Bly Castor's Book of the Body; accolades commonly called "Vens", priests "Venerators".

Revery of the Cane Saints: *ancient religion that personified a host of saints through the teachings of the Ten Prophets, later partially absorbed into the Ven church.*

The Movement of Knowledge: *secular revolution placing science and materialism above religion and magic (underpinning "Civilisation" and "Purity").*

Mortal Magic (or witlacing, flesh weaving, blood corrupting): *magical practice relating to living flesh and consciousness. Broadly grouped into four schools: intention, will, flesh and parsing.*

Earth-touching (or dirt-minding, mindlessness): *magical practice concerned with manipulating the physical world, of and relating to the environment.*

The Arbitration: *international regulators of safe and proper magic use.*

The Lock Gate Cavern: *elusive warrior-training commune in Azir.*

Leaders of Interest

General Macwest: *commander of Stanclif's 3rd Brigade.*
Colonel Vibrant: *commander of Fawn Battalion, Stanclif's 2nd Brigade.*
Captain Brade: *famed Stanclif adventurer.*

Notable Members of the 12th/5th Imperial Artillery (Stanclif)

Leaders: *Major Bluefern, Captain Crash, Lieutenant Jonus*
Rank and file: *Sergeant Pillson, Sergeant Harks, Private Unders*

Notable Figures in the Sober Sound Occupation

Drail 15th Division: *Dalton Terrifold (witlacer), Pitt Sonland (witlacer), Lieutenant Droll, Sergeant Kether*
The Axefell Family: *Rotus Axefell (mayor / patriarch), Chiara (daughter), Erol (son)*

Notable Members of the Blood Scouts Platoon

Leaders: *Captain "Tenacious" Tate, Captain "Wild Wish" Evans*
Magic support: *Emi (dirt-minder)*
Snipers: *Oksy, Dalliance*
Rawboys: *Macmiddan, Graveguard (medic), Latebite, Ptrangus*
Grunts: *Ohno (Urlian), Scraper, Crag, Grebe, Lugger*

Notable Races/Species

Cantalesian bandit dogs: *savage pack animals ridden by lunatics.*
Cirga: *large insectile centaurs with a hard carapace.*
Fenstarts: *utterly bizarre animals often cited as something unnatural.*
Giants: *enormous bipeds of various types, including skalk, hawk and swamp.*
Goblins: *green-skinned bipeds, about half human size and low in intelligence.*
Gonish (waders): *diminutive but intelligent race from the Emerging Isles.*
Grekkels: *part lupine (wolfy), part lacertillian (lizardy) bipeds.*
Grescinds: *huge crustacean (crablike) creatures native to Paradise Fails.*
Humans: *the prominent, powerful and most common bunch of bipeds.*
Matticks (trunks): *stocky bipeds with heads in their chests.*
Nevolk (the Stranded, the Strayed): *diminutive but scarily unusual diaspora (the fenstarts of the "civilised" species).*
Spidroms: *robust arachnid-featured folk principally from Azir.*
Urlians (ogres): *bigger bipeds, known for their great strength and less great wits.*
Wyrlings: *big flying worm things.*

1

*No one woke one morning and decided to kill thousands of
innocents. These were not carefully planned, calculated
disasters. The most devastating actions started with small
missteps, stemming from innocuous, often well-intended
beginnings. The problem was that by the time the scale of
the monstrosities became apparent, it was too late to stop
them.*

Atrocities Through the Ages, Buckman, p. 58

Kneeling in the slippery mud of a steep verge, taking in the wide
road and flat countryside ahead, with its singular farmhouse, Wild
Wish tried to pinpoint exactly what it was that was so unnerving
about the man she had been sent to find. In a war where every other
person, place and object had a colourful nickname, Wish had
initially laughed at being told she was to track down a ghost.
Apparently it wasn't a joke, though, as Colonel Vibrant had made
clear with his heavy scowl during the briefing. Artilli Ptrangus, the
mouthiest of her Rebel Rawboys, had since warned (repeatedly)
that the Lock Gate Cavern "ghosts" were famously made into
formidable warriors by removing their fear of death, in a process
that produced "utter lunatics". Over the fortnight they'd spent
sneaking around semi-abandoned villages on the trail of Ty
Gaussica, Ptrangus had suggested they'd find him eating babies or
skinning cats or dancing naked through a fire. Wild Wish, being in
charge and not really liking all the negativity, told him to stop
exaggerating. And weren't there plenty of unhinged soldiers in the
rank and file as likely to do such things anyway? The war was one
great melting pot for madness, after all. But now they'd caught up
to their target, Wish couldn't deny that he was, perhaps, a degree
stranger than average.

Ty Gaussica was an ex-Arbitration agent who they were due to recall and deliver to Major Bluefern; that and him being a ghost was all the information Wish had been given, bar a general description of a tall Azirian unlikely to be in uniform. It had been enough to get them here, but now it was apparent that even the "Azirian" part was unhelpful: the man was lean and had coppery brown skin, while Wish typically understood people from the distant continent of Azir to be short, pale and wide-headed.

Something about the way he stood in the open, painfully still, screamed caution. His bulky old leather riding coat, down to his calves, seemed unaffected by the light breeze. If he'd been leaning against a post nibbling a carrot or something, Wish might have just called out to him, but she had hesitated, seeing him hyper-focused on the farm building, his fists clenched at his sides, like he was eyeballing it for a fight. His back was to them, so they couldn't see his face, which she imagined was like a snarling dog's.

He hadn't moved for the five minutes they'd been watching. Possibly a lot longer before that.

"See, boss," Artilli Ptrangus said, at Wish's side. "You've got some talent for finding the absolute worst of this war's many, many psychopaths."

Wild Wish wanted to reprimand him, and remind him of her rank and his lack of one, but he wasn't wrong. Just looking at Gaussica's back, she wondered if she should've brought Emi and Ohno for a better show of strength, instead of Ptrangus and Quickness, because he'd seemed to know about ghosts and she'd happened to be closest when they set out.

"Lucky he's even alive for us to find," Ptrangus went on. "You want to knock him down soon or we might still lose him. Truss that one like a pig, I'm telling you."

Wish was trying to figure out exactly what the man was staring at. They were a few miles into Drail territory, without any major enemy fortifications nearby, but still might be spotted at any moment. The farmhouse was pocked with bullet-holes and had razor wire near the base and a military truck parked at an angle near the door, so it could have been occupied. It was hugely reckless for

Gaussica to stand in the middle of a road, on full show, and Wish expected a gunshot from a window at any moment.

"Is he actually one of ours?" Quickness asked, another concern they had all shared. Azir hadn't weighed in convincingly on either side of the war, and here he was with no uniform, not bothered about being seen by the enemy. And Wish had been instructed to bring him to Bluefern along with her whole (admittedly small) platoon. Was he going to come quietly?

"Probably murdered someone," Ptrangus said. "He's a killer if I ever saw one."

"If he was a threat, they would've said capture instead of escort," Wish sighed, rather than point out, *again,* that they were all killers. Maybe not Quickness; she was still new.

"That tattoo on his neck, you see that?" Ptrangus asked, peering through a miniature telescope that looked like it belonged on a toy rifle. Where had that come from? "Yeah. That's a gate. I'd bet a week of Latebite's rations it's the gate and eye. Fucking sign of a double-qualified ghost, alright. You know what, boss, we should just slide our arses back down this slope and tell Vibrant the lad was dead when we found him. No one else is gonna go looking."

"What's the big deal?" Quickness asked. "I can go say hello if you're that worried."

Ptrangus scoffed. "Be my guest. Your man there doesn't care if he dies. *Can't* care if he dies. You know what that does to a person?"

"Probably gives him more peace than the rest of us," Wish said.

"We had one of them work with us on the Raw Coast once, the guy was a –"

"Do you hear that?" Ness interrupted, rising slightly. They all fell quiet, listening to nothing, until she whispered, "Thought I heard movement. People?"

"In the house?" Wish hadn't anything herself. Quickness looked uncertain now.

"Boss," Ptrangus said, the warning clear in his eye.

Wish willed Gaussica to move. Give some clue to his intentions. Walk their way. Or just get shot already so she didn't have to risk getting involved. But he remained still. Glowering at the house.

"There's someone in there, guaranteed," Ptrangus said. "And if this ghost's looking for trouble, it's nothing good. You know that, right?"

"Yeah."

"You stick your head up, you're as big a target as him. Except we're bloody obviously not Drail. Draw any attention and, you know . . ."

"Yeah."

"So? How much longer do we wait?"

Wish frowned. It couldn't be *that* dangerous, with him standing in the road untouched. And if he wasn't going to move, she had to. She took a breath, and called out, "Ty Gaussica! Captain Wild Wish of the Blood Scouts. Stanclif 3rd."

Her own volume made her duck back into cover, the other two scooting lower, but after a moment of silence, they met each other's eyes questioningly.

"Fucking madwoman," Ptrangus said.

"Gaussica? Can we talk?" Wish slowly poked her head over the verge. He was in exactly the same spot, no sign he had reacted at all. No movement in the house. "What are you doing?"

"Maybe he's lost his hearing," Quickness suggested. "Shell blasts, gunfire, it's common –"

"Sure. Cover me," Wish said and stood. She intended to march out in a commanding manner, as bold as Gaussica, but her boot slipped and she planted a hand in the mud. She pressed on quickly, flicking the mud away and not looking back as Ptrangus and Quickness complained in hushed whispers. She blocked out their voices, continuing with her rifle lowered, one eye on Gaussica and the other on the farmhouse. The windows were empty. The gravel crunched underfoot as she got close, but the man still did not move. She fought the urge to crouch and hide as she called out again, "Gaussica! Ty Gaussica? Colonel Vibrant sent me."

For a long, uncomfortable moment, he continued staring ahead. Coming alongside him, Wish took in his long face, sharp nose, eyes that bulged a little. He had rough, black stubble that ran evenly from his scalp down across his face, and yes, that big tattoo on the side of his neck was a gate with an eye in the middle. His coat was open at the front and he had a wide variety of weapons strapped across his chest and secreted around his legs: lots of sharp-looking tools and pockets chunky with probable explosives. Under his threadbare woollen top, she made out the dull sheen of what looked like a plate of armour. This irregular weaponry, on an unclean tattooed man out of uniform, gave Wish a sharp pang of familiarity, not unlike the civilian soldiers she'd clashed with in the Saints Mire, Kasidee's Irregulars. But his expression was not malicious, just focused ahead. He was young and, if anything, looked a little worried.

"About another twenty minutes to nightfall, would you say?" Gaussica said. His voice was incongruously polite, deep and chocolate-smooth.

Wish replied eloquently, "You what?"

"Maybe thirty?" Gaussica's eyes slid to the side to take her in. His brow knitted. "You're a woman."

"Kind of," Wish replied, not sure why. "I'm here to take you to Major Bluefern." She remained acutely aware of four big windows across the lawn, all providing wonderful views from which to kill. "Whatever you're up to, could we step back a bit? Into cover?"

"They're not armed," he said, confirming that there were indeed people in there. "Couldn't use guns if they wanted to. Don't *need* to." That set off new alarm bells, which he compounded with: "You shouldn't be here. It's not safe."

Wish gave the farmhouse another look, and in the absence of obvious targets inside she checked the exterior and the lawn before it. The entrance door was broken around the edges, forced open and propped back in place. The grass was cratered from impacts, churned in a weaving pattern by some big animal. Or a group of them. Not ogres: she had an ogre on her staff, and, big and heavy as Ohno was, she rarely damaged the ground she walked on. Wish tried to race through what other race would be big enough to break the earth but intelligent and nimble enough to take shelter in a human-sized house. Not giants. Cirga would have made a lot more mess. And he'd mentioned nightfall. There was one obvious choice but it didn't belong here. Didn't belong anywhere near here.

"Trolls," Gaussica said as if he'd been waiting for Wish's thoughts to get there first. "Breaker trolls. Three of them. I hoped they'd get upset enough to face me out here in the light, but they've been especially cautious."

"You were . . . hoping three trolls would come outside to fight you?"

"While the daylight remains, yes. It weakens them a little. But now . . . Better I go inside, I guess," Gaussica said, as though this was a perfectly reasonable plan. He squinted and added, "No one heard them. Not as bad as it looked . . ." He trailed off, these added fragments making the already iffy situation that much stranger. It was exactly what it had looked like. He was a madman wanting to pick a mad fight.

But the question remained: *"Why?"*

Gaussica looked her over again, a woman in uniform with a huge foreign rifle, dirty from her journey and unable to hide the distaste in either her voice or expression. He said, "You really are Captain Wild Wish? It's an honour to meet you at last."

Wish was thrown, quiet with surprise.

"And all the more reason for me to stop them coming out now."

"Hold on. Why do you want to fight trolls? Isn't there some way we can . . ." She trailed off. She wasn't sure bullets were much use against trolls.

"There's no *we* here," he said. "You have a life to protect."

"Yeah, *yours.* Can't we just go?"

He looked up the road, not seeming to hear, checking something either imagined or not visible to her. "We have – we will. Time to get to it."

"What? What do you –" Wish started, but he was walking up the farmhouse path. She followed for a few steps before stalling. "Mr Gaussica, I need you to come with me –"

"After I eliminate these trolls," he said, without looking back. He was halfway there, and pulled his coat aside to draw a weapon. It'd have to be a particularly fearsome gun to – no, it was a hammer. Barely bigger than an ordinary household tool. In Wish's gawking surprise, he reached the door. He called out, awfully politely, "Please don't follow me!"

Then he kicked the door down and charged into the yawning darkness. Gaussica yelled a battle cry that was met by a chorus of grating roars that shook the building. The walls rattled harder as its oversized occupants converged on him. Wish dropped to a knee, bringing her gun up to scope the windows, but as the sounds of smashing violence came out she couldn't discern the shapes flitting through the shadows. The trolls' screeches grew worse, like pained mountains.

Panic hit Wish as she watched. This was her first serious command since the Blood Scouts had been reinstated by General Macwest. She had been specifically instructed to bring her whole platoon. The first time she'd needed everyone. They should've *all* been here, to support this crazed man who'd chosen to attack damn trolls. Instead, it was just her and she couldn't do anything and she was about to lose her charge.

"Mad damn woman!" Ptrangus shouted, huffing towards her.

Ness appeared on her other side and Wish realised it was the newer recruit he was shouting at. She dropped down beside Wish with her rifle ready, saying, "What've we got, boss?"

"Trolls," Wish replied as Ptrangus skidded down to join them, three soldiers now pointing guns uselessly at a quaking house. Big, indiscernible shapes sped past the windows as the fight escalated with more roars and crashes. Gaussica was still alive. Though possibly being ripped apart.

"Trolls?" Ptrangus echoed, with a rare hint of genuine fear. "He just went in there?"

"Should we follow?" Ness asked, despite a tremble of her own.

Neither warranted a response. It was enough to watch the house shaking.

There was one final, drawn-out cry of troll vitriol and the farmhouse shuddered with a last, echoing impact, crumbling at the edges, then it finally went still. The roar echoed over the countryside, far away from them.

"Drail are definitely gonna hear that," Ptrangus noted.

"Agreed," Wish said. The daylight was quickly fading. Half an hour of light, Gaussica had suggested, yet it was almost dark. The trolls might come out now.

They needed to leave.

"Movement!" Ness announced, and they trained their guns on the doorway.

"Hold!" Wish barked, the silhouette too small for a troll. Gaussica stepped outside, supporting himself on the door frame. Another step and he swayed to the side, almost falling over. Half his face was dark with blood.

Alive, but maybe only just.

"Should we . . ." Ness didn't finish. The house was quiet but that didn't make it safe. Might just mean the trolls had done enough to know he was done for. Yet he still had his limbs. He was upright.

"He did it," Ptrangus said. "That fucker."

That triggered Wish. "Help him. Fast. We need to move." In the next moment, she was racing up the path, but Quickness was already ahead, true to her name. As Ness slid under Gaussica's arm to support him, Wish moved past to cover the entrance. The hallway was a mess of rubble. Broken walls or broken trolls, she couldn't say, and she didn't care to take a closer look. The important thing was they get him out of here. Complete this mission. Get clear of whatever project Command had in mind that involved a man capable of killing trolls.

2

It is roughly agreed that there are twenty-three species on the Rocc of comparable sentience, popularly known as the Races of Thought, but this is a modern construct. Before the Movement of Knowledge sought to standardise such labels, it was variously considered that as many as a hundred or as few as one species could be considered civilised. Even within human history, there is disagreement over the equality of man: Boldarowian texts have claimed Azrian, Ringed State and Emerging Isle natives to be closer to other species than human. Certain Necostrian discords even insisted that only human males are truly enlightened.
A Primer of Modern Thought, H. Minant, p. 28

The way back involved a lot of hiding, crawling and willing their own people not to shoot them. It took an hour to regroup with the five Blood Scouts Wild Wish had left waiting, and another two hours to cross the line, to reach the rest. In their final leg, crouching through the shin-deep water of a broken waste-pipe to shelter from front-line gun nests, Wish quietly asked Gaussica, "How were *you* planning on getting back across?"

He paused to consider the question, then shrugged. He hadn't said much since they'd left the troll house, and wasn't going to start now. The suggestion seemed to be that he hadn't thought that far ahead. As if crossing a deadly border that separated warring empires was a minor inconvenience.

Wish offered him a nonplussed expression which he didn't seem to notice.

Out the other side of the pipe, she signalled a distant watch with a mirror and the moonlight, and got a signal in return. Everything in order. Unless it was a mistake or the post had been taken and it was a trap. She swallowed the concern and dashed the final distance through a refuse pool to the barbed-wire bank of their hopefully friendly line. A Stanclif soldier leant out of a gap, urging, "Through here, quick, quick!"

She struggled on, gritting her teeth as a barb caught her leg. Then she turned to help the others. Gaussica continued past with a lofty nonchalance, unhurried. As Crag, the last scout, raced in, huffing under her own weight, gunfire erupted nearby. They all dived into cover, rolling around concrete blocks and stumps of trees, scrambling to get weapons free, as a patter of reports followed, and the guards dived into their dugout, readying a machine gun. It took a moment to realise the shooting wasn't directed at them, as men began shouting further down the line.

Wish panted, trying to slow her heartbeat. Last thing she needed was a bullet in the back just as they got to safety. Especially now, ready to deliver their target with the promise of a break on the horizon. The Relight Festival was all but theirs, she told herself. A short march to get Gaussica the rest of the way, then they'd be dismissed for the end-of-year festivities. No one was going to fight over Relight and she was building a solid platoon to enjoy it with. In the space of only a couple of months, they had swelled to fourteen strong, and though she had reservations about there being seven men in what was supposed to be a female unit, she appreciated having all of them around. Quickness had been a particularly welcome find, somewhat inexperienced but always keen. Smiling to herself, Wish patted Grebes, her newest recruit. He flinched as she said, "We made it. Almost done."

They continued through a network of trenches, a procession of muddy misfits not especially noticeable in a maze of weary soldiers. Soon, Wish found her way to a clearing beyond the trenches, in a circle of tents, where the rest of her platoon were waiting: Ohno, Emi, Lugger and Dalliance were in the middle of a game of cards with a few strangers.

"Mission accomplished!" Wish announced, gesturing to her followers, tiredly traipsing in behind. Only Dalliance hopped up to greet them. "Did you get us transport the rest of the way?"

"No, we're walking," Ohno said, momentarily deflating her. "It's chaos out there. You might hang on the back of a moving carriage, but no one's putting us on a docket."

"Ah."

"Is that him, then?" a loud Rawboy voice asked, as Latebite sauntered in from the other side of the clearing. The cheery expression on his round face and his easy swagger hid all signs that he'd almost lost a leg in the Saints Mire. He'd more than made up for his downtime with chatter since, and Wish had learnt the man was adept at acquiring almost anything they could carry. She had left him here in Fawn Battalion as much to see what he'd turn up as to convalesce, and her eyes shone keenly on the pack he was carrying. He said, "Rat-goat. Good bit of meat but not a good meat, if you catch my drift." She didn't, but he went on with a pointing finger, "He doesn't look all that. Why the fuss?"

Gaussica remained at the edge of the clearing, hands in his pockets. The Azirian squinted at Latebite before scanning the rest of them. His eyes fell on Emi, their resident mage, who was notably quiet, darkly staring. She hadn't been happy since the start of this assignment, on account of the man being an ex-Arbitrator, a natural enemy to mages.

"Everyone," Wish said, "this is Ty Gaussica. We would've been quicker but he had to kill a couple of trolls."

That got a laugh from Lugger, but the big guy went quiet when no one else joined in.

"Three, actually," Ptrangus said. "Wasn't it, fella?"

Gaussica gave a quiet, non-committal noise, averting his gaze from Emi, who had not yet blinked, and looked like she might leap across the clearing and claw his eyes out.

"Emi," Wish said, sharply, and the mage jolted out of it to offer a mocking grin instead. It challenged Wish to go on, to offer an order that she knew the mage wouldn't follow. But Wish knew that the best tactic with an earth-minder was typically distraction. "Have you still got some of that whisky? I think we've all earned it."

"Not enough to share," she replied, with another look at Gaussica. Certainly not with *him*.

"Then maybe you can acquire some?" Wish said. "Say it's captain's orders."

Emi's grin stretched. Magic words that gave her permission to make trouble in Wish's name. Latebite was quick to jump on that, saying, "Sure I can help her with that. Long as someone cooks up this rat-goat."

Wish gave a smile and nod, because she was too tired to deal with them otherwise. With a sly Emi wink, the pair slunk off into the shadows. Hopefully they'd leave this camp far behind before whatever mess they were likely to create with the quartermaster caught up to Wish. If they couldn't get transport, it was another three days by foot to reach Major Bluefern's position, which she wanted to get done soon.

"Captain," Dalliance said, hesitantly, and she drew her attention back to him as the others started to filter out, hunkering down with murmurs while Quickness hurriedly told them about the trolls. Dalliance had approached with a restless stance, joined by a young, smaller soldier, standing next to him, and Ohno appeared, looming hugely over them. The ogre clearly knew what he was after and wanted to watch. "Can I introduce you to Iggy? We fought together on my last active assignment, before Rock Stable – honestly couldn't believe my luck that we ran into each other in camp here."

This felt familiar. It was Rock Stable where she'd first encountered Corporal Dalliance, then a private, a young Vasseer lad wanting to follow her, with his friend in tow. That friend had been cut in half by a monster's pincers, and here he was offering up someone new. She really didn't need another vulnerable man to protect. Between Quickness, Grebe and Lugger it seemed nurturing hopefuls was becoming her job.

But when Wish took in Dalliance's companion, she discovered the short soldier, barely up to her chest, had a soft, round face, large, eager eyes and a button nose poking out from under a helmet two sizes too big, padded by extra clothing. A mess of utility belts and pockets, laden with tools, almost hid her grease-stained skin. Her front teeth showed, a little too big for her mouth.

"You're a woman?" Wish said, hearing the echo of a hundred men addressing her the same way. Gaussica had done so only a few hours earlier. She quickly corrected, "I mean. You want to be a Blood Scout?" She glanced aside and found Dalliance smiling proudly, Ohno watching with amusement.

"Sir, yes, sir!" Iggy said, snapping her boots together and offering a sharp salute. A strange, lilting accent. Then her stiff posture collapsed as she leant forward, hands coming up apologetically. "Is 'sir' right? Ma'am? Captain?"

"Boss is easiest," Ohno advised. That was the term the Rawboys had adopted for Wish and it seemed to be sticking.

"Okay. Right. Yes, please, boss?" Iggy rattled out, with the energy of a nervous child. She looked like she might start hopping on the spot, and her higher-pitched accent was plainly foreign, drawing fresh attention from the others. Wish couldn't deny an immediate softening for her – this was turning into a good day.

"We met on the front line, at Passerlee Manor," Dalliance hurried to explain. "The 113rd Infantry were overextended and we almost didn't get out of there – Iggs single-handedly gave us a chance to retreat. She's incredible at fixing stuff and knows her way around all sorts of munitions and machines."

His rapid vouching hesitated Wish, and she looked up to Ohno for input, aware that Dalliance had a reputation with the ladies from before he joined their platoon. Hence his nickname. Was this a play to get with this woman? But Iggy didn't strike her as his type, short, stumpy and pale (where her skin was clean enough to see) in contrast to his dashing, dark-skinned charm.

"She saved my life," Dalliance finished, to be clear. The short woman was beaming, showing off her big teeth.

"You're an engineer, then?" Wish asked.

"Not exactly," Iggy said. "I'm just good with anything mechanical. Fixing and breaking them. And bombs. Most things that go boom have mechanisms." She clapped her hands for emphasis, making Wish flinch, and laughed too loudly. "Sorry. Force of habit."

"Where are you from?"

"Emerging Isles, boss. Tarrland, specifically. But don't hold that against me, ha."

Wish was unfamiliar with Tarrland but realised that was why she couldn't place the accent. Clear, bright, energetic. The Emerging Isles were distant and full of people said to be friendlier than most, removed as they were from the world's problems. "Why are you here?"

"All in it together, ain't we?" Iggy gestured expansively. "You don't get much opportunity to fix war engines and play with bombs on a farm, so I came over with the Tarrish 5th Engineers in the summer – mostly building bridges or knocking them down. But we got disbanded and I've been bouncing around divisions since. I'd like to get stuck in again, boss."

"You lived on a farm?" Wish asked – this was getting better.

"Oh sure, that's all Tarrland is. Farms and mines. There's only about twenty people living there so we've each got about two hundred acres." She laughed again, which was helpful because Wish had almost believed it. She was already seeing a little ray of light for the platoon in this woman, but tried not to let it show. Had to avoid looking too keen herself.

"Alright. So. We do dangerous work here. You really want to join a scout unit when you could be dealing with bridges?"

"Ah, you guys are making moves, you're somebodies, and it's more dangerous being a nobody in this war." Iggy smiled, and her buck teeth were too endearing to resist – Wish finally smiled back. Though she wondered which moves the woman was referring to, and how many people had died when Wish made them. As if guessing that, the young woman pointed to the dark hulking frame of Gaussica. "I can see it even here – you're escorting someone right important, ain't ya? Dalliance says he's a ghost, that right?"

"You know about the ghosts?" Wish asked, a little hopefully, because any outside source was likely to be more reliable and less dramatic than Ptrangus.

"Never heard of them before tonight, no ma' – *boss*. But they've been telling me about it – it true they break their minds so they can float and walk through walls and that?" Iggy sounded fully ready to believe it, and Wish sent a look across the camp, where a couple of the others were bowing their heads or looking away guiltily, having both passed on Ptrangus's rumours and apparently embellished them. She then looked the other way, to see if Gaussica had taken offence, but his eyes were turned skyward, apparently focusing on something far away.

"From what I gather," Wish said carefully, "no one's quite sure exactly *what* impact the Lock Cavern's had on these guys, except that it makes them very good at killing very dangerous things. You'd have to ask him about the specifics." She stepped in Iggy's way as the young woman's mouth opened, quickly adding, *"Don't ask him. We're just escorting him onwards – it's not our business. Okay."* She continued as officially as she could manage. "Never mind that, we're talking about you. If your commander allows it, I'm happy to have you. Dalliance, you can sort out the transfer – let me know if I need to sign anything or whatever. Now, I've got to rinse this crap off before it solidifies." Wish turned to walk away, in what she hoped was a decisive manner, her boots squelching as she went. The other scouts converged to introduce themselves in her wake and Dalliance patted Iggy on the back.

"So you like music, or what?" Ptrangus was demanding, as Wish ducked into her tent to grab some fresh, or at least dry, clothes. Unseen, she let herself smile more broadly. Their mission was essentially complete, she had another girl on the roster and a potential meal of rat-goat and whisky to look forward to.

She paused in shedding her mud-caked clothes as something exploded far away. More blasts followed, with shouts mingled in, but she pricked her ears and judged the distance. Not their position. Not their problem.

This was a good night. They were ending this year on a high. Weren't they?

3

There is No Harmony
Like Harmonial
Lake Harmonial slogan, coined c.695

Though there was an argument unfolding before him, Pitt Sonland was too busy appreciating his luck to pay it much attention. Standing outside Sober Sound's Great Wyrling Hotel, he was transfixed by the sight of the town's main thoroughfare. At the best of times, it would've been a dream to visit such a characterful retreat, with its timber-framed stone houses and arched tile roofs, cobbled streets and warmly glowing lattice windows. Wooden market carts stood down the road, there was a fountain with a set of fantastical statues, and beyond the main buildings sat the untouched lake, smooth as a mirror. It spoke of a more majestic time, when things were simpler and everything was crafted with care. The sort of place he never could've visited on a pipeman's salary. Not without a military mandate.

And after the last few months' hard work in increasingly chilling circumstances, Sober Sound was especially welcome: somewhere you could almost believe the world wasn't on fire. You would never know it sat so close to the fighting, and it was easy to see why the locals had refused to evacuate. A year and a half of global violence had skirted this town, thanks to its proactive mayor and a history of catering to important people. If they did their job well, it would remain at peace, and all Pitt needed to worry about was learning as much as he could from one of the world's leading witlacers.

Dalton Terrifold, a tall, handsome man whose mere presence commanded authority, was a mentor Pitt could never have dreamed of even meeting in peacetime, but by virtue of him being stationed close to Sober Sound when the call came, now they were practically friends. Terrifold was counting on Pitt as a second-in-command, an understudy, a crucial part of an important plan, and he had a vested interest in helping him be the most effective mage he could be. All while insisting Pitt rest as much as possible as part of their training, to help foster his powers, leaving Terrifold to the gritty business, such as calming down locals – which he was currently doing, explaining to a half-dozen irate Mattick fishermen that they must vacate their warehouses.

Pitt, in turn, was scarcely able to contain his gratitude and had been smiling too much for anyone in these difficult times. He couldn't help it. Two weeks ago he'd been worried about catching the arrex pox in the ruins outside Old Brazer, using his magic to weed out the terminally ill. The corruption was evident in the energy of almost everyone he encountered, and he doubted many of the thousands in the area had survived. They were dying in ways that made a gunshot on the battlefield seem pleasant, and he had been certain it would get him too. But here he was, in a spa town, with no sounds of distant bombs and gunfire, where people radiated healthy energy. This was, after all, where society's rich and famous came to recoup. Before the war.

"Pitt, focus please," Terrifold's baritone voice cut through his reflections and he stood to attention with a fresh smile as the man approached him. Dalton was perhaps two decades his senior, his close-cropped black hair distinguished by greying highlights, but he had the robust frame and energy of a man half his age. It didn't hurt that he knew how to dress well, in richly embroidered long jackets and high boots. He'd left the trunks not especially happy, from the looks on the wide faces sunk in their chests, but they were grumbling instead of shouting, defeated. The mage said, "They'll be well rewarded, in time, but for now they've contented themselves with the promise that we'll relocate their boats to the north-east of the town. They'll need to shelter in the woods."

"We're going to put boats in the woods?" Pitt said, smile turning bemused.

"*You* are. Consider it part of your training."

Pitt mugged surprise, half-serious – there wasn't much his

powers could do to help move large objects, nor with the logistics of safely storing anything in the wild. But no doubt Terrifold had an idea.

"Walk with me, I want to show you something." The mage strode ahead, towards the lake, and Pitt skipped to keep up. "I've got the basics narrowed down. Once the practicalities are taken care of, we'll be free to get back to your training."

"Okay." Pitt was in constant admiration of how organised and forthright Terrifold was, never faltering in decision-making or action. They'd only met three weeks ago and already he'd seen the man corral companies of infantry, armour and artillery, breaking down a large military camp fifty miles east. Now he was taking over and reorganising a whole town. In the two days since they had arrived, Terrifold had got a complete understanding of Sober Sound's layout, structural weaknesses and population, and had the hotel partially secured with reinforced windows and sandbags. The tavern had become as efficient a mess hall as any in the army; the Cherin Bank had reorganised their vaults to function as a secure command bunker; the Tin Pot cafe was given over to the regular custom of non-commissioned officers; and the shoemakers and blacksmiths were doing a roaring trade in uniform and equipment repairs.

At the end of the road, Pitt could see that a major piece of construction was coming along, too, as soldiers built a ramp down onto the lake. With only fifty men at their disposal, they'd already constructed the frame for one launch post as wide as a road, and were scuttling about the skeleton of another.

"That's the fish barn and the boathouse cleared out," Terrifold announced, pointing towards two of the biggest structures on the lakefront. Even those buildings, with their industrious purposes, were impressively ornate with arched wooden frames and lattice windows. "At least, they will be soon. You'll need help from Lieutenant Droll and I'd say about a dozen men. See the loading platform, top of the boathouse? That's where we'll make you comfortable. From there, you should have a view over the town and out across the lake. It'll also be our main supply store. I'll take the lighthouse." Terrifold pointed the other way, to a thirty-foot stone tower with a lantern cage on top. It looked like an old lamp post, but the structure was big enough to hold a couple of people inside. It was ornamental, Pitt realised, considering the calm of this isolated lake where there was zero possibility of stray boats on a foggy night. He wondered how much of Sober Sound was built for show. Then, did it matter if it was fake? The escape was real.

Pitt became aware that Terrifold had gone quiet and was watching him, waiting for something, and he tried to refocus. In those details, he'd essentially been given the bare bones of their plan for the weeks and possibly months to come, with his assessment now required. He squinted at the lighthouse, then back through the town, up the thoroughfare to the hotel and the crooked inn opposite it, onwards, past the east side and the market, over to the small dockyard. All given, a town perhaps a mile wide with a population of little more than three thousand, a good portion of whom had seen sense to leave earlier in the war. Fairly flat, protected from the elements by tree cover to the east and west, and by a rising set of hills to the north, with only the wide lake for an opening to the south. It wasn't a huge area to cover, but it was more than Pitt had ever had in the past. He was a pipeman, until a few months ago adept only at sealing leaks, seldom more than a few feet wide, and now he was faced with assisting a task given to the Empire's most accomplished mage.

A fresh concern crept in. He could see himself getting complacent here. He could imagine squandering this great opportunity. He swallowed.

"It's doable. We can easily cover the entire frontage of the town between those two vantage points; they're no more than a half-mile apart, and with no real elevation. You could easily cover the town yourself. And yes, I can do it, too. I know I'm a way off at the moment, but give me a little time. I can definitely do it."

He drew his gaze back to Terrifold and the man's contemplative look made Pitt shift his weight, a little awkward under such scrutiny.

"What? Did I say something wrong?"

"No. I just appreciate your optimism. Now do you want to tell me what you *really* think?"

Pitt laughed, taken off guard, and shook his head. He folded his arms as he considered the town again. If he could pull off a parsing job of this size, he'd be classed level three by default. He could have his pick of assignments. All manner of work waiting when the war ended. With a good reference, to boot, he figured.

Not bad for a kid from the Arrow who'd barely been able to afford pipeman training.

If he could pull it off. But Terrifold believed in him. The mage would make this happen, there was no question. Pitt exhaled, making himself serious, and nodded.

"I can do it. I will do it." He regarded pretty little Sober Sound and imagined the shield he'd provide it. No harm would come to this place, not with him watching. His sincerity broke again, though, as he couldn't help offering Terrifold another smile. "You won't need me to, though, will you? You've got everything under control."

Terrifold's amused glint in his eye was worth everything on its own. "That's right. But if I can come out of this having trained an alternate, then we'll have doubled our effectiveness here." He finally drew his analytical eyes from Pitt, looking up the road. "Next task, I think we need to double-check the atmosphere of the inn, what do you say?"

Pitt grinned. "I say lead the way, Master. I am your very willing pupil."

"Ha! Then it's time I taught you about Lomian Lake Wine. Do you know, this region has a very rare fermented spirit, combining grapes with deep-psalm weed?"

Pitt raised his eyebrows, having not known deep-psalm weed was a thing that existed, let alone a delicacy in wine-making. But before they could explore this possibility, they were interrupted by irate voices approaching, and the pair spotted the trunks returning. They had the town's mayor with them, Rotus Axfell. A businessman who owned much of the town and walked with more pomp than most army officers, head high, chest out. His suits were always crisp and his complexion perfect, aside from his thin, slug-line moustache.

"Apparently your fishermen hadn't quite contented themselves," Pitt murmured.

Terrifold straightened himself up as the mayor arrived. "Must we get into this again?"

"Yes, apparently," Rotus huffed. "We've only a few weeks until the solstice and I'm suddenly being told the fish barn is to be cleared out? Where are we supposed to store everything from the town hall to provide space for the annual Light Dance?"

Terrifold's brow folded with weary irritation and he offered a response that was quickly getting tired: "There is war on, Mr Axefell."

"Making it more important than ever we keep up spirits, yes?" Rotus said. "How many times are we going to have this conversation, Dalton? Sober Sound isn't merely a respite from the war; it's a beacon. Our resilience lets people everywhere know life can and will go on."

He continued blustering as Pitt let his mind wander, having heard this before. Quaint as the town was, its residents weren't half self-righteous with it. They truly believed it should remain exclusive, and would remain untouched, even with the war mere miles away and this occupation force now present. As he excused himself and started towards the inn alone, Pitt couldn't help considering the untouched houses, the normalcy on show, and hoped they were right. After all, in a few more months the war might actually be over, thanks to what they were doing here.

4

Downtime in the army was something all its own. We spent so long in waiting that our camps became hives of recreational innovation. We adapted games of chance to a level of complexity that'd shame the greatest Khib saga writers. We developed new languages, communicating through good-humoured references decipherable only by our close-knit collective. Our union was deep and personal, and woe betide anyone who threatened that.
All This Aflame: Memoirs of a Soldier, Lindon, p. 36

"So the rumours, like, of this all-women platoon," Iggy was saying, as they walked in a vague cluster through a field, "were they exaggerations, or talking about someone else, or . . ."

Wish knew that as their leader she shouldn't encourage such informality, but it hadn't taken long to warm to Iggy's easygoing nature. The smaller woman smiled a lot and her darting eyes appeared constantly on the lookout for some trick or joke. Wish said, "It was true. Things changed. We're working on it."

"Okay, cool, I mean, I'm not complaining – these guys all look like they can fight. Especially you, big man." Iggy picked out Lugger, the largest of their group after Ohno – but also the most shy. Wish sensed Iggy had chosen him deliberately for that, as he flustered, looking to Grebe for support, who merely smiled. "But I've not come across many other women soldiers and I guess I was curious."

"There's more out there," Dalliance said from a few paces behind them. "There were forty strong before they all went up into Low Slane. We're gonna find them."

"Low Slane?" Iggy whistled. "Rather you than me. And that's from someone who grew up poaching hunch beetles – those things grow three feet long. What the hell were you doing up *there?"* Iggy's beaming expression faltered as Wish's face hardened, and she added, "Boss, I mean, sir – respectfully if you don't mind me asking."

Wish didn't mind. It was just the memories she regretted. Three-foot beetles were nothing compared to the monsters that had torn apart Rock Squad. She said, "It was a mission, that's all. We got split up."

"So she says," Ptrangus called from further back, "but the boss is right modest. Once you've seen her in action you'll realise she probably tore up Slane fighting giants and riding volcano hawks."

Iggy laughed. "For real?"

Her smile was infectious and genuine, innocent. And Ptrangus wasn't that far off the mark. But as Wish started to speak, she noticed Gaussica watching her far too carefully from the group's left flank. He had that vacant death stare from the farm house, and the uneasiness stole Wish's enthusiasm to talk. She said, "No. Nothing that glamorous."

A few of the others followed her gaze to the ghost, and Iggy's expression further darkened. Head down, Wish pushed on faster to make clear this conversation was over.

For the final leg of their journey, Gaussica's presence had clouded the scouts' usually lighter dispositions. Wish thought Iggy's happy new addition might balance him out, but his awkwardness had spread to everyone else, including her. Aside from these occasional small breaks, there seemed to be an unspoken agreement to keep things quiet until he was gone. They had already taken turns asking the Azirian questions he wasn't up to answering. Macmiddan asked where he was from, Ohno asked about the troll fight, and Ptrangus made comments about the Lock Gate Cavern, all receiving single-word dismissals or cryptic comments that raised more questions. Emi helped add tension by keeping a wide, sneering distance in general.

Gaussica was hardly injured from his fight, and their medic Graveguard said he would heal fine, but Wish wondered if a blow to the head had left him dazed and less personable than he otherwise might be, as she'd got more out of him before the trolls than since. He now mostly appeared oddly nervous, constantly avoiding eye contact, except for moments like this where he suddenly had a grim, unnerving focus. Usually staring at her in particular, before catching himself and worriedly looking away. *You have a life to protect,* he'd said. The sort of thing you said to someone who was pregnant. And he'd recognised her name.

If his weirdness wasn't from a blow to the head, and he was just like this, she wondered exactly what his training had done to his mind. If it was true that the ghosts were trained to believe they were already dead, what did that do to a person? Was he not all quite there? And if not, then where was he? These questions felt well beyond her.

Not long, though, and things would go back to normal. But Wish resented how he was getting in the way even for this short time. She glanced back and found he was once more looking into the distance. Maybe if she could involve him in the conversation, they could all relax a bit. She slowed to walk by him and asked him, "Who do *you* report to, Gaussica? You must be attached to a platoon, or a division, something? It's crazy being out there alone."

His brow knotted and he shook his head, murmuring, "Only the task, not any person."

The tone suggested she leave him alone, but she replied, "Sure but didn't the task . . . come from a person?"

Gaussica's protruding eyes locked on her for a chilling second, either shocked or upset, before he looked away again. "You need to be able to see."

Not helpful, so Wish tried another angle: "You've heard of the Blood Scouts, right? You knew my name."

He eyed her again, sharply, wary of a trick.

"You said it was an honour to meet me."

"I did?" He checked the ground, his feet, like he'd dropped something. "It would be, I suppose. Yes. I know the Blood Scouts. Or I will." His voice trailed off and Wish saw Ptrangus over his shoulder mouthing, *What the fuck?*

She walked ahead again, another failed attempt. Better to push the weirdness to the back of her mind and instead imagine the coming break.

They were only a month away from the solstice and the festival of Relight, and she was determined to end the year on a high. This was likely to be their last major operation before the army as a whole hunkered down to wait out the worst winter weather. There would be a tacit agreement between the empires that this was a time for easing up on the violence. And combined with the rest her soldiers had already had, by the new year everyone would be fit and able. All that remained was this hike, taking them further from the fighting, and then they could bring on Relight.

Wish relished the stories of the Relight ceasefire last year: unlikely rumours of soldiers from either side shaking hands, sharing gifts, playing sports. Granted, they'd gone back to killing each other the next day, and there were general edicts already circulating about the punishments for fraternising this year (a bullet to the head for anyone daring to get friendly with a green-coat), but Wish was optimistic. The darker days would bring in a sense of cosiness and comfort even if it was just within their own ranks. She had a troop of fourteen allies now, and while it was half men and a long way from the lofty days of Tate's Blood Scouts, they were getting to be friends. Of the three new women, Crag was rather hard and stand-offish, but Quickness was a cheerful delight and Iggy was hopeful. And Emi would calm down with Gaussica gone. They could all have a proper meal around a campfire on the darkest day, with roasted nuts and spiced drinks, jokes, maybe music . . .

She just needed to get Gaussica to where he was going.

On their second night of travelling, the scouts made camp a good way from the front line, though the fighting was visible on the horizon as artillery bombardments began for the evening. They pitched their tents and Latebite started a low fire, no danger of being seen out here, then they settled into a card game that the Rae called "Spidrom Fingers". Its rules were expansively complicated and

Wish was quite sure her Rawboys had at least partially invented them, but it provided a much greater distraction than the simplicity of rolling bones. This was proven by Latebite and Ptrangus's attempts to teach Iggy how to play. She, all too seriously taking notes, compared it to a Tarrish game involving a fishing pole which made even less sense – until it was unclear who was trying to trick who and most of the platoon broke into laughter.

Wish lost her cheer quickest, though, as the double scrutiny of Gaussica and Emi staring from distant points in the dark dampened her mood again. Again, the others collectively picked up on her vibe and quietened down, attention shifting to the Azirian. But Iggy, apparently on a role with making friends, called out, "Ah come on, ghost, you not gonna join us for a hand?" He shook his head, gaze lowered, so she added, "Only get your kicks hunting big beasts?"

"I mostly hunt people," he said. "I find it regrettable, killing the myriad. There may be none left, when this war ends."

It wasn't so much what he said, which was bad enough, but something in his tone. His whole aura. The happy circle of soldiers from moments before was reduced to cautious quiet, and looked to Wish to salvage this. Their leader and designated madman handler, apparently. Last chance, she supposed, to engage the man before they let him go in the morning. She said, "You're worried we might kill all the myriad creatures?" He didn't answer, so she continued, "There's more humans dying than anyone, surely?" Except, there were more people to begin with. Trolls were very rare. Giants, grekkels, cirga, all the most formidable species, now she thought of it, weren't ever numerous. And this man was a reminder that they were always hunted with extreme focus.

"Mages, too," Gaussica added quietly. Apologetically? "It could all be gone."

"Yeah, and you wouldn't like that?" Emi snarled, readying herself from across the camp. Wish shot her a warning look, as the Azirian shied under the attention of so many people, looking like he wanted to disappear into the shadows.

"We've had wars before," Wish said, to refocus, "I'm sure the creatures will survive." But she didn't need a response to know that was naive. Nothing had ever been killed on the scale that this war made possible. By its end, might entire races be gone? Trying again, she said, "What brought you after those trolls, anyway?"

Gaussica shrugged.

"Just stumbled into it? Fair enough. I wouldn't like killing animals, either."

Gaussica frowned. She heard how it sounded. Like she didn't mind killing people. But you had to shoot enemy soldiers, coming at you with guns. She wasn't sure she could shoot a horse or even a rat-goat, innocent as they were. Were trolls peaceful if left alone? She settled her eyes on the red horizon. The violent flashes beyond the trees and hills lit it like a bloody sunset. Clouds of smoke formed a new skyline. That would be behind them tomorrow. Might Major Bluefern have some kind of bathing facilities nearby? A hot bath, that would be a dream.

"Do you know why we're escorting you?" Wish asked.

Gaussica took a thoughtful moment, before saying, "Somewhere I need to be."

"That's good and that, but . . . what for?" Ptrangus contributed. Gaussica's eyes swelled slightly in realisation that all the people squatting and sitting around the fire were watching him. Iggy offered an encouraging smile and the Azirian quickly averted his gaze.

"We're to assist Bluefern?" he said. "The Vulgar Division?"

"It's not a division," Wish said. He was dressed as a civilian, albeit a dangerous one, so perhaps he didn't know about the military. "The Stanish army has brigades, the Drail have divisions. But we're going to a single company, anyway – part of 2nd Brigade. The 12th Imperial Field Artillery."

"12th over 5th," Gaussica said, a polite and patient correction. "Two companies combined mid-last century, I believe. They call themselves the Vulgar Division."

Wish scowled to avoid blushing.

"Twelve over five," he reiterated.

"Yeah, I got it."

"How come you know that?" Iggy asked. "They mates of yours?"

"It is irregular for an artillery company to need my support," Gaussica said, side-stepping her question. "Do you know what they're up against?"

"I was hoping you might fill in some blanks yourself," Wish said. "But I guess it's none of our business."

"Like anyone ever tells us what we're dying *for,*" Macmiddan volunteered, sat away from the fire where he'd been more contently drinking and watching the others with Ohno. As the oldest veteran Rawboy, he was therefore the wisest.

"They ought to," Gaussica said. "Preparation is nine-tenths of any battle."

"Well we've done our part," Quickness said, brightly. "The battle's your problem now."

"You believe that?" Gaussica directed this question at Wish rather than acknowledging the wider group. She recalled now his initial question: hadn't he said *we* were to assist Bluefern?

"My orders were to get you there," she said. "I thought it seemed unnecessary to send all of us, until you attacked a house full of trolls."

"Mm. No, Command didn't know about the trolls." He hesitated, like he wasn't sure he should share, but at last explained, "I heard rumours of their defection nine days ago. A scout from the Khib 433rd Segment, outside Brandock, had gone as far as he dared, so I volunteered to finish the job. Three trolls in Drail hands could have done a lot of damage."

"They were heading west?" Ohno asked. "Where to?" It was a good question: trolls didn't belong anywhere near here, typically only found in the east.

"Only to the nearest command post."

The ogre was watching him for more, but when he didn't go on, she drew conclusions for herself: "I'm guessing they were originally here under Khib orders? An exchange of heavy ordinance and species support. We get that a lot across the Comity. A cosmopolitan time to be alive, in some regards."

"It makes my job harder," Gaussica replied, by way of confirmation. Still staring away, like none of them were really there.

"Your job being what, exactly?" Latebite said. "Extreme monster hunting?"

"Exactly. Though as I've said, the worst monsters are typically human."

"Mages," Emi hissed, and Wish picked out her silhouette walking around the camp's flank, arms folded. The dusk half-light caught her eyes with a nasty spark. "You should all be ashamed talking to him. Better if he kept his mouth shut. Or I shut it for all of our sakes."

"Mages can be monsters, too," he admitted, ignoring the threat but getting another nasty sound from Emi that didn't help her case. "But my attention's been on dissent stirring from the east. Defecting trolls is the tip of it. I thought that was why you found me." His eyes met Wish's again.

"What? Why?" she said.

"Because you're Captain Wild Wish," he said. This time he didn't look away, but squinted as he considered her, some confusion seeming to clear. "Yes. Captain Wild Wish. It is an honour."

"You remember now, huh?" Ptrangus scoffed and Wish clicked her tongue at him.

"I keep track," Gaussica said. "The most dangerous assets on either side of the line. Our paths had to cross." He searched for words. Or ideas. Then said, like it was a surprise to himself, "Something about you and Havikare Eens."

The name went through Wish like a shot. She swallowed. It'd been hard to push Havikare and the events of the Saints Mire from her mind. No one had held her accountable for all that had happened during the doomed journey to Drowndeep. She'd been lauded for her behaviour, even, as she'd stopped the advance of Kasidee's Irregulars and restrained whatever mad power Havikare had sought to unleash. It was less well known that Wish had actually played a part in Havikare unleashing that power, distracted as she was by the woman. A number of innocent priories had been utterly destroyed. Wish had a sneaking fear that it would come back to haunt her. That someone would stop and say, "Hey, wasn't the Mire your fault?"

Or, more accurately, "Let's talk about you and Havikare Eens." No one in the platoon had brought it up; only Captain Brade had noted that the pair had been "close", as he put it, and he, thankfully, had traipsed off to cause trouble for someone other than Wish, at last.

"They've been making things complicated for everyone," Gaussica was saying, and Wish wasn't sure if she'd missed something while in her thoughts. She cut in, hit by how sure he sounded.

"Wait. Stop. Who's *they?* You said Havikare. Is she alive?"

There was silence, caused by Wish's voice pitching too high. If any of them hadn't realised she cared too much about Havikare, they did now.

Gaussica said, "You didn't know?"

Wish bit her lip. She had *hoped*. She had imagined it, in her most secret thoughts. Seeing Havikare in the dark, at night, with everyone else asleep, slipping into camp unseen . . . She shook the thoughts off when they came. She had tried to convince herself that there was no way Havikare had escaped Drowndeep. With regret. But no one had mentioned the woman since. They had been *ordered* never to talk about the Mire.

"There's chatter," Gaussica said, "about what was uncovered in the Saints Mire. About a group of separatists exposing old lies. Rogue myriad creatures following a goblin horde. Havikare Eens is a part of it. I've encountered half a dozen desertions inspired by her. If I was closer to the Mattin Mountains, I would investigate the source myself. But . . ." He looked troubled again. "That's not what this is?"

"Definitely not," Wish said, with rapidly growing doubt. "Is it?"

"Not here. Not if we're to join an artillery company."

"We're not, you are," Quickness said, helpfully. "We're off to greener pastures."

"Greener than the grass of bloody Lome?" Ptrangus laughed. "Get this one, thinking there's any way things get better than this."

She went quiet, but Crag growled in her defence: "Didn't you bastards just come a hair's breadth from fighting trolls? A break's not out of the question."

"A break, are you fucking kidding and all?" Ptrangus sneered. "If there were trolls this time, next one's gonna be grekkels or something."

"If there were trolls," Latebite noted. "Still not convinced it happened."

"Alright," Wish cut in, as their voices were rising and going off-track. "Save your cheery thoughts for later. Or not at all, maybe?" She ran Gaussica's words back through her mind. "You're going to help Bluefern, aren't you? You're not going to run off or attack our own people?"

"I am not military," Gaussica replied, "but I support the Comity. I do what's needed. You didn't come from Major Bluefern yourself, did you?"

"No, I told you, the orders came from Colonel Vibrant. Why?"

"Because if you'd already been there, you wouldn't have needed to come with me."

Emi barked a laugh from out in the field, a random point she'd wandered to, and said with theatrical exaggeration, "Oh Wild, I *said* he was trouble. Why don't you ever listen? And now we get to find out together what thankless task warrants both a mage-killer *and* the Comity's most unhinged scouts."

"In the service of an artillery company," Gaussica added, with ponderous quiet.

Wish took in a breath. Probably a good time to show solid leadership and shore up their doubts. But there were no good promises she could make. Instead, she opted for distraction and demanded, "How the hell did you kill those trolls?"

It was just sharp enough that it snapped the platoon out of their momentary slump and a chorus of agreeing calls followed. The Rawboys threw in a few insults too, and it was enough that Gaussica's eyes finally took them all in, shining with worry in the firelight before he looked away again. As they simmered down, he replied, "I killed them like anything else. There's no material that can't be broken. You just need to know where to strike it."

It was an answer precise and grave enough that it silenced the platoon. He had brought the darkness back, but nodded as though he'd provided a great pearl of wisdom, then at last turned away, muttering to himself.

"By Bly," Latebite whispered, "how's he do that?"

"Makes you shiver like a ghost, you mean?" Ptrangus asked. "Told you, their lot are all deeply wrong in the head." He deliberately looked to Wish, as though there was something she could do about it.

5

GENERAL DIAMOND: Of course they followed orders blindly. They didn't know – no one outside Command knew, half the time, why our strategies were necessary. They couldn't know, or else give the damn game away. Only we understood the bigger picture, and the best soldiers trusted in that.

JUDGE WATT: And what percentage of your orders, would you say, were fully informed?

GENERAL DIAMOND: All of them. All of my orders were based on the best information available to us at the time, in the best hope of victory.

Transcript from the Hingbarman Trials, 734

The chilly morning provided grass that crunched with frost, as the platoon crossed great stretches of empty fields and passed a series of farms long-abandoned by the war. They followed a road through a town billeted with soldiers on leave, and continued into the countryside to crest a hill that revealed the camp of the 12th/5th Imperial Artillery.

Having learnt the Vulgar Division's more common name, over the final half-day's march Wild Wish had developed expectations of a raucous crowd of ne'er-do-wells swinging from beams and swigging beer as they shouted insults and fired guns in the air. Men who played harder than they fought. Bluefern had an adventurer's name, after all, likely another globe-trotting Brade, oozing knowledge and charm.

The actual Vulgar Division, however, sat in misty calm with a quiet, ethereal quality. No bivouacs and trenches here: they were miles from the front line, in reserve, so had constructed a village of semi-solid square tents, tall enough to stand in. Supplies were stacked at the sides, the thoroughfares between the tents clear, and the men visible were gathered in inoffensive huddles around fires in metal barrels. For the hundreds that the camp must've contained, it was eerily still, and the soldiers present offered only gentle nods as the Blood Scouts entered.

Corporal Dalliance commented, "Who do you think died?"

"Hopefully not Bluefern," Wish replied. The loss of their commander could mean a failed mission. As they passed more soldiers, she saw them rubbing their hands for warmth and drawing their coats tighter and wondered if they were just conserving their energy. It was hard work traipsing across the country with their packs, so the Blood Scouts were warmed by the march, but they might be less energetic themselves once they felt the cold.

Leading her tiny parade to the centre of the camp, Wish took in the company's banner flying near a wooden, barn-like hut, likely an ammo dump. Near it were three large guns covered with sheets camouflaged by leaves and foliage, the treads of big wheels showing and the slant of their long barrels unmistakable. The artillery this whole company was here to serve. Wish looked for more, but those three guns seemed to be it.

"Major Bluefern?" Macmiddan's voice cut into her thoughts, the Rawboy having pulled away to address one of the nearby soldiers.

"Big tent up that way," the man volunteered. "Follow the shouts, you won't miss him."

That wasn't a great introduction, but there were no shouts apparent so far.

"Wouldn't happen to be bringing orders, would you?" the soldier added, given an opening, and Macmiddan moved closer, pulling out a pack of cigarettes. Quickness sped after him with a little coo at the opportunity of a smoke.

"Why do you ask?" he said, offering up the pack. "Thought you had work for us."

The soldier scoffed and his comrades joined in with humourless laughs. "Sure you're in the right place?"

"You said Bluefern's here," Quickness said, taking a cigarette herself. "Must be."

"Guess you'd better tell him that."

Macmiddan sent a look Wish's way. She nodded to (hopefully) silently convey that he hang back and get the lay of the land, then continued up the path. There were two men billeted outside a circular tent that had the clear aura of command, and Wish paused at a good distance to ready herself. "Well, Mr Gaussica, let's meet the major."

Approaching a leader, Wish was aware she couldn't take her whole platoon, but always liked to have at least one companion, if only to double-check her understanding of the orders. And every new manoeuvre required a rapid assessment of who to bring. Not Emi, she was already sauntering away, studying a pile of boxes, or pretending to, with her back to everyone. Ohno was too intimidating and the Rawboys were too controversial – their people, after all, were historical villains of the Stanish Empire. Dalliance had an easy air of confidence, and Lugger was a bull of a man, but she preferred to put the female pride of the platoon forward, never mind the quicker legitimacy a male soldier would provide. Quickness was lingering with Macmiddan, the pair happily muttering and smoking with the others now, and Crag had wandered aside to share unimpressed remarks about the camp with Ptrangus, generally too surly for a good impression anyway.

Wish's eye went to Scraper. The slender, lank-haired scout so often managed to go unnoticed. Plain, quiet and secretly terrifying. Always good as back-up. "Scraper. Come with." Then, as an afterthought, "And Iggy. Why not."

The shorter woman stiffened in surprise.

"The rest of you find someplace warm to rest and get some food."

"Ask them where the mess hall's at," Graveguard called back to Macmiddan, and with that Wish continued with Gaussica and Iggy, who was smiling in confusion as to what she had done wrong. Scraper hovered further back like a spectre.

Iggy asked, "Where should I – what would you like me to do? I can stand beside you, or behind you, or outside? Should I –"

"Doesn't matter," Wish said, but that only made the young woman look more worried. "Just. Be there, I don't know – represent the platoon. Maybe you can connect with them about bombs."

Iggy took that in, nodded and fixed her expression with determination. As eager as Scraper was reticent.

Ten metres from their destination, a shout came out the tent. The first sentences were muffled but plainly angry. The next was audible: "How about I ride up there and give you the message personally? Maybe you'll hear it better if I shove that fucking receiver far enough up your arse? Hello? Are you – bloody shitting hell, he's gone again."

Wish stared blankly at one of the guards outside the tent, a sunken-featured young chap without much muscle. Not reacting to the shouting behind him, he frowned at the three women.

"You some kind of relief outfit?" he asked in a rough Stanish accent. "Don't need medical supplies right now and the major's busy."

Wish pulled back the lapel of her travelling cloak to reveal the captain's stripe on the breast of her uniform. On a man, it would get guards to jump to frightened attention. On her, it made both soldiers lean closer with deeper frowns.

"Captain Wild Wish Evans and Ty Gaussica!" Iggy announced, abrasively loud. "To see Major Bluefern on the orders of Colonel Vibrant!"

That startled the men into standing up straight, and they looked to one another. Iggy was grinning with her uneven smile, which undermined the attempt at making them look important.

"For Castor's sake." Wish walked between the men into the tent. They gave a plaintive "Hey!" as she entered, the warm interior a balmy contrast to the morning frost. There were three men inside, bent over a device with many tangled wires, and they all looked up with surprise. The tent contained multiple desks, organised with piles of paper, and a low-burning sconce. Of the three men – one tall and slim with spectacles, one square and hard-faced with a scar through his lower lip, and the third short and rotund with a bushy moustache and a frizz of untamed curly hair – she picked out Scar Face as the likely major, and looked at him as she repeated Iggy's announcement.

"You're Captain Wild Wish herself?" the short man said,

shifting around the desk to get a proper look at them. The other men deferred to him, and she recognised his croaky voice from the shouting. Then she saw the major's stripes on his arm. He looked like an affable librarian, not a hardened major. Then: *Havikare was a librarian.* "And Gaussica, fantastic. Pleasure to meet you."

Major Bluefern offered his hand first to Gaussica, who shook it hesitantly while looking to Wish. The major then pumped her hand hard in his sweaty grip. He was a head shorter than her, standing close enough to make it very apparent, which made her feel uncomfortable. He backed up with a glance at the other two women.

"With your famous Blood Scouts? How many are you?"

"Fourteen, total. This is Corporal Scraper and Private Iggy," Wish said, realising then she might not know their actual names. "I've also got four Rawboys, an ogre and an earth-minder."

"Bloody hell, there's a mix. Don't know if I should be more impressed by the Rae or the Urlian?" He directed this question at Scar Face, who showed no more emotion than a stone. "Sounds like enough, anyway, I reckon."

Having unthinkingly given inventory, Wish realised he'd had a reason to ask. "Major Bluefern. Do you have orders for us, because I was under the impression we were just to escort Gaussica here?"

The short man gave a guffawing laugh, as hearty as his earlier shout had been vicious. He plodded around the desk, saying, "Yeah, you sound like you'll fit in. All I've been bloody hearing these days, *have you got orders.* Well, shit and damnation, at last, we can answer that. I should bloody well hope I've got orders for you, and it's not a moment too soon. I've had it up past here" – he pointed at the contraption on the desk, rather than indicating a height – "with Command and their faff. We've been on the bench six weeks, blast it, and your arrival means we can finally get bloody moving."

"I'm sorry?" Wish said. "We just came back from over the line –"

"Right, right, sure, you'll get your rest and rations, whatever you need. But my men have been itching for action and we don't have all winter to get the job done. This is bloody good, at last." He rubbed his thick hands together. "I can finally get off that damn crackle-box."

"Is that a wireless transmitter, sir?" Iggy blurted, like she'd been struggling to hold the question in. Wish shot her a look but she was gazing at the wire mess with oblivious bright-eyed fondness. It earned another laugh from Bluefern.

"When it wants to be," he said. "Temperamental as a flano lion with a broken tooth. Funny, the thing has a habit of cutting out just as I'm getting into it with someone who needs a good hiding."

"I'd love to take a look at it. Maybe I could help?"

"Private Iggy is a technician, sir," Wish came in, to justify the interruption. "She'll fix anything you give her."

"Appreciate it," Bluefern replied, "but you're in the Vulgars now – we're all engineers here. I taught science in Dransic University before I took up this life of luxury." *Professor,* Wish silently kicked herself. Not a librarian. He indicated the tall, bespectacled man. "Though your girl and Sergeant Pillson can compare notes later if you must. I've wasted enough time on this thing to last the whole war." He paused. "I suppose you heard that kerfuffle, coming up? My apologies, you caught me on a bad call. Now where's my manners? Introductions. I am Major Bluefern, you've met Pillson now, and this is my second, Captain Crash."

Crash, the mean-looking soldier, was eyeballing Wish hard. Not the first time she'd had an officer regard her with instant disdain; he probably hated women. Or just people.

"You're younger than I expected," Bluefern went on, "but everyone's bloody younger than they should be out here. Give it a year and they'll be younger still, with the rate they're killing our vets. But if you're good enough for Command you're good enough for me. And by hell, I'm done waiting."

"Why've you been waiting for us?" Wish asked.

"Because I had to, of course, bloody hell," the major snapped, with a hint of his former angry shout. He ran a hand over his moustache to calm himself. "They wouldn't give us the go-ahead without an escort. Which is fair, despite my bluster, in honesty. Just didn't like sitting here doing nothing with a war on. We've had six weeks that could've been spent shelling the enemy, understand?"

"Not really, sir," Wish said. "Honestly. Not at all. What do you need us for?"

Bluefern looked at her carefully, like he was deciding between aggression and charity. Shout her out of the tent or put on a friendly smile. The choice hung for a painfully long moment before he grinned. "No one's told you the mission?"

"They did – it was to deliver Ty Gaussica to you." She glanced aside, noticing Gaussica was yet to say anything, staring into a corner that held nothing worth looking at.

"No, they *didn't*," Bluefern corrected, a little snidely. "It was to deliver Gaussica *and* the Vulgar Division safely to Sober Sound. Lake Harmonial. Roughly twelve kilometres into Drail territory. Well, let's say seven for us and twelve for you."

He paused to let that sink in, and Wish needed it. Her first thought was that twelve kilometres was *a lot*. In her tumultuous career as a scout, she'd made dozens of short trips over the line but rarely further than a few miles. The one distance of special note, all the way to Low Slane, had been a disaster. Then an entirely new worry emerged: he wanted her to take an entire company into enemy territory? She exclaimed, "With those cannons?"

"That would be the point," Bluefern said.

"That makes no sense. Why would we want our artillery to cross the line?"

"Two reasons. One, because we must, and two, because we can." The major held up two fingers, as if this explained everything. Then he continued, "It's a unique situation. Like most things in this bloody war. We've got a chunk of no man's land where there's a town that needs shelling before Lake Harmonial freezes over. Otherwise the Drail could advance while everyone else is hibernating. We don't have the resources to push the line north here, nor does anyone especially want to, nor can we cover a space as wide as that lake once it freezes. But we do have three big bloody guns that should be able to batter in their entry point, if you can get us close enough without being seen. A little bomb-and-run job."

"With an entire artillery company?" Wish said. "If stealth's an issue, wouldn't sappers make more sense?"

"Sure, have you got some sappers with enough ordinance to take out a town?" Bluefern said. He let the sarcasm linger like a smell, before going on. "The greens have plans for Sober Sound, we know that much, but they don't *know* that we know, or they'd be moving faster, pushing south so we can't get to them. We have to remove that position, entirely. That's the job."

"Twelve miles into no man's land," Wish said.

"Our guns can fire five, if you can get the rest of the way to direct them and confirm the job's done. While keeping the enemy at a healthy distance."

"And . . ." Wish looked to Gaussica again, aware there was more. Some ugly detail that required this particular man.

"There's a mage." Captain Crash spoke for the first time, voice as rugged as his appearance. He took apparent relish in telling her the worst of it. "A very powerful parser who we need dead."

"A mage," Wish echoed, as Iggy failed to contain a surprised "Oh!"

They even had Gaussica's attention at last, as the Azirian's eyes narrowed at Crash.

"That's for him to deal with, if necessary," Bluefern confirmed. "We have special orders for you from Command." He nodded to Pillson and the sergeant hurriedly rummaged through their papers to produce a crisp black envelope. Solid black with a red wax seal. Iggy made another surprised sound as Pillson held it out to Gaussica. The Azirian turned it over in his hands, then pocketed it. Everyone watched, even the major wanting to know what was inside, but Gaussica did not react. Bluefern harrumphed. "You'll let us know if we can help with that, yes? I'm actually hoping we can take care of the mage at a healthy distance. You're a sniper, aren't you, Captain? Ideally, we put this man down before we start shelling."

"Because he could defend the town?" Wish asked, only slowly drawing her eyes away from Gaussica and his black envelope.

"That's right. And we have to do a very thorough job here."

"Right." Wish wasn't liking this. Parsers were arguably the most powerful, and militarily desirable, of the witlacing school of magic.

Defensive parsers, those who could cast shields to limit ranged attacks, were particularly sought after on the front lines, and could make a huge difference in any battle. It also made them hard to kill at a distance. "Anything else to complicate matters? Do they have giants in reserve, dormant grescind?"

"Yeah," Bluefern replied, seriously. "This area of no man's land is more in Drail hands than ours. There's a company of the Stranded patrolling the woodland."

"Oh fucking hell," Wish said before she could stop herself. She shouldn't have been surprised. Command were getting good at finding ways to put her on collision courses with all the world's most dangerous creatures, many of which most people hadn't heard of, let alone seen. Though in this case it was something *everyone* had heard of. In a world of monsters, the Stranded were the race so frightening that many genuinely believed they were from a different world. "Pardon my language, sorry, sir – but isn't the best advice with tackling the Stranded to never go anywhere near them?"

"That's where you come in," Crash said. "They're your problem. The mage is his."

Wish glowered, because *actually* Gaussica had killed trolls so it'd be best if they were both his problem. This, at least, she managed to keep to herself.

"We've been assured you're well-qualified for the task," Sergeant Pillson added, a little more polite than the other two. "Of all the scout platoons, Command said you had the best experience in these environments, against such . . . creatures."

Wish took in a big, unhappy breath. She couldn't exactly deny it. The Stranded were tribal warriors who sat somewhere between the reclusive, hostile communities of the Mire and the inhumanly nasty monsters of Low Slane. But she didn't *want* to repeat past successes. Mostly because she knew there was a great deal of luck and a greater deal of heartbreak involved in the horrors she'd survived so far. She said, "I guess that's still not everything, then. What exactly is this environment we're supposed to be comfortable in?"

"And what's his name?" Gaussica spoke at last. It made the air heavier somehow, his voice, his eyes sharp, in contrast to the quiet, uncertain man of before. He was already imagining duelling a powerful mage, Wish could see it.

"Terrifold," Bluefern said. "Dalton Terrifold of the Drail 15th Division. He's –"

"One of the strongest they've got," Gaussica interrupted, getting a look of disdain from the major. Unbothered, the Azirian added, "You definitely need my help."

6

Though the popular image of the front line is one of systems of trenches, it was also sporadically divided by urban centres, including entire towns where civilians refused to evacuate and attempted to continue life as normal. Many of these attempts to ignore the war ended in tragedy, but some, miraculously, survived untouched.

The Great Ebb and Flow: Reflections on Modern Trench Warfare, Sommer, p. 326

The army were starting to appear in earnest, first with the arrival of finely turned out infantry and then with truckloads of munitions, and then a group of stiffly important officers. Pitt watched them taking over the picturesque town, marvelling at how many people it could accommodate. How much weaponry they could pack in the small stock houses. This drawn-out preparation promised a decisive strike, and his heart swelled to be a part of it.

It helped that he was making progress with Terrifold's lessons, despite a few hesitant starts. The principles behind parsing were simple, really, but putting them into practice took work. It was a question of shedding everything Pitt had learnt before: he had been raised with an understanding that witlacing was made possible when you pushed hard to meet a need. He sealed pipes by willing spaces to close. Wrong, Terrifold said, again and again, when Pitt attempted to raise a shield. The arch mage at one moment lost his patience: "Stop trying to *think* it into happening. Thought is what's getting in the way."

But if he wasn't supposed to think, what *should* he do?

The question frustrated Pitt as they progressed, making him think more, and Terrifold had to take frequent breaks or risk losing his cool. He wasn't a natural teacher, but he was always apologetic when he returned. And besides, the demands of increasingly unhappy townsfolk and newly arriving soldiers provided plenty of distraction. Pitt was able to get a little further with his efforts when the mage wasn't around. He could produce a shield, by now, even if it would barely cover a person, let alone half a town.

Being less available throughout the day, Terrifold invited Pitt to talk over dinner with extended conversations about where he came from, what he enjoyed, music . . . anything but witlacing. Pitt couldn't help feeling there was a manipulation in that, deliberately done to distract him, and despite himself it added more pressure knowing Terrifold was trying to clear his mind. Still, he enjoyed these fine wines and meats, a class above anything back home, in another world to the filth most soldiers enjoyed on the front. The company wasn't bad, either, with Terrifold offering gentle smiles and smoothly-voiced stories of his own. Kind eyes. He must've been a real charmer when he was younger, Pitt imagined, though he also detected a sadness there, too – weary, perhaps, from a life of heightened responsibility.

Terrifold's attitude improved as they better established themselves in town, with windows shored up and more uniforms than civilians visible. Rotus Axefell became a less frequent visitor as he had other officers to harangue, and alongside the military adornments Sober Sound was starting to look more festive for the coming holiday. Pitt watched from his loft-space perch in the fish barn, with its open front overlooking the town, as the locals hung colourful vines and glittering paper from their windows and balconies, and an enormous Relight tree was placed in the town square, slowly getting decorated. The soldiers helped out, singing and drinking like this was a holiday. But this peaceful town could change everything. A breakthrough here and the Drail could route the enemy, push back the Comity, end this damn war. The best Relight present anyone could ask for, achievable before the snow thawed.

Pitt was drawn from his reflections on this particular cold morning, though, as cheerful voices rose from the barn floor behind him. The men stacking cases of shells were unmistakably hooting to celebrate a woman's presence, and he twisted around to see for himself. Civilians shouldn't be coming in here, but there were some lovely young ladies in town, and damned if he was going to miss an opportunity to –

He yelped and fell on his rear as a face appeared coming up his ladder, just as he was about to lean over it. She didn't pause, but smiled at his reaction as she climbed the rest of the way into his nook. Pitt hurried to dust himself off and tidy out his coat, trying to stand but tripping again, and there he found himself cringing, on his knees, looking up as the prettiest and most inaccessible girl in town tutted.

"No, by all means, stay there," Chiara Axefell said, a hand on her cocked hip. "I like a man at my feet."

Pitt sat on his haunches, smiling uncomfortably. The mayor's daughter was a force of her own, flirty, fierce and a raven-dark beauty. She stood in leather trousers, heavily strapped boots, a frilled white shirt that showed off her cleavage, and a glistening thick sable coat. Her black hair flowed in waves over her shoulders. He'd enjoyed seeing her from afar, and hearing her silky Lomian accent – a fairy-tale beauty, fitting to this setting – but he'd also seen the spark of fire in her eyes and knew she'd chewed out about as many people as her father. A familiar feeling set in, which he hadn't got to enjoy since leaving the Arrow: he really *shouldn't* humour this woman, and was likely to get in trouble not just with Terrifold and the army, but on a personal level. Yet he knew just looking into her eyes, drinking up her sly smile, that he *would*.

"If you're looking for Dalton," he started carefully, "he doesn't come up here."

"Oh I know that," Chiara said, crouching and resting her elbows on her spread knees. "It's you I want today."

Pitt swallowed. He was no stranger to the attention of beautiful women, but it always gave him a thrill. His voice peaked a little as he tried to keep cool. "Really. What would you want with me?"

"I require an escort," she said, leaning closer. Deliberately lowering her chest, so he had to strain not to stare. Warmth stirred in Pitt, down low. "To Haven. And you are it." She poked him in the chest and he almost fell over again, but recovered with a laugh and finally stood. She rose with him, close enough that their breath mingled.

"Are you going to tell me why, or . . ."

She smiled and he soaked it up. This was a game, of course. She knew the effect she had on all men and revelled in it. He didn't mind if she intended to use him; perhaps this was the distraction he needed to unlock the next step of parsing. He winced even as he thought that, though, sure he'd jinxed the process.

That made Chiara frown. "Something wrong?"

"Oh no, absolutely not. A walk is just what I need. Let's go." Pitt whipped up his great coat and swung it on, gesturing for her to lead the way. She gave him another sly look, considering this had been too easy, why hadn't he resisted or asked for details – but she went ahead of him. As they climbed down the ladder, he enjoyed the jealous looks and hushed comments of the soldiers below. Leaving the fish barn, pausing only briefly for Chiara to take a basket she'd left below, Pitt scanned the road, hoping not to see Terrifold or her father, both equally likely to ruin this. Neither were visible, but he enjoyed more lingering looks from lowly soldiers watching Chiara pass.

"It's a long way, perhaps you'd like to take some supplies?" she said, without slowing.

"I trust you know what you're doing," Pitt replied, preferring to get out of the open.

"Good choice. There will be refreshments when we get there. This way." They slid between houses to reach the western path out of town, a walking route that hugged the shore briefly before passing into the cover of the trees. When they were away from prying eyes, leaving Sober Sound behind, Chiara pulled her coat tighter and said, imperiously, "You may speak now."

Pitt laughed. "Thank you, Your Highness. It's an honour to serve the town's royalty."

She looked at him sidelong, the playfulness in her eyes delicious. "You're not going to ask why we're going to Haven? Or why *you* are coming with me?"

"Wasn't planning on it." Pitt shrugged, rather than show concern, and that got an adorable little fold of her brow. "Like I said, I trust you have your reasons."

"You know me, do you?" she said.

"I've met your father, so yeah, I have some idea of what you might be capable of."

That got a wry smile. She held out another moment before giving in and explaining herself. "You won't have met my brother. He is a very gifted but somewhat troubled soul. That's who we're going to see. He couldn't stand this busyness in town, so he is one of the few left in Haven."

"It's not so safe out there," Pitt commented, regretting at once how obvious it sounded.

"Please," Chiara scoffed. "You have men stationed there and you have those wretched nevolk prowling about. Haven is perfectly peaceful. Or at least it will be."

Now Pitt saw she had a clear purpose for this visit. Not just a game. "Miss Axefell, you should know, I have a pretty specific and limited position in –"

"You're the right hand of Dalton Terrifold. The Drail will do what you tell them."

He let that lie for a moment as they continued. It was possible, he supposed, though not something he'd tested. Everyone looked at him differently here. He had respect. But . . . "What is it you want me to do?"

"Tell your men that the nevolk are to stay away. Far away. They are not needed here and they're causing my brother a great deal of distress."

"The nevolk," Pitt echoed, not liking the mere mention of their wilder allies. He hadn't seen them, but he knew the Stranded were out there in the woods. They kept well clear of Sober Sound, but evidently not Haven. He slowed down, considering that the price of this woman's company might be too high after all. "I've got no desire to deal with the Stranded."

"You won't have to," Chiara said. "Just instruct the sergeant in Haven. You can do that for me, can't you?" She offered her smile again and he had to smile back. He was tempted to ask what he'd get in return, but she lifted her free hand to brush his shoulder and said, in a sultry tone, "Now that's settled, shall we talk of more pleasant things? Where are you from, Pitt Sonland? And where are you going?"

His load lightened at the sound of his name on her lips, known without him giving it to her. He took a breath as she walked on with the sway of her hips. It was a bright day, pleasant, and he appreciated that this hike through these woods was another luxury ordinarily enjoyed by only the most fortunate. Though the trees were thorny and tangled, the Harmonial Woods were a marvel in themselves. And he was here in them with the finest company.

He told her freely, unashamed, of his upbringing. She delighted in his account of the Arrow streets – where he joked that they stole apples from street carts and ran from lawmen. Was it true, she asked, that the walls of the houses were blackened by more chimneys than a man could count? He described the winding streets of the Metal Farm district, the walkways and machinery, and she curled her nose with disbelief. She laughed with shock as he described travelling between buildings using rusted girders four storeys or more above the ground. Her attention lit a warmer fire in him than Terrifold's studious nature ever did.

Somehow two hours flew by, the walking easy, hopping over rocks, enjoying views through the trees to the lake. They came to Haven, the evacuated village in the woods, and Pitt was in a breezy mood as he was introduced to Sergeant Kether and his small group of watchmen. The sergeant was young and smiley, and Pitt noted how his and the other men's brief concern for Chiara's arrival evaporated as they attempted to please her. One man offered her a seat, another a coffee, and Kether quickly enquired about her day, but she brushed them all off to say, "I'm here only in escort to Mage Sonland, Sergeant. It's he who needs to speak to you."

Pitt watched her carefully, more impressed than put out at how easily she twisted the situation. He said, "Indeed. Sergeant Kether, I'd like to ask –" He paused, cleared his throat, Chiara's eyes warning him hesitance was not becoming of an officer. "That is, I have orders to relay. You have open communication channels with the nevolk?"

Kether's cheer disappeared, he and his squad collectively paling. "You could call it that, sir. They occasionally come to requisition supplies. Truth be told, our actual contact is limited."

"Well, I'd like it to be even more limited," Pitt said. "Can you inform their leader that as of now, they are to stay away from Haven and the main road? Their watch is to cover only the western side of the Haven Woods."

Kether's face grew a little paler, mouth down-turned. "You want me to give orders to the Stranded directly, sir?"

"You're not issuing them, only relaying them. Is that a problem?"

The sergeant and his men shifted nervously. If he was looking for an excuse, he failed to find one and shook his head. "No, sir. I've no love for the thought of talking with them, but it's a command we'll be happy to share. Certainly be easier on our nerves if they keep their distance. We'll agree a point further out to leave their supplies, will we?"

"Absolutely," Pitt said, riding on the wave of this remarkably simple success. He gave Kether a congratulatory nod, keeping this brisk and professional. Though he itched to know more about this situation, and what they'd seen of the elusive race of nevolk, he resisted asking, in case the curiosity undermined his authority. He was already aware the orders had come out a little too much like a request. He was distracted anyway by Chiara turning to walk away, the task apparently complete.

"Good day, gentlemen," she called out over a shoulder as she approached the base of the village clock tower. Pitt moved to follow her but she paused as she reached a door, giving him a look with the slight shake of her head. "I'm visiting my brother. Wait here."

Thrown by the sudden dismissal, her tone oddly cold, he stood mute as she entered and left him behind. Pitt watched the door for a moment, considering following her anyway, but he turned away and avoided meeting the nearby soldiers' eyes, sure they'd be amused at his expense. He waited, looking aimlessly out between the buildings, with the sinking feeling of having been used. Had issuing these orders been more contentious than he'd realised?

Soon, Chiara exited the tower with a brief smile – a flat one, now – and a simple instruction, "Let's get back shall we?"

And just like that, the deed was done and they were returning through the woods, the sun creeping down. She walked ahead, saying nothing. Pitt asked, "That went well, I suppose?"

She hummed agreement, not looking back.

"How was your brother? Well?"

"Yes," she replied, nothing more. Wow. Still, he pressed for engagement.

"It's a lovely area. Have you lived here all your life?"

"Yes."

"And you like it?"

Chiara finally stopped with a tut. "Quiet time for the way back, perhaps?"

And he was left to fall behind again, hurt and unsure. Was it all a put-on, the journey there? He'd expected manipulation from the start, but she'd seemed to enjoy his company. He pushed down the disappointment. Contented himself with the fresh air and the view of her walking ahead. A good chance to clear his mind, he considered, before trying again to conjure a shield. Except the closer they got to town, the bigger his anxiety grew again. He would be no more able to parse than before, having blundered into issuing orders he probably shouldn't have.

Never mind. A day well spent in fine company was enough in itself. He would let it lie – after he gave it one more try, anyway, determining to ask Chiara if he could get her a drink. See her again. She might say no, but maybe she was just tired, or needed time to warm to the idea. They reached the alleys of Sober Sound, and he was about to ask, when Dalton Terrifold's angry voice called out, "There you are, you foolish child. What have you been doing?"

7

Popular perceptions of the nevolk in western Boldarow were, in the early eighth century, principally formed through the comic character of Mr Skimister, a devilish figure who appeared in the Stanish broadsheet, The Vasseer Times. Mr Skimister was famous for his catchphrase, "I'll sever your gizzards!", regularly shouted after the inevitable thwarting of his nefarious plots.

Though comedic, these depictions reinforced a strong impression of the nevolk, seldom seen in the flesh by ordinary folk, as an inherently hostile and malicious race.
Shifting Perceptions of the Myriad
Creatures, Ukele, p. 65

Wild Wish left Major Bluefern's tent with a familiar feeling that things were once again taking an unpleasant turn. A lifetime had passed since she'd left her home in Swelig, sneaking through the Stanish countryside to join a military effort that she'd believed to be sleek, professional and unstoppable. Hard to even recall now her evenings by the fire reading books, chatting with her parents. She wasn't sure how well she remembered their voices. Their faces. She remembered her father mentioning the Stranded, though, quoting a comic from his newspaper. A joke, how unusual and absurd the angry character was. How funny, when you didn't think you'd ever actually encounter such creatures. Her parents were quietly spoken, soft people, unaware of how hard things really were out here. She had been soft too, then.

It was a lifetime, even, since her time in the Blood Scouts had taken a nosedive and she'd lost everyone she'd come to care about. Shot and stabbed and crushed and burnt. Even the ones who had survived, she had lost to the wilderness. She'd asked Command repeatedly to find them, before and after the Saints Mire, and always they told her things were moving. Keep up the good work and she'd be rewarded.

Well, she'd braved Low Slane and decimated a holy land, and she'd brought a Lock Cavern ghost back from duelling trolls, only to be told that they were due over the line again, where they might (definitely would) face the Stranded. She'd lost Newk and wasn't sure if she'd ever hear Oksy's annoying voice again, while Havik, the worst of the people she'd mistakenly cared about, was the only one who apparently wouldn't die. Relight Festival was supposed to bring a break. She needed the rewards *now,* and there didn't seem to be any.

There was only the Stranded.

Worse than that, probably. What she'd been told wasn't everything – it was never everything. Leaving Bluefern's tent behind, walking with Gaussica and Iggy, she said, "What's with the black envelope?"

"Ooh," Iggy responded first. "It's black paper! Super rare – only a real skilled witlacer can make it, using spidrom ink. The way they do it, only specific people can read it. Something about storing emotion in threads."

"And you're not going to open it?" Wish demanded of Gaussica.

"I will. In private," he said.

"Great. So we've got a troll-killing one-man-army hiding his orders."

"I'm not hiding them. I will consider them in private."

Wish grunted, tempted to wrestle the envelope off him. It probably said something like, *Wait until all her friends are dead then send Wild Wish in to fight the mage alone with a spoon. And burn her Relight decorations.*

"So you know him?" Iggy cut through her thoughts. "This Danny Terrific? The mage?"

"Dalton Terriford," Gaussica corrected, but Iggy gave him a disbelieving look.

"Are you sure? Danny Terrific's better."

It quirked Wish's smile. She preferred Iggy's version, too. But

Gaussica, not seeing the humour, said, "I'm sure. The Arbitration monitors any parser that registers on the class system, and he's a first-class mage."

"Then, like, have you met him?"

"No. I usually only meet a mage because they have to die." He looked unsettled as Iggy googled at him, her stare demanding more. He added, "I had one friend, Lerol, but we were twelve. He's dead now, anyway." Another pause. "He was my only friend."

Wish stopped. The man had gone from total caginess to awkwardly personal in an instant, with the same effect of thoroughly discouraging more interaction. "You mean *ever?*"

He cast his eyes down. "Sorry, you didn't need to know that."

"Hey," Wish said, "we're all friends here."

Iggy patted his arm, limply, with an attempt at a smile. But her eyes went to Wish with concern. Wish nodded to indicate they carry on.

Gaussica said, "I would like to say something. To everyone."

"Everyone in the company? Or just our platoon?"

He nodded.

Wish swore under her breath. This was going to be a long mission. "You can talk whenever you want. No one's stopping you." He could learn for himself the price of conversation with the unforgiving Raw Boys.

They arrived at a mess tent, following the sound of familiar voices, and on entering caught the tail-end of Latebite speaking far too jovially: "I'm just saying, I don't get how none of you even went in to check. When I've got a man claiming to have killed three trolls with his bare hands, I want to see the evidence!"

He had his back to them, sitting on a bench at a table with most of their platoon for an audience, only Ohno and Emi sitting separately. There was laughter from some, but all of them stiffened at the sight of Gaussica. Quickness, who was also facing away and hadn't seen him, cheerily replied, "We didn't need to see anything, we heard it well enough! And you want to pick over troll corpses, you be my guest."

"Potential troll corpses, they might've just been –"

"Cane's teeth, shut up man," Ptrangus said, throwing a severe glance over Latebite's shoulder.

The soldier twisted around, smiling like he expected a trick, a curse ready in his mouth. His face fell. "Ah. Fucking typical."

"The wrong person always turns up when you run your mouth *all the time,"* Wish said, walking through the tent. Passing the table, she checked the food spread. Lifeless as this camp appeared, they were apparently well catered for, with a great steaming cauldron of stew bubbling alongside stacks of tins. All left out for whoever came along. She took in a deep breath of the meaty aroma but turned away, resisting. For now.

"Look, I'm not saying I don't believe it," Latebite said, holding his hands up to Gaussica. "I'm saying it's something I would've *personally* liked to see."

"Keep going, for the love of the Flesh," Ptrangus said. "We'll get a demonstration soon enough."

"He's right to be sceptical," Gaussica said, though. "I didn't kill them with my bare hands. I had a hammer."

There was a moment's stillness, because it was said so factually, as if this information might allay any doubts. *Innocent,* was the word, Wish realised. There was something weirdly innocent about this hunter. She noticed Scraper, beyond him, lurking near the entrance, and wondered if the pair had a few things in common. The Rawboys, so generally loud and on show, were dangerous in a very clear and noticeable way. Wish was apparently collecting less obviously mad killers, though, and she needed to be careful about how she read them. And how she used them. What was the appropriate leadership style for unpredictable weirdos? She said, "Anyway. We've got orders."

That killed the cheer even deader than Gaussica's arrival – and as if summoned, the tent flapped open again and Macmiddan entered, Graveguard just behind him, completing the platoon. The medic huffed, "Did she say orders?"

"She said orders," Ptrangus replied, icily.

"The morning keeps getting better." Graveguard wandered past to investigate the buffet table too, as Macmiddan held back, folding his arms and giving Wish a significant look.

"Something you need to tell me?" she asked.

Macmiddan replied, "After."

She huffed at another impending problem. Everyone was already waiting on her, though.

"Okay," Wish said, forcing her lightest smile. "Good news and bad news. Let's start with the positives: we know what our mission is, and I'm fairly confident we'll have it done by Relight. In fact, the timing is kind of crucial, so we *have* to be done by then."

"Great, we were really worrying about that," Ptrangus told her, drily, and she scowled. She'd have words with him separately about pretending not to care about the festive period.

"Anyway, the mission is a mixed bag. It involves a first-class Drail battle mage and a possible company of the Stranded, but the idea is to stay hidden so you don't have to worry about them." She had to raise her voice for the last part because the platoon erupted in shocked curses.

"What kind of mage?"

"Did she say the Stranded?"

"We're not fighting fucking magic!"

"You can shove those orders right up your fucking –" Ptrangus cut himself off because he'd gone too loud and everyone else went quiet.

"Yeah, a bit much," Wish said, and for once he looked abashed.

"That's what he's here for?" Emi called out from her perch on a table, knees up and staring darkly at Gaussica. "We really did bring a mage-killer to kill a mage?"

"Yes," Wish said. "But –"

"I'll accept apologies on a printed card with chocolate."

"It's a *good* thing," Wish countered. "Unless you want to kill this mage yourself."

"It's a witlacer, isn't it? You said first class, so it must be one of those pratbags. I would *gladly* kill him. Any day of the week. I'd spoon out his eyes." The earth-minder demonstratively lifted the dented metal spoon from her stew and twisted it around. "You know I would."

"A spoon?" Wish echoed quietly, thrown by how closely it mirrored her earlier worries.

"Do you even hear yourself?" Latebite said. "Oh no, don't bring a mage-killer, I want to kill the mages? Pick a door, Emi."

"I'd kill any *witlacer* for sure," Emi said. "But he doesn't discriminate."

"He's a bloody Arbitrator! Discriminating is *all* they do! They're famous for it!"

"Alright, stop digging holes, Bite," Wish sighed. "And it doesn't matter, he's coming and I am happy to delegate the problem to him. Now, I'll give you the gist of *our* job."

With a few final smart comments, and more serious, ready glances, the platoon grew quiet, and Wish did her best to try and recall everything that Bluefern had told her.

The western front line, stretching from Farne down through Lome to the Most Blessed Sea, was shored up nearly all the way along a thousand miles of trenches, forts and natural barriers. All except for occasional random blips. Lake Harmonial and its surrounding area, including the resort town of Sober Sound, was one of those blips. The dense woodland around the lake was nearly impassable for any sizeable force, which left a stretch of uncontested no man's land some thirty kilometres wide and twenty deep. As there was nothing especially worth securing there, and it was a long way from the more substantial fighting, with its few narrow paths easily guarded, the Comity and the Drail had established defences on either side and otherwise focused their efforts elsewhere. There was a bare-bones system of trenches and watch-towers some miles south and a short way north of the Harmonial Woods, with no serious defences in between. It was, after all, easier to guard a tree line across an empty field than to secure the woods themselves.

"So, another big stretch of land all the death-happy empires don't dare touch?" Ptrangus put in. "Wonder if there's a sick and ugly reason they're leaving *this* place alone. And sending us in, I'm guessing?"

"It's not deeply historical or religiously messed up, no," Wish said. "Just too many trees for anyone to care about."

"I think your man there has a point, still," Macmiddan volunteered, more seriously. "Anything that can be blown apart as easy as a tree doesn't tend to stop Stanish progress."

"Okay. Well, perhaps there is a reason. Shall I finish?"

The two Rawboys shared a look then shrugged, like, if she must. So she went on.

"What's actually notable about this uncontested region is three points of interest bang in the middle. There's three roads through the woods connecting the lake, the town of Sober Sound on its north shore, and Haven, a village in the woods. All three are idyllic holiday locations for the wealthy elite. Usually."

"Ah, we're talking gilt-frame torching!" Iggy cut in with excited realisation, drawing plenty of odd looks.

"What the hell does that mean?" Wish said.

"You know, gilt-frame torching? Where you burn out a part of town but some miraculous force turns the rioters down another street just as they're about to hit the rich nobs."

"What rioters? Who's burning out a town?"

"As a general thing. It's an expression." Iggy's enthusiasm waned only slightly before the roundly confused audience. "Ain't it a thing in Boldarow?"

"Not in common parlance," Macmiddan answered, "and I don't know for riots, but I get what she's saying. Money talks, even in a war zone. Reddy's Rebels lost a lot of favour two odd decades ago with the bombing of the Slopland dockyard when they only set off half the charges they were supposed to. They tried to pass it off as a mistake, but it turned out Reddy was friendly with the men whose boats and warehouses got off unscathed. Restrained himself where it might help his pockets, see? Know what they say, war's for the poor to endure."

This got murmurs of agreement and knowing nods, though Iggy looked a little put out, saying, "My example made sense, too."

"Our fault," Quickness assured her quietly. "We don't know Tarrish politics."

"Yeah," Dalliance offered, "I've got zero idea who Reddy's

Rebels are either."

"Anyway," Wish interrupted the rapidly devolving discussion. "With the situation we have here, Haven, on one of the artery roads, was evacuated at the start of the war, but Sober Sound was reportedly still functioning as a town – until recently. Both places are likely to contain Drail troops now, even though their main defences are north of the woods. There's some tacit understanding that the Drail has greater control of the area, if only because the Comity can't be bothered to wade in. Our latest scouts saw guards in Haven, a long way into the woods, and figured they were welcome to keep it."

"Until some fucker decided we should go in and change that?" Ptrangus said.

"Not exactly. There's a pretty specific issue we're up against. With winter coming in fast, a little ice is about to transform this otherwise useless position into something more convenient. While everyone *should* be looking to shore up their positions to wait out the cold, and enjoy some Relight festivities, when Lake Harmonial freezes it'll create a wide and undefended gap in our line. As the south shore opens onto farmland on our side, but the north funnels into the woods, this is more useful for anyone coming north to south: Sober Sound will create a launch point for the Drail, and a choke point for us. *But* for them to take advantage of this, they need to pass a sizeable force through that town. Hence, they've been quietly moving into the area, and our side have been quiet about stopping them, so they don't get too secure. Bluefern's men don't even know why they're here, in case rumours leaked out. Though that's going to change this evening, when he finally issues orders."

"Orders involving us," Macmiddan prompted.

"Yeah. Our job is simple," Wish said. "You've got half a day to get some rest, gather some supplies and all that, then we sneak the artillery into the woods, close enough to blow Sober Sound to hell. If the mage is there, we have Gaussica to take care of that. It shouldn't take more than a few days."

The last part came out like a question and left the platoon watching her with uncertainty. All the time she'd been speaking, she'd been wary of Macmiddan's steel gaze and however he was going to complicate matters. It was Corporal Dalliance who lifted a tentative hand, though, more polite than most of her men, and she waved at him to speak.

"Were you joking about the Stranded, or . . .?"

"Oh right, yeah, that." Wish grinned, because bad news was better with a smile. "No, there's reports of between fifty and a hundred nevolk in the woods, and we'll need to keep an eye out for them. It's a lot of ground to cover so we might not even see them. I think we'll be okay."

"While transporting a whole artillery company unseen up the road?" Ptrangus said.

"Yes. You're Blood Scouts. We've faced worse things than the Stranded. Right, Scraper?"

Her lank-haired soldier squinted back. Everyone waited as she appeared to think it through carefully, then said, "In Low Slane, a pack of dog-sized lizards attacked us. We didn't have a name for them. Their teeth melted things. Two people died."

Someone coughed.

"See. The –" Wish started, but Scraper added, "Actually, Larkin did say, *'At least it's not the bloody Stranded.'"*

Wish glared daggers at her as Latebite suppressed a laugh. Helpful. She turned to Gaussica. "How about you? You had something you wanted to say. Some advice, maybe?"

His eyes widened and he mutely shook his head.

"Seriously? You just said on the way here . . ."

He shook his head faster and she exhaled. Wish flapped her hand. "Whatever, then. Dismissed."

"That's it? A hundred Stranded and we're just dismissed?" Ptrangus said.

"That's it," Wish said, and walked to one side, down the food table, to be clear she was done. She glanced Macmiddan's way. Why hadn't he said his bit yet? He approached her as the others started complaining to each other. "What is it?"

Graveguard slunk up beside him with a plate piled with food, broody with his bald head and sunken eyes. Double serious, great.

Macmiddan said, low and private, "Been talking to a couple soldiers. This company's had owt to do but sit soaking up gossip from all over. The favourite topic of the hour is something you'll want to hear."

"What?" Wish found a sudden lift. "Have you heard something about my scouts?"

She was brought right back down by Macmiddan's pitying expression. If it was about the missing Blood Scouts, it wasn't *good* news.

"It's Havikare," he said, both men carefully watching her reaction. "Gaussica was right. Seems pretty definite she's alive. These rogue goblins have taken a town and they're drawing in deserters from all quarters." He shared a look with Graveguard before finishing. The medic clearly disagreed about telling her this. "They're saying this human lady is leading them in a myriad rebellion. An ogre-killer who's fighting for the little guy. Queen of the Goblins."

"That sounds like Havikare," Wish said.

"I was against telling you," Graveguard growled. "Bad bloody idea."

Wish glowered – she was their *leader* – but his hard face was unapologetic. As an able medic, everywhere in demand, he had even less fear for authority than the other Rawboys, though he was thankfully, generally, more respectful and mature. In fact both these men were older and more experienced enough that she could tolerate a little insubordination. She said, "You think I can't focus, knowing she's alive?"

"I think your mind's prone to wandering," Graveguard said. "And thoughts of that woman aren't gonna be healthy thoughts, are they?"

Wish grunted inelegantly, because he was right. But the niggle was obviously already there, since Gaussica had mentioned Havik. She *was* alive. What was she doing with goblins? They'd been on opposite sides in the Mire. Wish knew the general answer, though: Havik was causing trouble. She hadn't entirely understood the woman, but she knew that much. Causing trouble was her main motivation in life. She'd fit right in with goblins.

"So?" Macmiddan said. "What're we gonna do?"

Wish paused. "What do you mean? Now? We'll get on and finish this mission."

The two Rawboys shared another look, neither expecting this. Graveguard said, "You don't want us to look into it?"

"How? Divide the platoon? Go AWOL? That's what you were worried I'd suggest?"

"Not exactly, but, I mean –"

"Doesn't matter. Focus, gentlemen." Wish smiled as she found she quite liked how she sounded. This was a good reaction, surprising them. "We've got our orders, and no time to follow idle gossip."

They stared at her like she was a bog creature. A distrusting, unconvinced look they both shared. The confidence left her smile.

"Alright, yeah, keep an ear out for any news, but we've got enough worries as it is."

8

At any one time the front line covered a minimum two and a half thousand miles of territory, spanning an extraordinary variety of terrain and circumstances. The most popular surviving images come from conflicts like Fever Forest, Palicier and the Dust Basin, each covering only a few miles of heavily contested territory crowded with men and fortifications. The unsung greater majority, however, was controlled by lonely, overlapping watch posts, often manned by young, inexperienced soldiers who saw combat only when it came to claim them.

The Great Ebb and Flow: Reflections on Modern Trench Warfare, Sommer, p. 326

The Vulgar Division's mobilisation got off to an inauspicious start as Wild Wish discovered they could be noisy when they wanted. Scores of men exited the tents to set about breaking camp, loading up carts and a small herd of pack beasts. Night had fallen and her team were snoring in a peripheral tent while they had the chance, but she couldn't sleep with this activity outside, and the prospect of the road ahead. Walking through camp, dodging grubby soldiers tossing supplies about, Wish scolded herself for not demanding more time to prepare the operation.

This was a company of hundreds, used to fighting from way behind the line; they were not used to stealth and it was too late to start schooling them. She should've asked for a few days and the chance to map out their route. She should've asked, in fact, for the opportunity to go in ahead and clear the way. Though she could imagine Bluefern's response, from some of the comments he'd already made: they'd only get one clear shot at this mission, and if there was a risk of any advance team being discovered, it'd be better if they were all there to fight.

Something like that.

She spotted him in the midst of the busyness, the short man waving a hand about barking orders. She started towards him but jumped back as a couple of soldiers waddled in front of her hoisting a bundle of canvas. Her yelp drew the major's attention and he squinted at her.

"Don't need you yet, Captain!" he called out. "Another hour before we're ready, so you and yours keep out the way."

"I thought we might discuss –" Wish started, but she had to spin aside again as another man passed, shouting for someone to give him some wire. No apology. Brushing that off, Wish skipped ahead and tried to pick out Bluefern, but in the moment's distraction he'd started instructing Sergeant Pillson on the order of the pack beasts.

Wish paused to consider what she could actually request. Fewer pack beasts, for a start. Or none at all. Better to leave all unnecessary supplies behind than create a train of animals that could be spotted a mile off. There were eight of them, by her count, each the size of three wagons combined. If anything spooked them, they'd bray loud enough to be heard from a long way off.

They also surely didn't need this many people. They could move faster and quieter in smaller numbers. But Major Bluefern was apparently preparing everyone and everything to go without any concern. She tried to follow as he dipped out of view into a group. Instead, she found Captain Crash glaring at her over the heads of some soldiers. The look of disapproval was severe enough to stop her dead.

Fuck it. They could deal with who to leave behind closer to the woods.

Wish turned and spotted a friendlier face. She couldn't help smiling as she weaved through the crowd towards Quickness, perched like a bird atop a barrel, watching the activity like a show.

"Ness," Wish said. "What are you doing? I told everyone to get some rest."

"I did, boss," Quickness said. "But it's energising seeing these boys at work. They're efficient as hell. You couldn't sleep yourself?"

"I don't think I'm allowed to until after the mission," Wish said. "There's a rule about it in the officers' manual: once you reach a certain rank, it's your duty to worry too much to sleep."

"You have a manual?" Quickness offered a playful look.

Wish leaned against the barrel next to her. She watched the men turning one of the great guns, half a dozen soldiers barking orders at one another as they pivoted it towards a beast harness. She struggled to think of a witty response for Quickness, so instead said, "I'm not sure it's especially efficient to take an entire company. I really hope we don't see all these men die."

Quickness didn't reply at once, giving her grave tone the respect it demanded. Then, she said, "Not a problem if they don't see us coming, right?"

Poor girl. Quickness hadn't seen much of the reality of this war. Wish had picked her up only three weeks earlier, interrupting her first days in the trenches, where she'd been assigned as a runner and barely transported a handful of messages. She'd excelled in training and had a solid attitude, but she didn't know yet how bad things would get. Though her optimism was welcome.

The artillery gun clanged into place loudly, with a flurry of self-congratulatory cheers, and Wish cringed at their volume. Someone slapped the pack beast's flank and it rumbled forward, dragging the big weapon over the uneven ground.

"How are they not going to see us coming?" she muttered to herself.

"The first step," a voice cut in that made Wish spin – Emi suddenly standing by her shoulder, "is to separate *us* from *them.*"

Wish growled, trying to calm her rapid heart. "By the Saints Emi, what've I said about sneaking."

Hands in the pockets of her oversized coat, Emi tilted her head and stretched her froggy face to a wicked smile. "Sneaking is our greatest weapon? *Don't make so much noise, Emi.*"

"Great, you can be quiet when you don't need to be," Wish said, but as she did, she realised this was maybe the first time the mage had crept up on her since the Mire. A rare glimpse back to her former cheekiness, mostly absent since she'd been shot and captured, falling under a cloud. "What are you up to?"

"Following you," Emi replied frankly. "I thought you might trip and hurt yourself and I could say *I told you so*. Save waiting until that Arbitrator prick kills us all."

"If it's going to be this big a problem you can stay behind, you know? I can sign you off. It's only been a few months, you didn't need to –"

The mage made a harsh clicking sound, eyes flashing with anger, and Wish's heart leapt with more genuine fear, as Quickness likewise flinched. Emi said, "You need me more than ever, Wild. Trust me, I'll be watching him every step we take."

"Please don't," Wish said. "You're going to make things weird."

"No." Emi placed a hand on her shoulder and Wish's eyes bulged with alarm. "I wasn't there when you fell under the spell of that bog witch. I will be there this time. *Trust me.*" Her unsettling grin was made worse in the bouncing lights of the camp in motion, and the mage backed off merrily into the shadows.

"Dammit. Why is she always so *Emi?*"

"Typical mindless crazy, isn't it?" Quickness said. Wish narrowed her eyes, and the young woman hurriedly added, "No offence, boss. I know she's your friend. But they're all like that, right? Not quite . . . with it."

Wish wanted to disagree, to remind her their mindless mage was one of the greatest assets they could want. But Ness wasn't wrong. As uneasy as it felt to be setting out on a stealth mission with a clambering mass of noisy men, it was equally troubling to have both a mage-killer and a volatile mage in her command. And all this before they'd begun.

"Hey!" Quickness said brightly, freshly inspired. "If she's watching your back, you know, I can watch her for you. If you like?" After another moment, she added, "Boss."

Wish couldn't help smiling, but replied, "No, don't do that. Not unless you want to die."

***

It took most of the night to reach Harmonial, with dawn cresting the horizon when Major Bluefern called for a halt and requested Wish's company at the front. They had been camped a good distance from the line, in case anyone should guess their intentions, and it meant there was now no cover of night to slip into the woods. She pointed this out as Bluefern marched through his troops, Captain Crash and Sergeant Pillson in tow, leading her to a concrete box in the middle of an earth-churned field.

"Won't matter, will it," Bluefern huffed, putting in extra effort to keep ahead with his stubby legs. "From here, we're counting on no one being nearby to see us. Understood?"

"Sure," Wish said. She understood, also, that it sounded wonderful in theory and naive in practice. Especially as they drew up to the pillbox and she saw, beyond it, there were hundreds of metres of grubby fields separating them from a thick treeline, presumably the Harmonial Woods, with almost no cover. There was another pillbox off to the right, a rickety wooden tower a way off to the left, and a rugged, wide road ahead.

A lanky, pock-scarred soldier stumbled out of the concrete box to greet them with an imprecise salute. "Corporal Cole, sir. Welcome to Harmonial."

"At ease, Corporal," Bluefern said, ducking into the bunker. Wish followed with the others, discovering a very cramped, low-ceilinged space inside. There were a couple of chairs and a table messy from old food wrappers and used playing cards. Despite the wide open slit at the front, the air inside was thick with the scent of unwashed men. Cole had a single companion inside, leaning on a mounted machine gun aimed at the woods. He tried to stand and salute, too, but banged his head. Crash snapped at him to get back into watch position.

"Report, soldier," Bluefern said. "Where are the Drail right now?"

"Huh?" Cole replied and the major's moustache twitched with irritation. "That is – well, we've had no recent sightings."

"But you know where they are? You're keeping track of any troops in the woods?"

"Yes, sir. I mean, no, sir. That is –"

"Bloody hell," Bluefern growled, leaning closer to the slit as if to spot the enemy himself. Crash shook his head but Wish offered Cole a sympathetic smile. He was plainly not the quickest or most able soldier, having been positioned here to watch a place expecting to see no action. The major picked up a pair of binoculars from the ledge next to the gun. "When was your last sighting at this location?"

"Um." Cole looked to the gunner for help, but he was studiously staring ahead to not get involved. "Not since I've been on rotation here, sir?"

"Is that a question?"

"No sir, that's a fact. I've been watching those woods for two months. The enemy haven't touched that road. There was a skirmish on the east road about two weeks ago, a dozen or so men who quickly retreated. And we had a couple slip through a month back, found down in Cassward."

Bluefern threw him a questioning glare.

"That's a town two miles south of here. Well behind the line."

"Then what the fuck do I care about it? I want to know where the Stranded are."

"Ah." Cole lit up, something he *could* answer. "We never see them. No one *sees* them. They say if you do see the Stranded, it's already too late, you know?"

"Corporal," Wish came in before Bluefern could explode, "your job here's to keep track of how safe that road is, right?" A hurried nod. "So – briefly – how safe is that road, and how do you know so?"

"Ah. Very safe, ma'am, sir, sorry? Captain?" He recovered, kind of, noticing her stripes. "As far as the tree line, and getting in the woods there, I'd say it's totally safe. The Drail have kept back for a while. And we can hear the Stranded coming from miles off – we haven't heard them recently. Not in the last" – another glance to the gunner, who continued not to help – "must be about week?"

"You're not sure?" Captain Crash demanded and Cole startled, pointing at the desk.

"There's a ledger, sir! It'll say in there."

Pillson apologetically squeezed past to the table and picked through the garbage to get at a grubby notebook, which he flicked through.

"We've got a system," Cole explained, pointing at the gunner. "Unders came up with it, see, from listening and watching. Talking to the other boxes. When you start hearing them, they're generally about five miles out or so, we think. Gets noisier and noisier until they reach you. It usually takes about thirty minutes for them to pass, sometimes a bit quicker. That is, they'll get within about a half mile in thirty minutes then move off again."

"How'd you calculate these distances?" Bluefern checked, softening now he had an actual, unwelcome detail to chew on.

"From the timings, sir," Cole said, "by getting all the bunkers along the line to record them. I mean, they're maybe not going parallel to us, but roughly speaking, we think that's how it works."

"Sorry," Wish said. "What do you hear? Are you saying they're always making a noise?"

Cole's face got sombre. "Yes, ma'am. There's no mistaking them. It's . . . like nothing I know? Foxes kind of scream that way, and I've heard fenstarts are similar, but I don't know for those things. I've only heard these ones. It's not exactly animal, though. Almost like a chant. They want anything nearby to know they're coming."

"Part of the fun for them," the gunner, Unders, muttered, fear evident in his quiet voice.

"And you haven't heard them in a week?" Bluefern checked.

"Yes, sir," Cole said.

"Six days," Pillson corrected, tapping the ledger. "Passing east to west. Another twelve days before that. They don't come this way often, it seems. Not this far south, anyway."

"Assuming there's a lick of sense to this," Bluefern said. "You lads have the latest maps, any other notes?"

"Yes, sir," Cole said. "We've got maps of everything we're aware of around Haven, as far as Sober Sound, and there's –" He was quietened by Pillson's loud shuffling, gathering up whatever papers the outpost had to offer.

Bluefern waddled past, patting Crash's arm. "This is clearly no kind of science but if there's no noise now we have a potential window. Fast, I want every man, gun and screw in those woods before the sun tips the trees."

Crash twisted to leave, but Bluefern clicked his fingers for him to wait, turning to Wish.

"You can send your people ahead but we're not waiting. We'll make a proper plan once we're inside. Can't stay in the open a moment longer than necessary. What do you say?"

Wild Wish floundered, feeling as suddenly overwhelmed as Cole looked – they hadn't made a plan, hadn't considered their options, and didn't know where the enemy were. She *should* go ahead, but his orders were coming too fast.

"Right, got it," Bluefern decided in her hesitation, looking to Crash again. "Tell her lot to go with the rest, we'll catch up with more orders when everyone's in tree cover."

The captain glanced to Wish in annoyance at having to manage her platoon too, then turned and stiffly left, his boots crunching through the frost.

"Here, Captain Wild Wish," Bluefern said. "Let's see what we're dealing with."

She itched to dash out and join her own people, to have some part in managing the start of their mission, but she heard Crash shouting, an unlikely distance away. The company were moving.

"This is good," Pillson said. "They've got enemy patterns down. We can work with this."

"You did this?" Bluefern asked the gunner, who cringed. "If you've got a head for the Stranded, you can come with us. Tell Captain Wild everything you know." Unders' face cast with horror, but the major bowled on. "What are we looking at in terms of choke points?"

Wish was then witness to a better demonstration of the Vulgar Division's efficiency than she'd seen in the night. As the men began racing up the road in tight formation, passing their pillbox to blend into the woods, Bluefern and Pillson exchanged rapid-fire comments about potential enemy positions, numbers, movements at different times of day, likely locations to set up their own attacks. Mostly, they traced the trails of a map, where she saw the three main roads and a handful of snaking paths marked intersecting the forest. She barely got a word in herself, though they occasionally asked her input: it was enough to agree, thankfully, because she was distracted by the large animals and guns moving into the woods. Lumbering pack beasts dragging hunks of weaponry and even a few horses trotting past. Her own girls were with them, she saw with a pang of jealousy – there was Quickness, marching with Iggy, chatting like old friends.

"That'll do," Bluefern announced, watching the tail of the exodus himself. "Pack it up, Pillson. Unders, why isn't your kit ready?"

The gunner startled, rattling the weapon in his hands, sitting like he was hoping they'd forget about him. Cole looked equally frightened.

"Your mate will be fine on his own. Quickly now."

"But –"

"There was no question there!" Bluefern barked and stomped out of the pillbox. Unders looked pleadingly to Wish and she shrugged, then ducked out after Bluefern rather than get involved.

She almost slammed into someone coming the other way, and jumped to the side. Wish found herself looking up at two tall men in crisp, lean uniforms, both with gaunt, sunken faces and stubbly hair. They straightened up importantly, rigidly, but were catching their breaths, having rushed to get here. One had dry crusty skin and the other very thin lips.

"Captain Evans?" Dry Skin said, and she noticed Bluefern watching, a few paces off, having apparently avoided them. As Pillson and Unders hurried out of the bunker, the man opened his uniform jacket to show a metal shield badge on his hip. He went on, a little breathlessly. "I'm Officer Castin and this is Officer Vash, CEF. I'm glad we caught you in time. Can we have a word?"

"CEF?" Wish was only vaguely aware of the abbreviation's meaning but knew its purpose. The Empire's military police. She looked from them to Bluefern. The major's expression hardened. Beyond him, Pillson and Unders were jogging up the road with their arms full.

"We are looking for a woman who may be in your command," Castin said. "Wanted for crimes against the Empire."

Wish laughed before catching herself. *Crimes?* The word sounded like a joke, as they were crossing the front line, amidst a war with thousands dying daily. What was a crime out here? She stared into Castin's cold eyes, neither of them blinking, and from the straight line of his lips felt this was not a man who appreciated, or perhaps even understood, laughter. She didn't apologise, though: the rest of her platoon were already moving into danger without her, and Bluefern was going to be angry at their own delay. She took a leaf from the major's book, decisive, unabashed, and said, "I don't have time for this. If we make it back alive, you can find me then."

As she turned, Castin stepped closer, blurting out, "That's unacceptable, ma'am, we're –"

"Captain," Wish snapped. "Which, unless I'm mistaken, outranks *officer,* so don't tell *me* what's acceptable." She pointed towards the trees. "We're going to risk our lives for your bloody empire, so back off."

She marched quickly past Bluefern. The officers made some complaining noises, but Bluefern offered some final unpleasant remark that shut them up, before he came running up beside her. She gritted her teeth, expecting a reprimand. He said, "In point of fact, depending on their remit, officers of the CEF theoretically have authority over any rank of civil or military society."

Wish kept her eyes ahead. Did not know that.

"But I respect your fortitude." He slapped her shoulder with the back of his hand, making her jump. "Mission first, before that bureaucratic crap. I assume you'll keep the situation under control."

He was looking at her sidelong, wanting reassurance. She offered a weak smile. She had no idea what the situation *was*, now he said it. Should have asked who the men were after before dismissing them. But the woods beckoned, and her point stood. That fresh question mark wouldn't matter if they didn't survive this place.

9

To effectively parse is not, as many assume, to push your energy out. Allowing your energy to stretch beyond your physical body is only half of the skill. It is in the control of that energy that parsing becomes tangible.

Essential Witlacing Theory, Kilmack, p. 76

Pitt was bleeding around the fingernails. It seeped out in an unnatural, thick ooze that made him grimace more from disgust than pain. He wiped it off against his cloak, dark enough that the stains wouldn't show, old enough it didn't matter anyway. Why the nails? It stung almost as much, though, to recall Terrifold's judging eyes as the arch mage insisted it wouldn't hurt if he did it right. Well, fuck, he couldn't do it right, could he? But Pitt pushed that bitterness down as it arose, as the old man's other smooth admonition crept in: "The most important step to success is believing you can do it."

Pitt took another deep breath, blew it out in a cloud, and tried again, looking past the houses and the tree tops, and through the clear, starry sky. He watched the wisps of his own breath turning, damn cold up in the open fish barn loft. But a good place to avoid Terrifold. He couldn't stand another casual dinner with the shadow of his failure over them, compounded by the quietly stern way the mage had responded to Pitt's walk with Chiara. There had been a succinct lecture on fraternising with the locals, particularly *that* local, but the bulk of his anger had been reserved for him issuing orders to the soldiers in Haven when he had not earned his position. Terrifold's words stuck firmly with him: "When you can do what I do, you can make decisions for yourself. Only then."

As if Pitt was some unruly child. An apprentice tugging at his robes.

He closed his eyes, breathed deeply again. That was exactly what he was, wasn't it? And seeing as he was struggling, and didn't even know why it was a big deal for them to instruct the Stranded to avoid Haven, he guessed he didn't know better.

Just needed to relax. Just needed to *do this.*

He pushed the energy out, body vibrating, shell expanding, as he'd been taught. Just like blocking a pipe but bigger, filling the space, shoring up gaps. He felt it growing, sliding out through the loft. Further, further, he had a hold on it, expanding like a bubble. It widened over the barn front, curved over the roof – he was doing it! He opened his eyes, grinning, and caught a glimpse of it in the air, shimmering like a heat wave. Then it burst, lost from his grip, and part of it dissipated into the air. The rest shot into him, a gut punch that knocked him back. He gasped, winded, blinking hard. *Lost it.* He clenched his fists, but held his frustration down. No.

That was good. The best so far. He'd almost covered the barn.

Pitt pushed himself to his feet and swayed, light-headed. Enough for one night. He needed food and drink. Sleep. He staggered to the ladder and climbed down, to find Lieutenant Droll bent over a crate.

"Still here, Lieutenant?" Pitt asked, voice muggy like he'd been sleeping.

"Still here, sir," Droll murmured back. He had a clipboard in hand. "Trying to keep on top of the inventory, seeing as we're fixing to stow half the Empire's ammunition here."

Pitt hummed agreement, considering the state of the barn, packed floor to ceiling with crates of munitions. It was hard to recall how big the space had seemed when they cleared it out, nor how much weaponry such a cache represented. He said, "You don't sound like you approve."

"Not my place to approve, sir," Droll sighed. "Just feels like an awful lot of supplies to put in storage when we've got lads elsewhere who need it right now."

Pitt frowned. "But when we move, we'll push the Comity back. It could make the difference."

"Oh, I get that, sir. That's why I'm here and not out in that inn with the big stripes – I'm handling the details, they get to deal with the bigger picture. But how about yourself? Bit late to be practising, isn't it? You'll wear yourself out."

"Maybe," Pitt said, not wanting to get into it. "But I'm done, anyway."

"Have you nicked your hand, sir?" Droll gestured, and Pitt quickly hid his fingers, folding his arms.

"Yes, no – it's nothing." He left the barn with a rushed good night.

Pitt walked up the road, flexing his bloody fingers and wiping them off again. He had almost shielded the barn, but he'd bled a lot more, he saw. He'd need to get in early tomorrow and clean the ladder. But for now, food. He approached the town hall, which, after some arguing, had been co-opted for the growing number of soldiers coming in, serving as a semi-permanent mess hall on the proviso that it be emptied, in immaculate condition, for two hours each day, in preparation for the town's Light Dance. They didn't need two hours a day, as most of their decorations had already been hung and what else was there to do? But Rotus Axefell drove a hard bargain seemingly for the sake of it. Ruthless like his daughter . . .

The central hall was imposing, tall like a church with a bell tower and big arched doors. Its lattice windows glowed invitingly with the gas lights inside, and it was alive with the noise of scores of soldiers enjoying their downtime. Pitt was glad to have somewhere he could slip in for a casual stew, rather than a sit-down meal in the quiet inn where the officers congregated. Maybe he'd report to Terrifold afterwards, let him know he'd made progress, but he didn't feel like it now. Fortunately, the street was empty, and he'd soon be in the shelter of ordinary soldiers, where the head mage didn't go.

As he reached the hall doors, though, a voice froze him: "Pitt!"

Pitt cringed. This was worse than running into the mage. He turned and forced a smile to greet Chiara as she came out from an alley. Had she been waiting? Watching for him? Her smile was thin and purposeful, about all that showed from her expansive fur coat and flowing hair.

"Fancy running into you here. They won't serve you in the inn?"

"I'm more used to working man's food," Pitt told her. "And I should get to it, before you get me in more trouble."

"Trouble?" She laughed, charmingly genuine, and tilted her head to one side. "Was it really so bad? That blowhard wouldn't actually punish you, would he? You're his protege, his project – I've seen how he looks at you."

Pitt frowned, not liking to hear it put like that.

"Besides, they only refused to relay those orders before because *I* requested it – Father was using it as a bargaining chip to get Saints-knows what else." She waved a flippant hand. "Let them keep their Stranded nearby in exchange for an extra fifteen per cent on the warehouse rent, that sort of thing. Didn't fit his plans. But Erol sends his regards. He can paint again, you know?"

"No, I don't know, that's the thing," Pitt said a little hotly, not appreciating her casual tone, her easy nature, when he'd been straining so hard all day. "I'm here to do a job, not get caught up in your politics."

Chiara arched an eyebrow, thrown by his tone. But her smile returned. "My apologies if I distracted you, then. You do have my gratitude."

"Didn't seem much like it. You disappeared into the shadows the second you got what you wanted. Didn't even hang around to see me get an earful."

"Oh, that's not true." The sparkle of her laugh again. "I had a good view from the cafe –"

"What do you *want,* Chiara? Because I'm damn tired and not in the mood to play games."

She stopped, mouth slightly open in surprise, humour momentarily broken.

"Sorry," Pitt said, slumping. "Excuse my language. And my nature. I know you're not talking to some low-born pipeman out of charity though, so if you don't mind –"

"We *did* our business, Pitt," Chiara cut in, sashaying slightly closer. Her eyes flitted down, a quick assessment, and he made sure his hands were hidden in his coat. She noticed the movement, of course, and snatched at him. Pitt tried to evade, but she caught his wrist and lifted it, inspecting his fingers. Pitt's pulse raced as her warm fingers gently touched his. "Is that blood? What happened? What do they have you doing?"

"It's nothing," Pitt said, snatching his hand away.

"Come with me," Chiara said, already stepping away.

"What? No, I'm not going anywhere with you. I'm hungry and –"

"I will *feed* you, but first we'll take care of your hand. Saints knows, it doesn't look like anyone else is taking care of you. I have somewhere discreet, and I won't bite. Much."

Pitt gave an unhappy grumble, but her backwards glance shattered any resolve he had left. Who was he trying to kid – annoyed as he was trying to be at her, it wasn't an offer he could refuse. He followed, and she took his hand again, to guide him through the alleys. Only a few houses down, she unlocked a door and took him up a short staircase, where she turned on a gas lantern to reveal a cosy wood-trimmed apartment. She sat him down on a bench and went through a cupboard as he took in a small, tinsel-decorated tree and garlands over the windows, a plush bed in one corner with hand-woven blankets.

"You live here?" Pitt asked with disbelief. She laughed.

"Heavens no," Chiara said, sliding onto the bench next to him, their legs touching. She had rubbing alcohol and cotton and took his hand to dab at it. "This is one of our holiday rentals, but I use it sometimes. Erol has his clock tower, I have my nook."

"It's lovely," Pitt said. "Not what I'd imagine for you."

He winced as the alcohol hit his fingernails, and she held his hand tighter with a satisfied smirk. "Yes, I've been told I belong in an ice palace. Or a cave. How did you do this?"

"I don't know, exactly," Pitt replied honestly. "Just part of the process."

"Bleeding from strange places for the sake of the craft," Chiara murmured, focusing on cleaning it all off. She was gentle, attentive, and he appreciated the care, never mind that he could easily have done this himself. "I could imagine bleeding from the nose or ears, maybe the eyes, but at least an orifice. Why your nails?"

"That's what *I* want to know!" Pitt found his smile again. "Unnatural, isn't it? But I guess that's why not everyone is a mage.

Or, I mean, why everyone with the gift doesn't get much further than fixing pipes. It hurts."

Chiara offered that questioning eyebrow again. "Sure, that and the fact that most people can't afford the proper education. Or to get ostracised by certain communities."

"Ostra-what?"

"Cast out," she said, as she finished dabbing his fingers. "You need money to get into the magic schools and if you don't have the schools' support you're likely to get taken advantage of at best, lynched at worst."

"I don't think anyone lynches mages anymore," Pitt said. "But the idea's close enough." He could imagine it, in his own neighbourhood; it was all very well to call out a jobbing pipeman for a broken sink, but a scholastic mage would be unwelcome in any pub he knew. "Then, I guess I've been taken advantage of anyway. If I'm not being used by the military, it's pretty locals . . ."

"You would *love* to get used by me," Chiara scolded, tapping his nose with a finger. He batted it off half-heartedly, and she stood to clear up. Finished, hands clean and safe.

"Thank you," he said, and she leant against the sink. There was that assessing look again. "What?"

"I want to thank *you*, actually. Properly. You might think it was all a little fun, going out to Haven and getting you in trouble –"

"Not much fun."

"Yes. Well, Erol really has been struggling, and the nevolk, on our land? It's an ugly business. I know they've been selling us the line that we're all in it together, and there's people – *races* – from all over the Empire helping to win this fight, but Haven was always supposed to be exactly that. Sober Sound, the Harmonial Woods, all of it, is a retreat, a place of peace. Nevolk don't know the meaning of the word."

Pitt hesitated. He didn't know much about the Stranded, except that they were best avoided, and didn't fit in to ordinary society. Too violent and unstable. But something in the way she said it rankled him. He said, "I don't belong here either, do I?"

"No, I suppose not." She wasn't smiling. "But some of the

unexpected doors this war has opened are more fortuitous than others. It will be quite the story to tell, after all, to see a lowly pipeman from the Arrow slums rise to the right hand of the great Dalton Terrifold."

"Instrumental in the action that changes the tide of war?" Pitt added. "Though less of the 'lowly', huh?"

"Do you believe that, though?" she replied, still serious.

"Alright, calm it. I might not come from money –"

"About the war, I mean," she cut in. He paused, seeing her real concerns come to surface. Was there a touch of fear in her eyes? She went on quietly, "It wasn't supposed to come here."

"It still won't," he assured her. "By the time the Comity figure we're here, it'll be because we've broken the line. This is good, Chiara, I promise you." He stood up, moving close to her, this time taking her hands in his. She retreated, nervous suddenly, but couldn't go far. "Sober Sound's in the thick of it already. It isn't just on the line, it's between them – I'm surprised anyone stuck around. But I admire it. I respect that the town's been preserved and I'm glad to meet you here. And I'm glad we're gonna move things on at last. Glad that I can help protect you. Between Terrifold and me, no one's getting near this town."

Chiara's sly smile was back at last, and her fingers caressed his as she studied his hands again. She looked up to his face. His lips. "You promise?"

The silky tone hit him with a mixed jolt of desire and a pang of doubt. Was she after something else from him now? Personal protection?

Did it matter?

"Sure. I promise."

"And your master, won't he be upset to hear you're spending time with me?"

"He's not my master. And he doesn't need to know."

10

Tales of the "danger of listening" can be found within almost every mythological system. Everyone knows the story of Prince Orfun braving the deafening Horns of Heaven, but fewer know there is a near-exact parallel in the Necostrian Ballads of Yurpyn, in which our hero almost claws his own face off when forced to listen to the Blood Call of the Stranded.

Legends of the Kleb Range, Brade, p. 120

Wild Wish had been through a number of forests during this war. She'd seen gunfire and artillery blasts tear woodland apart, with the army rarely allowing trees to get in their way. Yet until entering the Harmonial Woods, she hadn't encountered any woodland too dense to fight through. She marvelled at trees, and how they intertwined. This was precisely the opposite of the Midwood in the Mire, with its channels between gargantuan trees: here, the gnarly, spiky trunks stood crookedly to twenty or thirty feet at most, narrow but tight together, linking leafless branches in a messy, impassable tangle. Around their bases was a great mess of dry vines, riddled with finger-length thorns. The phalanx of soldiers and animals was penned in by walls of foliage.

Bluefern stormed past his waiting men and Wish tried to keep pace with him, the man fast considering his height. He flapped a hand about as he summarised what they'd learnt from the maps in the pillbox: "We've got five miles up this road before we reach Haven. We take that village by lunchtime and there's an eastward fork in the road. We'll hit our destination before nightfall. We'll cross three intersecting paths before Haven, so I want you ahead to scout them."

Getting near the front of the procession, they passed the pack beasts, supply wagon and covered cannons. The more erratically dressed Blood Scouts stood out amongst the uniforms.

"You want a horse, get there faster?" Bluefern suggested, but Wish shook her head. She had ridden a horse precisely once and it had scared her.

"We'll be quick enough without," she assured him.

"Sure. You'll take my men, though – 2nd, 3rd and 8th Squads. Reach Haven as fast as you can, but leave a squad each to guard the paths. We'll cover the first one ourselves. Understood?"

"Yes, sir," Wish replied automatically, while trying to picture it all in her mind. She was warmed by the familiar faces of her scouts watching her approach and offered them a smile. Quickness smiled back and Iggy gave a wave, which she lowered under Bluefern's scowl. Firming up her voice to sound confident alongside the major, Wish said, "Blood Scouts, with me. We're marching for the village, double-time! Boorah!"

She sensed from their expressions they didn't all take her seriously, but they fell into line, shouldering their packs and readying rifles, at least pretending to be an orderly platoon.

"Forward!" Macmiddan added his voice to her order, and he got a loud "hut!" as the others followed. If their efficient stride was mocking, it was the same as if they meant it.

Satisfied, Bluefern turned to relay orders to his own men, and a couple dozen soldiers raced out of line to join Wild Wish. He rattled off the names of a lieutenant and three sergeants, which she immediately forgot, and off they went up the road. The rest of the company continued not far behind them, so Wish quickened her pace, reaching Ohno and Macmiddan at the front.

"It's a good road," Macmiddan said. "But not much for cover. Drail come this way, we're cooked."

A crack sounded, far off. Off to the west. Another, and another, rolling together like distant thunder. Wish was no good at guessing the distance of artillery blasts, but she had a feeling it wasn't in their woods. Wasn't anything to do with them.

Macmiddan said, "That direction's the Islace offence. Must be a hell of a barrage if we can hear it from hear. Guess they're eager to get things done before the cold sets in, same as us."

"Mm," Wish agreed, as the blasts continued. Islace was where the fighting was really concentrated in this part of Lome, further west than where they'd picked up Gaussica. A tremendous distance. She hoped any local Drail advance would be equally audible at a distance, because Macmiddan was right about the lack of cover in this funnel of a road. She said, "What's up with these damn trees? Forests are supposed to be good for hiding in."

"Lover's vines," Macmiddan said readily, and when Wish mugged ignorance he went on, "Or strangle-thorns. Someone renamed them to sound nicer. Hard to get through unscathed, harder to get out of once you're in. They're popular in designer horticulture, dense enough to create corridors and such."

"Cute," Wish said. "And the whole forest is like this?"

She looked up at Ohno, that much taller than everyone else, but the ogre shrugged. "You see what I see."

Wish squinted at the shameless lie, but on a scan of the flanking forestry, trying to spot gaps, she supposed it might not look any better from a few feet higher. If they were forced off the road, they'd get cut to ribbons. Scratch that, they *couldn't* be forced off the road – the only options were forward or back. And those intersecting paths Bluefern had mentioned. It meant there were very limited routes the enemy could use to get through, but it also meant there was no hiding from a confrontation. Again, she had a feeling of being unprepared, moving into all this too fast. Pushed into a woodland death-tunnel, escorting animals, Gaussica with his black letter – and she hadn't even had a second to consider yet that the CEF had almost cornered her.

Wish twisted to the other scouts, walking in keen-eyed pairs behind them. "Girls. Are any of you wanted for crimes against the Empire?"

Most of the troop were thrown, but Ptrangus answered, "You really want to go there?"

"No, not you guys," Wish replied, "I asked my *girls,* specifically." Quickness and Iggy looked surprised, Crag and Scraper wore darker looks, and Emi was leering. Not Emi, the mage swaggering slightly to the side – she was always a threat to the Empire, but if they wanted to punish her they'd send more than two stick men.

"I am Tarrish," Iggy volunteered uncertainly, regaining a cautious smile. "People sometimes confuse Sanctuary Island with Tarrland?" Sanctuary Island. A famous prison colony in the Emerging Isles, far, far away from everything that mattered.

"That's not what this is," Wish said, checking the others. Crag shook her head, disdainful of even being involved, while Scraper stared ahead like she didn't want to be noticed. Yeah. There was potential there – but what could she have done recently? They'd been together for months, and Scraper had been under Tate and Larkin's watch for a while before that. Wish considered Quickness instead. She looked nervous now, guilty. "Did you do something?"

"I'm . . ." Quickness hesitated. Cleared her throat. "I might not be as *old* as I said."

"Fuck," Wish said. Well, she barely looked like an adult. But no one was hunting underage soldiers, were they? Stanclif would be out half its manpower, if so. Then again, a young woman was more of a scandal. "Are you someone important, Ness? Wealthy family?"

She shook her head. Wish considered her a moment longer. It could still be that. But it had to be something worse, didn't it?

"Never mind," she said. "You're good. You're all good. Forget it."

"Was that what those men wanted?" Ptrangus asked. "Fucking CEF chasing after us, is it? Anyone's pissed them off is good in my book."

He got murmurs of agreement from the other Rawboys.

Wish pushed the concern aside – if it was Quickness they were after, it might just mean a trip home early for her anyway. Though Wish figured she'd better work harder to keep her alive. There were bigger questions to worry about, anyway. Like the Gaussica matter. She looked around and saw him walking on the other side of the troop, Emi's opposite. "Gaussica, have you read that black note?"

"Yes," he said, peering up the road. "I would like to have a word, Captain."

"You'll actually talk this time, will you?" Wish countered, and he looked hurt. Losing patience, she gestured ahead, picking up her pace to pull out into the lead. She kept her eyes on the trees, but saw no sign that this was anything more than a wintry stroll in the forest. Far enough ahead for a little privacy, she demanded, "What is it?"

"It's not exactly here."

Her hackles rose at once. Straining to keep her anger down, she said, "Some advice? If you don't want to say something then don't tell people you want to say something, Gaussica."

"Yes. I struggle to . . . keep track. Of what should and shouldn't be said. Or what has and hasn't. I don't see a straight line. Do you?"

"Where? Branches all over, the road's –"

"In time. Do you see things as they come?"

Wish had to give that a second, first to check that yes, he had just said that, then to consider what the hell it meant. She said, "Does this have anything to do with the black note?"

"I ask because there's a barrier I navigate, that of life and death – you lean closer to my side than most. But more and more, during this war, I see the line shifting." His voice matched his glazed-over expression, eyes off somewhere else. Wish felt that cold tingle done her spine again. "I cannot witness all journeys' ends, Captain Wild Wish, but I know you'll face fire in these woods. On your flesh. Close. Very close. I should have been there, perhaps, but I wasn't."

Wish glowered at him, wondering if there was a chance he was just trying to freak her out. Emi wasn't above grim prophecies like this, but she usually gave it away with her smile. Gaussica hadn't shown much evidence of humour so far, and his phrasing was that little bit too strange to be deliberate. She said, partly to convince herself, "Well, we're in in a war zone, it's a pretty safe bet we'll see some fire. You know, we had a menafis mage at the Swelig annual fair who told fortunes, and even us simple country folk understood their tricks."

"It's no fortune. The smell haunts you."

"You *what?*" Wish exclaimed. "Look, what the hell are you trying to say?"

"We spoke on the road south of the woods. I didn't come, I

should have, but you insisted. And your flesh . . ." He trailed off with a pained look, which drifted towards confusion. "Haven't I told you?" Wish didn't dare reply, fearing he might be a hair's breadth from snapping. He took a few breaths to regain control, and whispered, "I will."

"Do you need something?" Wish ventured. "Some water, a break?"

"It's because we're closer, that's all," he said. "Where life and death thin, I see more. Like I exist again. And when *you* see *me*, and push the barrier, it gets easier. I feel like I almost *can.*"

Now truly out of her depth, Wish regarded him with fresh concern. Emi was erratic, but at least the earth-minder was coherent, outside her magic-induced mania. She had to wonder what exactly the Lock Cavern did to people to make them monster killers. They'd broken his mind, for sure, setting him on a wavelength she couldn't follow, and she wasn't sure he could make sense of it himself, let alone plainly tell her what his orders were, now. She said, quietly, "Is there some way I can help?"

"You already have. Or maybe . . ." He screwed up his face. "Yes, this is why – it's coming now. Wait. Just a second. The balance is shifting. Here."

A bird-call cut through the trees and made her jump – much louder than the patter of Islace artillery fire. Another call followed. Wish frowned at Gaussica as the sound built, layers of voices adding to it. Had he heard it before her or predicted this? She found her troops' eyes widening, listening with alarm as they closed the distance to her. Those weren't bird-calls. They were jeering screeches. Their biting, wavering pitch was more antagonistic than any natural woodland creature.

Gaussica sighed loudly, almost relieved.

"Oh god, oh by the Saints," a young soldier uttered in fear. "Oh fuck oh fuck."

Wish spotted him: Unders, with one of Bluefern's squads, watching the trees with jittery nerves. Further down the road, the company was still in view, spreading out in concern. The noise grew louder, like a whooping, circling party of angry animals, tearing at each other, cackling with inhuman laughter.

"We have to go," Unders said. "We have to get back. We can still leave, we –"

"Shut the fuck up," one of Bluefern's sergeants snarled him into silence. He turned to the others. "Keep your shit together. Weapons ready."

Eyes shot to Wish for orders, and she nodded: follow that command. Her scouts threw down their packs and lifted their rifles.

"Off the road," she said. "Get what cover you can."

"Defence formation!" Captain Crash's voice shouted over hers, joined by the galloping of hooves. He was riding towards them, kicking up dust as the company split down the middle, racing to the edges of the road, some already crouching or lying down. Behind him, one of the pack beasts made a braying noise in answer to the sounds of distant terrors. Wish waved at her soldiers to scatter as Crash reared his horse around. He ordered, "Dig in! If they come this way, be ready."

"If they come this way," Wish echoed, reconsidering the trees. The gaps between trunks and branches. Something making sounds like that didn't seem like it would be bound by roads.

"Hold the line," Crash snarled. "That's the order."

He turned the horse back as men pulled each other down. Unders was all but thrust into the thorns by the sergeant. The pack beast made another frightened sound. Understandable: the screeches were sounding increasingly like something from the caves of hell. Crash hesitated on his horse, even this veteran shaken.

"They might not come this way," Wish told him. "Keep everyone down. Quiet."

He gave her a sideways glance, not appreciating the suggestion, but he was almost thrown from the saddle as his horse stamped its hooves with a whinny, responding to the pack beast's next moan. Crash tugged at the reins, looking darkly down the road, and Wish followed his gaze, to where the pack beast was stomping unhappily. Her heart sank as she sensed his thoughts. There were three men rushing around the big, daft animal's muzzle, trying to calm it and lead it aside. Failing.

"No," Wish whispered, but Crash whipped his reins to go back.

The noise of the Stranded, undoubtedly now what was coming, became more discernible as it got louder, closer. Screams, shout and howls. Wish half expected to see them already on the road, but there was nothing ahead. There was no one around her, either, the rest of the platoon having taken up low positions in the tangled tree lines. She couldn't spot Gaussica at all. She trotted over to Ohno's massive form, barely shielded by a mess of thorny hedges and jutting branches. The ogre's patchwork clothing was dark and scrappy, though, blending in with the shadows. Wish shed her rifle bag and readied her ornate gun, the extended Coaerm 0.44 Automatic. She looked over the scope, judging the distance. Adjusted it for the furthest point of road visible.

Wish twitched as a particularly long and sharp screech broke the air, followed by the crooning of a half dozen animals, like wolves mad at the moon. The Stranded's shouts were inhuman, but there were actual animals joining in, too. The pack beast took in a breath, big enough to hear up the road – an inhale for a very loud, frightened sound – but a dull, hard thump cut it off. Wish jolted around. She watched the beast fall with horror, pulled down by a group of soldiers as one backed off, lowering his gun. It'd been pressed in hard enough to barely make a sound. Her mouth dropped open. "No."

Unders was groaning again, but the sergeant gave him a blow and hissed, "Keep it up and that'll be you, next. Fucking *quiet.*"

That stilled the man, at last, for all the difference it made with the Stranded growing closer. Wish raised her rifle again, watching for movement. There had to be scores of them. It could have been a thousand as easily as fifty. And here she was at the very front, just Ohno for company. When they came, they'd reach her first. She steadied her aim. So be it. She doubted she could run from them. The screeching escalated, invaded her senses, almost forming words, though they plainly weren't Stanish. Promising death, torture, pain. All with sinister laughter, a game to these monsters.

Let them come . . .

It dragged out, the interminable noise, sending birds squawking from trees. Another soldier gave a low whimper, tension bubbling out. It shook through them all.

Then is quietened.

Wish looked up over her rifle, not believing the scope. The road was still empty.

The noise was receding. Breaking up in its violence. There was laughter within the screams. It rushed off quicker than it had come. Soldiers began to calm behind Wish, with mumbles like they scarcely believed it. The sounds circled hazily around her head and she wasn't sure if the Stranded were still audible, far away, or it was just the memory of their screams.

She got to her feet, legs shaking from the fear that had pumped through her body. Ohno stood alongside her, subtly coming close enough to support her weight against her thigh, and whispered, "Guess we'll get them next time."

Wish forced a smile. Had to. She gave the ogre a companionable pat and turned back, pausing to make sure she wasn't going to collapse. Past the worried men now making a quiet joke of their fear, her eyes found the great bulk of the pack beast, shot dead in the panic. Grimacing with anger, she stomped back down the line.

11

The innovations that came out of thrusting so many different cultures together to accomplish unique daily tasks were as diverse as the peoples involved, from how best to preserve footwear through to horrifically creative traps and improvised weapons. Such things were a mixture of both the genius of necessity and the permissive madness of desperate fools.

A Fine & Baffling War, Flegherty, p. 18

"You didn't have to bloody kill it!" Wish said, almost a shout, as Bluefern's men scattered like frightened rats. Captain Crash alone stood his ground as she bore up to him. "There was no need! It was for nothing!"

"They didn't come," Crash replied flatly. "If that beast made a sound, they would've."

She bared her teeth, fists clenched at her sides, wanting to hurt him. To drive his face into the dead animal's gore. It bled profusely around its thick wrinkled neck, wet nose pressed to the ground and leathery eyelids closed. By its side stood a sullen bulbous man in riding leathers, the pack master.

"Captain Wild Wish, calm yourself," Bluefern ordered, approaching from the tree line. "What do you think –"

"You Saints-damned brought these animals!" Wish reeled on him. "You knew we needed to keep quiet and you brought them here, and now you kill them for being scared! I did *not* agree to this! We should have stopped and bloody well planned and –"

"Enough," Bluefern cut in firmly. His face was blank, with calm worse than mere anger.

Wish saw she'd left her platoon behind, running here. Surrounded now by the artillerymen, with Crash closest, she stepped back. She looked from his miserable scarred face down to the great dead animal again. She wanted to shout, still. To make it clear this was not okay. People could die, people *should* die, but leave the damn animals alone.

"It would have given away our position," Bluefern told her. "But your point stands. It was a mistake to bring pack beasts. Horses, too. I thought we'd be a large enough target their size wouldn't make a difference, and failed to consider their other liabilities."

Wish was disarmed by his forthright response. Something in his eye said this was a gift. He was making it sound like she was concerned only about their safety, not losing her shit over a dead animal.

"I'm sending them back. We'll go on by foot. Two teams to a gun. It'll be slower but we can guarantee quietness."

"We can hitch them here," Captain Crash suggested. "So that –"

"They could still give us away. Even if we're not with them. No. Captain Wild Wish is correct. And we've all been made well aware of the need to move quickly now, haven't we?" Bluefern locked his gaze with Wish's again.

"Yes, sir," she murmured, trying to sound obedient. "I apologise for my . . ." *Empathy? Love of animals?*

"They were too damn close for comfort," he went on, not waiting for her to finish. "And even without seeing them, we've got enough soiled pants here to testify that we best not meet that force head-on. Crash, get the animals out of here and ready us to continue. Captain Wild, walk with me. I need you to get ahead *now*. Pillson, you too."

His sergeant stepped forward, Unders' papers in hand, eyeing Wish carefully as he did. As she calmed, she became aware of how many unhappy faces were watching them.

Bluefern began striding up the road, leading her away from his men and towards her own. She took a second to appreciate this was over, and she was free to leave this unsettling crowd without having got herself killed. Crash was glowering, and she managed to shoot him an equally mean look before skipping after the major, with Sergeant Pillson. Bluefern huffed along until they were clear of the others' earshot, the Blood Scouts and their escorts spread across the road ahead. Dalliance and Scraper had crept closer, guns in hand, and she noticed Gaussica some way beyond the platoon – had he gone somewhere and come back?

"Everyone's on edge," Bluefern grumbled, "but you want to chew an officer out you do it in private, Captain. Am I clear?"

"Yes, sir."

"The last thing I need is for anyone in my company, or yours, to question our leadership." He looked at her purposefully, and she understood he meant they'd be doubting her, not Crash. "Try that again and I'll strip your command, understand?"

Her face flushed with shame and frustration. "Yes, sir."

"But it *was* my mistake. I hate to see the animals hurt, too." This, he sent aside to Pillson, as if to confirm it, and the sergeant nodded bland agreement. "It was also damn good sense Crash acted as fast as he did. I don't know about you, but I would rather not see the monsters that can make sounds like that. Our company isn't equipped for that kind of fight."

"Absolutely," Wish agreed, and that brought them to the edge of her platoon and the accompanying squads. Wish noted the grim expressions on her scouts' faces, like they'd been expecting a fight. Except for Emi, who looked more bright-eyed than she had in days.

"Listen." Bluefern raised his voice, drawing them all that bit closer. "We can't say how close a call that was, but we can't leave it to chance next time. Those fuckers" – he pointed off towards the trees – "are already closer than we might've hoped. If they happen upon us, this falls apart. Might be there's no avoiding them, though, so we have limited choices, don't we Captain?"

He looked to her to complete the thought, throwing her another bone. A chance to regain the appearance of order. Or an opportunity for her to take responsibility for a damning proposition? She guessed retreat wasn't a choice, so said, "We could get to them before they get to us. Eliminate the threat. But if we're forced to fight them, I'd want to secure the village first, to have a defensive position. Considering getting there is the challenge, though . . . we'd be better off drawing them further away."

"How?"

"We could run a diversion, actively move them off to the west. Meanwhile try and seal off the paths so they can't come back. Emi could manipulate the trees, create blockades."

"I can do that," Emi said happily. "These trees might look like dead, brittle husks, but they'll do what I say." She punched a fist into her other hand as if to suggest she was going to beat the woodlands into submission.

"Okay," Wish said, "but if we somehow end up on the back foot we need those paths to escape ourselves. And there's a chance they won't be as impeded by these trees as us anyway. How big are the Stranded? Can they do things we can't?" Wish threw that to the group and a lot of eyes looked away.

"Smaller than humans," Ohno volunteered. "Goblin-sized or so, I'd say."

"So we'll have a tougher time obstructing them. As for a diversion . . ."

"Map." Bluetorn snapped his fingers at Pillson. The sergeant unfolded the big map they'd taken from the pillbox and spread it out on the dusty ground, flattening it with a shaky hand. "Unders?" Bluefern called out. "Where's the kid?"

The gruff sergeant came forward, pulling Unders by the collar, and thrust him in front of them. "Almost got us killed, sir."

Unders stumbled, white with fear. Wish felt for him: until this morning, he had a position where he never expected to see action, most likely because someone, somewhere, knew he wouldn't cope.

"How far away were they?" Bluefern asked.

"I – I don't –"

"Take a breath dammit. Think. Meantime, everyone look here." The circle of onlookers closed in, shoulder to shoulder, as he pointed. "They were off west, at least, which is a good thing. We keep them that side of us, we don't need to pass them to reach Sober Sound. The closest path west loops south, not much use to us or them. The next two connect to a few places a pack of Drail scum could congregate. And they were congregating, weren't they?"

"There are clearings at Petitioner's Rocks," Pillson said, reading from the map, "Church of the Light, Serene Fields, Ladies' Walk."

"They were further than Ladies' Walk," Unders mumbled, and flinched when Bluefern snapped a look at him. "At that volume. We've heard them louder without seeing them – we're already closer to the Walk than our pillbox was to the tree line. They had to be at one of the other sites." He was saying it with more hope than confidence: the alternative, that they might actually be closer, was too harrowing to consider.

"That's good," Bluefern said. "Good lad. Now, I agree with you, Captain Wish – if this was a regular Drail patrol we might just seal the paths, but that's likely to hinder us more than them. Better if we can keep them in the west side of the woods."

"Better if they fucked all the way off entirely," Ptrangus commented, not quiet enough to be private. The major didn't respond but it earned a frown from Pillson.

"Captain." Bluefern puffed his chest out. "How can you divert them?"

Wish froze. He'd been talking so assuredly she had been waiting for a clear solution, not an expectation of a plan. She cleared her throat to buy time.

"If we send a couple smaller units further west, they can lay traps, draw them away," Wish thought out loud, not appreciating the implications until she'd said it and a couple of men whispered unhappily. "But, respectfully, sir, my platoon is not here to be used as bait."

"Agreed. And we don't know what we'll find in Haven, so I want you there, Captain. But these westward routes could take our chaps south before any such traps might be sprung. Sergeant Hark, if you have a half dozen fast soldiers – I should think it possible to get as far as the church before retreating back over the line. I'd expect you home safe before we start firing our guns."

"Sir, yes, sir," the gruff sergeant replied without hesitation, stamping his feet together. Between this eagerness and his aggression towards Unders, Wish suspected he was at least half mad, and the major was aware of this. She doubted the chosen half dozen would be equally keen.

"Who of your people can lead them?" Bluefern said to her,

though, shattering any suggestion that her platoon was safe. Wish's eyes bulged, so he elaborated, "Fast and subtle. Not the ogre or your dirt-minder."

"If there's any resistance," Emi said, "you might want the full power of the woods."

"I'm going to stay optimistic," Bluefern replied, "and suggest the company needs that protection more."

"Is that a rock formation, the Petitioners'?" Iggy cut in, chirpily out of place. "A big one?"

Bluefern looked to Unders, who bristled again at being noticed. He stuttered and shifted uncomfortably before nodding. "It is – or isn't – I don't know, what's big?"

"Taller than a person?"

"Um. Yes, then? It's ornamental. Or fake, built there – the whole area is, like, for leisure. Those rocks are supposed to imitate a Tikan prayer formation. The smallest are eight or nine feet tall? It's pretty impressive."

"We can use it to amplify a sound," Iggy said with a grin directed at Wish. "Use their own scare tactics against them. I learnt a bit of basic acoustics working on the Tarrland Hornhouse. For operas and that. If we position a few explosives in the right place, we can send a noise through the rocks out over the forest like those monsters did. It's far enough west to send them away from here, maybe – but even better if we can direct the sound off like a horn. They won't know exactly where it came from, especially with how tightly all the trees are packed in around us, and the hunt should lead them further away."

Wish wasn't liking that *we,* drawing her back into it, but was taken by her confidence in the unlikely plan. Ptrangus, ever the voice of reason, asked, "Have you been smoking something? You think because there's rocks out there you can throw a bomb's sound?"

"Yeah. Haven't you seen how the Hornhouse works?" Iggy exclaimed like she couldn't believe he wasn't familiar with an obscure cultural icon from an island on the other side of the world. "They use these man-sized pillars to warp sounds around, redirect them, amplify them – it's all about creating channels."

"Like the Horns of Heaven," Wish said, recalling her time in that marvel of the world, where the gales produced music through mountain caves. Where she'd been tied to her friends, walking together, and hadn't at all appreciated how quickly she'd lose them all.

"That's exactly it!" Iggy laughed. "That's where it gets its name, modelled after the Horns. A lot of that going on down in the Isles – we copy great things and put our own spin on them."

"But you don't have an opera house to work with here," Ptrangus pointed out. "Just some random rocks you haven't seen."

"I'm not saying it's a perfect plan, but it's worth a shot."

"Not perfect?" Ptrangus continued. "It's not even sane."

"You think it's possible?" Wish asked Iggy quickly, sensing Bluefern about to scold him.

"I can certainly try." Iggy beamed, but, a few paces to the left, Dalliance shifted, fearing for her safety, and uttered, "Iggy, wait . . ."

"The clearing's close enough," Sergeant Pillson said. "And if the map's accurate, it's nearer to the western road than this one. Any disturbance might lead them that way rather than here."

"Thinking we're trying to cut through, avoiding the settlements?" Wish said, running with the idea. "At the least, it should buy us time."

"Sergeant?" Bluefern addressed Hark, who gave a one-shouldered shrug.

"Should distract the bastards, one way or another. We could set some bombs and trip wires nearby to catch them when they come, or just a timer, and fuck off ourselves."

"And you can navigate?" the major directed this at Iggy, whose smile disappeared.

"I can," Dalliance blurted out. "I'll go."

Wish wanted to say no, she didn't want *either* of them to go, but Hark got in first with a nasty scoff, "Got enough trouble in these woods without us watching out for a ringer, too."

Dalliance was statue-still, expression hateful, as Ptrangus bent sharply forward to say, "What's that, prick?"

Macmiddan pulled him back as Hark snapped, "I said I got no interest watching my back for this fucker."

Then half the men were jostling and Wish was about to shout at them when Bluefern spoke over the rabble, "Enough! You want to fight each other it'll be in a cell." This, though, he said with a look to Wish that suggested she settle this. As the men split apart, the more reasonable ones holding back the hotter ones, she realised she needed to send *someone* with this unpleasant bigot. A Rawboy presence was as likely to upset him as Dalliance. Quickness was a safer bet, fast and nimble, but her face was averted, unenthusiastic, dreading the company of such men. Iggy shouldn't be going either. More than anything, she needed protection.

"Macmiddan, are you up for it?" Wish said. He nodded without feeling, and she picked another name by virtue of the man standing next to him, helping block Dalliance: "And Grebe."

"That'll do," Bluefern announced with finality. "Saints' speed to you all. I'd appreciate it if you make sure we never have to hear those wretches again."

The path to the Petitioners' Rocks was about an hour's walk further, made more unpleasant by having confirmed Sergeant Hark was horrible and the promise of an approaching suicide mission. They quickly left Bluefern and his company behind, delayed as they were by cutting free from their animals and organising teams of men to drag the artillery. Wish was curious to see how many men it would take to replace one pack beast, but they couldn't wait around. They reached the first path on the map and almost missed it thanks to how tight it was. It *had* to be the path, as the only thing resembling a passage through the trees, but it was barely shoulder-width wide with roots and thorns sporadically sticking across it. It had been recently used, indicated by cracked branches and paw prints in the dirt. Lots of paws.

"They're riding dogs," Ohno said. That made sense of the mix of animal calls in the earlier cacophony. "From the size and those sounds, Cantalesian hounds."

"Bandit dogs?" Graveguard clarified.

"That'd be right," Ptrangus said. "How else do you make the damn Stranded more horrible than by putting them on a hell-mount?"

"These tracks are old," Ohno said. "Days since they came this way."

"Meaning it might be about time they returned," Latebite suggested helpfully, as Wish happened upon a more unsettling niggle that she didn't voice. Cole, in the pillbox, said it had been a week since they heard the Stranded come close, but they should have heard them make these tracks. Presumably they *could* travel quietly.

Not dwelling on it, they continued towards the next path. Wish tried to prep her team as best she could as they walked, calling Iggy, Macmiddan and Grebe forward.

"Don't take any unnecessary chances," she said. So far so obvious. "If in doubt, run."

"Outrun a Cantalesian bandit dog, sure," Macmiddan said.

"Shoot them first, if you prefer," Wish suggested and he smirked. Grebe eyed her unhappily, though. He was a fresh soldier, unblemished by cuts, but with skills proven in the trenches, well enough to be recommended to her. She was yet to see him fight.

"Should be alright," Iggy said, chipper despite a little shake in her voice. "If it all goes to plan, they won't even know we're there."

Her cheer, however forced, was infectious, and Wish wondered if they were all so positive out in the distant Emerging Isles. That accent and have-a-go nature reminded her now of the Isles companions she'd met in Low Slane, tiny people who'd joined her in assaulting the horrific Reeve Abbey. She said, "Hey. Did you know any waders back home?"

"The Gonish?" Iggy perked up more. "Sure, Gonland's only a ten-hour boat ride from Tarrland, we all know each other."

"Oh."

"No, I'm sprigging – we've got waders in Tarrland," she laughed. "I love those little guys. Couldn't eat a whole one though."

She laughed again, the volume making Wish cringe. "Sorry, bad Tarrish humour. *Obviously* I could eat a whole wader."

Wish smiled as Macmiddan chortled.

"Why'd you ask? Got any mates out there?" Iggy said, though, killing Wish's humour. The image of a stormy night in Slane came back to her. When one of the Gonish had killed Pound.

"I've met a few," she said, more solemnly. "Colm Hightower, his brother . . . I thought maybe, if you've seen any out here . . ."

Iggy's lips stretched to a crooked smile again, but her next joke caught in her mouth, as she read Wish's sincerity. She shook her head. "Sorry, boss, been a while since I seen any flogs at all, let alone a wader."

Wish nodded, not knowing what a flog was but getting the point. They fell quiet.

Not much further, and the path revealed itself with a break in the trees wider than the previous one. Also marred with dog tracks and crisscrossed with vines. Wish considered the foreboding tunnel of thorns as Sergeant Hark readied his six "volunteers" and Macmiddan double-checked the lightened packs of Iggy and Grebe.

"Explosives, ammo, light rations, water. That and a prayer should get us through."

"Good luck," Wish said, with an instinct to pat his arm. She held it in, but Ptrangus and Latebite came to see him off with efficient hugs. Dalliance was whispering to Iggy, looking infinitely more concerned than she did.

"Don't worry, Captain. You're gonna need that luck more than us," Hark said from the path's entrance. "Ready, ladies?"

Macmiddan gave him a look that confirmed they were not going to get along. Wish glared too, wondering if this gunnery officer had ever served on the front line, let alone crossed it. But she turned away, with one final idea to help. "Gaussica. Come here."

The Azirian slunk closer, having kept a distance since their creepy chat that preceded the screams. Hark sneered, worried she would send this foreigner with them.

"If you have anything useful to say," Wish said, "any advice, now's the time."

Gaussica looked from her to their expedition force.

"You can hunt anything," Wish prompted. "You kill monsters. If anyone knows how to handle the Stranded, I'd bet you do."

Gaussica nodded, accepting that fact. "The Stranded are easy."

"Ha, didn't see you racing out there to meet them earlier!" Emi erupted with a laugh and Wish threw her a look. Then she frowned at Gaussica, because he *had* gone somewhere when the sounds started. He was watching the mage himself, choosing a response carefully.

"Doesn't it remind you of the Standen Ball?"

Wish, along with everyone listening, had to process that. The month name of Standen sounded close enough to Stranded that it *might* have made sense. And his words had quietened Emi, who was staring with an intensity Wish had seldom seen from her. Maybe the slightest fear?

"What the hell would you know about that?" the mage demanded through clenched teeth.

Gaussica was silent, studying her like it didn't quite add up to him, either. Like he'd just picked some random troubling comment about Emi's past out of the air and it wasn't what he'd intended. He corrected himself abruptly, "No. Later. Wait. I can help." He paused again, as Emi continued glowering, her distrust at a new level but the disquiet apparently enough to silence her. "Yes. The nevolk have very brittle bodies. You could kill one with a blow from a good-sized stick. There's only one problem you have to overcome. Be faster than them."

The words hung over the platoon for a moment before Latebite blew out a breath and said, "Nice knowing you, Macmiddan, you slow bastard."

Ptrangus added another quip, but Wish's focus drifted to Iggy, who was sharing a brief hug with Dalliance. Grinning again, unfazed. Whatever qualities her latest recruit had, she sensed Iggy was not fast.

"Drop your pack," Gaussica added, a bright afterthought that quietened everyone again. He was looking specifically at Iggy, and she gave him an uneasy smile in return.

"Think I need it, mate."

"Not now. When they come. Let go."

Another grim silence.

"You could open a church, man," Ptrangus said. "The wisdom from this one."

"Aye, fuck this," Hark grunted. "We'll deal with them the same as anyone. Aim for the head, shoot fast."

The soldiers started turning away, accepting his bravado with nods and murmurs of false confidence, but Wish kept staring, increasingly disliking Gaussica's unpredictable thoughts the more he spoke. It was easier when he was quietly foreboding, instead of voicing ill fortunes.

Macmiddan approached the path, alongside Hark, indicating it was time they go. He nodded to Wish, no fear there at least, as Iggy shuffled up alongside him. She was hit with sudden, unexpected grief. She trusted and relied on this man, perhaps more than any of her soldiers, and he was taking her newest hopeful recruit into hell. She wanted nothing more than to order them to stay, to continue with them. She only managed an apologetic smile.

12

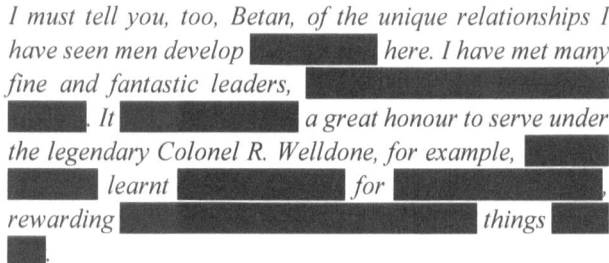

I must tell you, too, Betan, of the unique relationships I have seen men develop ▮▮▮▮▮ *here. I have met many fine and fantastic leaders,* ▮▮▮▮▮▮▮▮▮▮ ▮▮▮▮. *It* ▮▮▮▮▮▮▮ *a great honour to serve under the legendary Colonel R. Welldone, for example,* ▮▮▮▮ ▮▮▮▮ *learnt* ▮▮▮▮▮▮ *for* ▮▮▮▮▮▮▮▮, *rewarding* ▮▮▮▮▮▮▮▮▮▮▮ *things* ▮▮ ▮▮.

**Extract from the Letters of
Corporal T. Sander, Balnia, 720**

"Yes, that's it!"

Pitt tensed, losing control. Had to keep it up. Had to *relax*. He held his eyes open, watching the shimmer of his shield spread over the fish barn. Almost there. A growing audience of soldiers were pausing from drills and shifting supplies to watch. He doubted they could see it, not the way he did, but they knew something was happening from Terrifold's uncommon excitement, standing next to him. Just a little further, even if his skin was tingling like it might start peeling back. Brain throbbing.

He pushed the pain aside, the thoughts out, and breathed, as Terrifold had told him.

Deep breath in. Long breath out. And push . . .

"Excellent, you've got it!" Terrifold exclaimed, too sharply, and Pitt winced, barely able to hold it. But he did. He watched, not believing his own eyes, as the shield shimmered over the building. "You there, take a shot at that door!"

"Sir?" Droll replied and the mage barked, "Shoot the door, *now!*"

Pitt twisted away as he saw the lieutenant drawing a firearm.

Hadn't planned for this. Still clinging to the power, he started, "Hold on –"

But the pistol fired, its crack echoing through the town, and the audience gasped as he felt its impact, the blow hitting him almost as hard as a shove. Pitt staggered to stay upright, and snapped his gaze back to the barn as the bullet clinked against the cobbles. It had bent against the shield, bounced back, *stopped* in the air. Pitt's mouth fell open, but as he realised *he had stopped that bullet*, the shield popped. He gagged as the air rushed into him with a hard chill, and almost fell to his knees. Terrifold's hands were suddenly on him, the mage holding him up by the shoulders, patting him companionably.

"That's it, there it is, yes," he said into his ear. "Drink that in. Know it, embrace it. Get used to it. Well done."

"I couldn't, though . . ." Pitt strained to speak. *Couldn't hold the shield longer. Couldn't spread it further.* The crowd were commenting in wonder as Droll retrieved the spent bullet. There was scattered applause.

"Not *yet*," Terrifold said. "But you're closer than you think. Good work, my man. This calls for a celebration. Something special. I have just the thing in my quarters."

Pitt struggled to contain the feeling of overwhelm that the shield left, unsure of the mage's hands still on him, rubbing warmly. Then, through the onlookers, who were starting to return to their business as usual, he saw Chiara, a way off, watching with her father. Rotus looked determined to be unimpressed, but Chiara caught Pitt's eye and subtly raised her hands to give a slender, private clap. He relaxed, the tension easing out of him. Terrifold's hands softened too, rubbing more gently.

"Yes, there it is," the mage soothed. "You have it."

"Necostrian ice wine," Terrifold announced as he poured the syrupy blue liquid into a pair of crystal glasses. They were sitting together on the leather sofa in his luxurious apartment, where Terrifold had produced the bottle from a frost-box with a light fog. Pitt watched with an awkward smile; he was impressed by the wine's gentle glimmer, but was sure it would be wasted on him. Terrifold held one glass out and lifted the other. "To the Empire's next great mage."

"Oh, I don't know about –"

Terrifold slapped his arm, taking a big gulp of wine at the same time, and said, "Confidence, Pitt. Believe it and it will be."

Pitt kept his doubts in, to take a sip for himself. He let out an undignified noise and Terrifold laughed. "What is . . . I've never tasted anything like that."

"In a good way, I trust."

"The best way." Pitt nodded quickly, taking another sip, stunned by the complexity of flavour, the silky texture. They had enjoyed a few expensive drinks here in town, but he hadn't known alcohol could taste like *that* – fruity and sweet, but with a peppery bite. "That must cost a fortune."

"It's not cheap, no. If you have to pay for it. I received a case from Prognane Natiller after resolving a spot of trouble in Signess last year. And you should get used to it – your skills will soon be very much in demand from increasingly important people. I see a bright future for you."

Pitt let himself enjoy the wine and the compliment. Things *were* looking up. He'd turned a corner, training with the best, and met an incredible woman way above his station – and the war was sure to end soon. He raised his own glass. "To a bright future for all of us."

They drank deeply, together, and Terrifold let out an appreciative exhale. He looked into his glass and murmured, "This was always Tomask's favourite. He'd have been proud of you."

Pitt's brow folded. The first he'd heard that name, but an immediate understanding came with it. Though he often asked Pitt personal questions, Terrifold rarely spoke about his own life, or much that wasn't related to magic-wielding or the war. He carried a maudlin tiredness and in that look, those few words, Pitt understood he'd lost someone special to him. Not only that, but mentoring Pitt somehow lightened that burden. He asked, "Was he your apprentice?"

Terrifold gave him a sharply confused look, then coughed a forced laugh, shaking his head. "No. Just a good man taken before his time. A long time ago. I'm sure he smiles on us, yet. Will you have another?"

It wasn't really a question, as the mage began refilling their glasses, and Pitt tried to enjoy it. Terrifold circled his glass in the air as he made promises for what would come next: a matter of days to spread that shield across the town, he was sure. Commissions to divisions elsewhere along the front, if there was a need, then most likely a contract with one of the great houses of the Arrow – that was the best path forward. There would be trouble enough after this war ended that a defence mage would remain in high demand, especially with the lords and ladies of the Drail Empire scrambling for their piece of the Comity's ruins. With the other countries vanquished, they'd be nipping at each other again, and there was little more lucrative for a parser than providing shield-work to an estate in the Drail's most exclusive reaches. With a little more experience, and a lot more clout, they could then establish Pitt in the Arrow itself, as a consultant or aide to some very important government official, from which position he could accrue private interests: business investments, property. Terrifold had a road map in mind for an entire life that Pitt might play out, and the more wine he sipped the faster it came. Often framed as *we;* the mage saw himself actively involved in all this.

Pitt started picturing himself a year, two, ten years down the road. Brushing shoulders with the Empire's greatest. Going where he wanted, wearing what he wanted. Hell, it wouldn't be long before he'd be more than worthy of a woman like Chiara. Of Chiara herself, even – there was wealth in his future, a family, power . . . But as his mind drifted over these things and they drank more wine he became increasingly aware of Terrifold's eyes not leaving his, the mage sitting close to him on the sofa, legs touching, just as his had touched Chiara's that night in her apartment. Then Terrifold's hand was on top of his, in his lap, and he was asking, "This is what you want, isn't it?"

Drawn back into the moment, Pitt wasn't sure exactly what the question referred to – his future, their partnership or this instant, right now. An older man gently touching him with quiet, mournful longing. Pitt didn't dare remove his hand for a moment, but as he stared at Terrifold's resting on his he felt something pulse between them. A connective energy, a spark as strange and special as that first sip of the ice wine. It arrested his instinct to recoil as he tried to understand it – was this something only mages could do? – so Terrifold withdrew first, his aged face creasing with concern.

"Forgive an old man," he murmured. "I get carried away."

"No, that's . . . It's fine," Pitt hurriedly replied. "I do want it – everything you're saying, you've no idea how much I appreciate it. I'll do everything I can to take advantage of these opportunities you're offering me. I won't let you down."

Terrifold had gone quiet, though. He went to take another sip of wine, but the glass was empty, and his eyes narrowed in thought. Mood rapidly shifting. Was it something Pitt had said? Something he felt, in touching him? Or had all this reminded Terrifold too much of an old protege, or friend – something he didn't want to recall?

Pitt scrambled to fill the silence. "Dalton, I –"

"Don't mind me," Terrifold said, with a weak smile. "Wine's gone to my head, I suppose. And at this time of day, what am I thinking? You . . . you should take a break. You have earned it. Perhaps go for a walk, clear your mind of the town and people."

Pitt hesitated. Was this a dismissal?

"Yes." Terrifold straightened out his coat. "Yes – you've been straining here, in constant company, penned in by the buildings and the people and, I dare say, myself. Take some time outside Sober Sound, alone, and you'll find your mind can reset. The area is quite wonderful."

Pitt nodded uncertainly. "As you wish."

Terrifold smiled more broadly, settling on his decision, but still looked a long way from happy. He patted Pitt's arm again, standing. Pitt stood too and went to leave, pausing only for an overly officious handshake from the mage.

"Good work today. Very good."

"Thank you, sir."

That "sir" seemed to hit Terrifold like a blow, but he smiled again, gesturing to the door. Pitt left, slowly walking down the corridor, unsure what had just happened, but knowing he had messed up. He'd disappointed the man. And if he'd felt a charge of energy at that touch, something mildly electrifying, then Terrifold must have felt something too. Only, with a better skill at interpreting it.

Never mind, Pitt told himself. A walk sounded good.

Though he'd much rather it be in Chiara's company.

13

*The **Stranded** or **Strayed** (sometimes nevolk) are a species not of the Rocc; named as that which is trapped on a world where they do not belong. There is nothing natural about the biology of these violent alien nomads, who roam without roots, and for centuries their origins have eluded the brightest scholars of earth and sky.*

Encyclopaedia Bestialis (vol. 16), **Hawn, p. 456**

While almost every race bar the dominant humanity shares some feeling of Otherness, it was the nevolk who unsettled early writers enough to be accused of alien origins. The irony in this deliberate and systematic Othering is that archaeological finds consistently point to nevolk tools as the earliest in Boldarow; in all likelihood their ancient civilisation was erased precisely because they were an existing obstacle to burgeoning human tribes.

Over the centuries, however, it is hard to say to what degree their lasting reputation was manipulated to encourage persecution or a result of how terribly they resisted it.

***Shifting Perceptions of the Myriad Creatures*, Ukele, p. 13**

Both wanting a distraction from having sent three scouts to face terrific danger, and to convince herself there were practical ways to get through this situation, Wish called for Unders as she led the scouts on. "What else do you know about the Stranded's hunting patterns? How likely are they to double back?"

"I – uh – it's not exactly a science. But they don't often come this far east now. Less than before."

"And they scream like that the whole time?" Latebite asked, walking behind them. "How does it not drive them all mad?"

"They *are* mad," Ptrangus said. "That's the point."

"That, actually –" Unders twisted back, trying to catch their eyes. "That's a really interesting point. It's like a song to them, I think. Or a chant. There's an order to it that I don't think we can quite understand. They're not all chanting all the time, as the sound moves through the group in a wave, at different pitches. It's rather clever; they create a great deal of sound from surprisingly few people."

"The Blood Call," Gaussica said, almost inaudibly, from the flank. All eyes to him.

"If you had more to share," Ptrangus growled, "the time was before our people left."

"It's what they call it," Gaussica explained, without apology. "The chant of the Stranded – the song of the nevolk. The Blood Call is a technique practised from childhood to draw their communities together. They sing for hours every day, hunting or not."

"One of many reasons they're not welcome down the pub, I guess," Latebite suggested, half seriously, but Ohno answered that:

"They never wanted to join civilised society. Most of their interaction with people has been in reaction to us, by which I mean *you*, trying to drive them away."

"It's true," Gaussica agreed. "You – humans – have a perception both created and distorted by your own influence on it."

"Bully for the ghost over here," Ptrangus said, "A fine philosopher who doesn't consider himself human."

"I don't count," Gaussica said. "I don't exist as you do."

"Bly's bones," Ptrangus huffed. "How long have you been out of the cavern? Has no one actually told you you're not *dead* yet, you deranged beanpole?"

Gaussica gave him an uneasy look and Wish readied herself to intervene – but Unders blurted out to interrupt: "They don't belong here!" He winced in surprise at himself, before going on quietly, "This woodland has been free of the myriad for decades. Maybe centuries. The wildlife is cultivated for guests to hunt or enjoy nature. It's famously *peaceful."*

"Peaceful," Ohno echoed with a disagreeable rumble. "For humans. Excluding anything different to you, that's a certain kind of peace."

"I didn't mean – it's not *my* forest, I just live here –"

"You lived here?" Wish exclaimed, making him flinch again.

He nodded. "Yes, in Haven. We're going – I mean – that's my home?"

"You joined the army and they sent you five miles down the road to watch the trees?" Ptrangus laughed, and Unders' face fell, the poor man aware of his privilege, now stolen away.

"Would've saved us all some bother if you'd established defences north of the woods instead of south," Bluefern's lieutenant came in, the first contribution from one of the strangers in the group. He was a leathery man with thin strands of hair hanging out of his helmet around his ears, skin blotchy and uneven. He spoke with a kindly, north Stanish accent, more thoughtful than upset, in welcome contrast to the sergeant they'd sent into the woods.

"We didn't have the means," Unders muttered. "Most of the men of fighting age served and died on the fields of Comlas." That got some regretful murmurs: the name of the great Lome plain separating southern Boldarow from the Valley of the Drail, where the Lomian military had been annihilated – a location synonymous with death since the start of the war. "By the time the Drail reached us here, there wasn't any hope of resisting them, with the Comity refusing to take the woods. And the mayor of Sober Sound, he negotiated with both sides – he worked hard to preserve this territory. To avoid fighting."

"Then how the hell did he let them bring the Stranded in?" Corporal Dalliance demanded hotly. He hadn't taken Iggy's departure well.

"Probably *because* the woods are usually empty," Ohno suggested. "The Drail wanted somewhere to put them out of the way. I expect Mr Mayor was very well compensated."

"And meanwhile your village was tossed out of their homes, told to spin," Ptrangus said.

Unders hung his head.

"Ah not to worry, we'll pop in while we're there, pick up your things. You can give us a tour."

"Alright, Ptrangus," Wish sighed, sparing the young man.

"Captain Wild," Bluefern's lieutenant said. "If I may, since we're talking. I'd like to offer my apologies for Sergeant Hark. We are *not* unwelcoming in the Vulgar Division. Our ranks include ringers and trunks."

"It's in the past," Wish replied before Ptrangus could make an obvious comment – none of his welcoming men had stood up to Hark at the time. "But I appreciate that and hope your sergeant will be reprimanded when this is done. Thank you, Lieutenant . . ." She failed to recall his name.

"Jonus, sir. And, not to diminish Hark's responsibility, but we're all on edge after the news we've heard the past few weeks. Hearing those creatures, together with that . . ."

"The news being the rebellions in the east?" Wish said carefully, trying not to let too much interest show. She glanced aside, and, yes, Graveguard wasn't far off, definitely paying attention.

"Indeed," Jonus said. "They say there's a monster army – myriad creatures uniting against Civilisation. And not just other species; it's men, too. Fighting over being different, I suppose."

"Sounds about right," Wish said, recalling Havikare's mad drive for violence in the Saints Mire. As the priory at Drown Deep crumbled above them, Havik had tried to convince her that the chaos would be fun. She'd said they could do whatever they wanted under the banner of war. Was that the goal, then, to wage war on humanity itself? If such a force really was amassing, never mind if it was a thousand miles distant, she could see why coming close to the Stranded was especially troubling.

"Can I ask, Captain . . . did you know her?"

Wish paused; there was more to Jonus's concern than distant rumours. She had an urge to remind him she was his superior officer, and maybe he shouldn't be asking anything, but he was awfully polite and looked ten years or more older than her. He reminded her of Mr Rumnass, who cheerily packed their groceries in the Swelig store. She said, "Unless I'm mistaken, the rumours have this goblin army near the Mattin Mountains. I've never been further east than the Blessed Sea."

It didn't sound convincing to herself – especially as she realised that referencing the Most Blessed Sea was too big a hint towards understanding the Saints Mire region itself. She expected Ptrangus or Latebite to make a joke, but the Rawboys' faces were stone, serious when they needed to be.

Jonus considered his men following them, also listening. He said, "I doubt anyone's held onto the pamphlets, but these goblins have somehow been printing propaganda. Sharing unbelievable stories, frankly. Things about the Saints Mire and old powers, bizarre legends. But one of the claims they like to make is that the Stanish military are sending women soldiers over the front line. That seemed outlandishly specific, but . . ."

"I turned up," Wish said, thoughts whirling through her mind. Havik and her goons were writing about her? Printing *leaflets?* Straining to keep calm, she told Jonus, "We're not in league with or even especially aware of this goblin army, if that's what you're worried about. Either they've heard rumours themselves or made a very lucky guess. Me and my girls, all of us, are here to secure peace for Stanclif, that's all."

"Of course," Jonus said, nodding as though it was what he expected. She suspected he knew it wasn't that simple, but he added, "My apologies again, if my men have shown any doubt. We're honoured to serve with you."

Dalliance made an unconvinced scoff and she threw him a sharp look. He stared back, unrepentant. He'd been thoroughly obedient since joining her platoon, always eager to please (at least, when he wasn't reeling from the horrors they had faced), despite a slight cockiness. She held his gaze and he held his obstinate look. She tensed, fearing she was going to have to say something regrettable, commanding. But at last he averted his eyes. "Apologies, Captain, sir. I just would've liked to keep an eye on Iggy. It's fucking –" He took a breath. "Apologies *again,* Captain. But she only just joined us and I can't imagine what we've sent her to do."

"Uh-huh," Wish said. It wasn't enough; from his sullen slump, this was going to be a big distraction. To draw him out of his head, she said, "She saved your life?"

"More than that." Dalliance sighed. "We were in hell, at Passerlee."

He was quiet as they walked a few paces more, reflecting on the memory. Choosing whether or not to go on. No one interrupted.

"It was the Palicier front line," he said. "We were overstretched, and ordered not to withdraw. Command had a hard-on for this position we'd taken and I lost pretty much all my friends over it. Friends from back home, this was. We'd signed up together and when things fell apart I was a mess. Iggy kept me from doing anything stupid and getting killed myself. She also saw a way out for the lot of us – with her charges again. You might think her idea out there's mad, but she knows what she's doing when it comes to blowing things up. She's also a bit too brave for her own good though, I reckon."

Wish found herself warming, again, to their absent new recruit, definitely a Blood Scout by nature, but she noticed some caution in Dalliance's tone. There was more to his story than a heroic retreat. She said, "What else happened?"

Dalliance shook his head. "Nothing much, Captain. We lost the position, is all, and Command weren't happy about it. Iggy's plan worked alright, but she wasn't exactly . . ."

"Careful?" Wish suggested.

Dalliance gave her an unhappy look, but nodded. "I was going to say subtle."

"Really, I didn't get that," Latebite said. "Did you guys notice?"

That got a few laughs, as Dalliance smirked less happily.

"Yeah," he said. "So, Passerlee happened just before I found you at Rock Stable – we were separated in the confusion and, in all honesty, I came to you hoping . . . I thought if Iggy had gone anywhere it might be to the Blood Scouts we'd heard about. She didn't just save me, see – she's the reason I'm here now. If I can still protect anyone in this war, I wanted to look out for her."

"Ah, there's your problem, Dally," Ptrangus called out, as Wish let that revelation sink in. "Saving people's the last thing any of us can promise to do." Dalliance threw him a vicious look, but the Raw Boy went on, "And *besides,* we're the ones most likely to get in trouble out here. She's better off. Macmiddan is gonna watch out for her, and if that bigoted prick acts up *he* won't get executed for hitting a superior officer."

Wish gave Jonus a significant look and the lieutenant took this insubordination impassively. Maybe approvingly. Good.

"That was my thinking, by the way," Quickness cut in, slinking through the group, seeing an opportunity to join in. "I want to say sorry too, Captain – I could've gone. I'm fast, I could –"

"By Bly, what is this, agony hour?" Ptrangus cut in. "Like a bloody Flesh Confessional in here. Maybe we oughta get a song going, before everyone falls to their knees grovelling for Forgiveness of the Body."

Wish smirked, appreciating she didn't have to deflect all this herself, but she was the leader and had to do something more. Quickness genuinely looked worried, the situation weighing on her as much as it was on Dalliance. Maybe rightly so, considering she'd shied away from the possibility of going – there was no room for hesitation in the trouble to come. Yet Wish said, "It's not your place to volunteer, Ness. If I'd thought you should've gone, I would've sent you."

"Yeah, but . . ." Quickness chewed at her lower lip.

"Iggy's going to be fine," Wish told her. "But I'll make sure to put you both in peril next time the opportunity arises." That got some smiles, so good job Wish. And *now,* time for a deflection. To Dalliance, she said, "Just how close are you and Iggy, anyway? I hope you're not using my platoon to impress women into bed."

"What? Iggy?" He laughed, so surprised by the suggestion that Ohno made a warning sound, only a few days in and already protective over the new girl. He raised his hands, backtracking. "She's just a friend. We made a good connection during a bad experience, that's all. And I think she deserves better than me!"

That got a few more laughs, and a deprecating comment or two from Lateguard and Ptrangus, but Graveguard cut in more seriously: "But you've seen first hand she knows what she's doing?" Just when they were starting to relax.

Dalliance nodded. "For sure. She's good with explosives."

"Just not careful? Because it sounds like you're trying to tell us the woman we just trusted to set off some strategic bombs might not do so strategically. Is that what you're saying?"

That killed whatever mood had been returning, though Dalliance was smiling sheepishly. "Well. Yeah."

Wish took in a big breath as Graveguard levelled her a questioning look. Not sure how this would backfire, except that it would be her fault. There had been far too much rushing into things without planning ahead, hadn't there? She shook it off, though. "It doesn't matter. Macmiddan will keep her in check, he's got enough experience for the lot of us."

"That's reassuring, boss," Latebite said. "You know he's the man they think responsible for destroying the Dorae Poll Tower?"

That got a few laughs from Jonus's men, but they were uncertain, and rightly so. Wish was never sure whether the Rawboys were joking or not at the best of the times, but especially whenever they brought up outrageous claims from their rebel pasts. The Dorae Poll Tower bombing was something every Stanish child learnt about in school: a devastating bomb that destroyed a Stanish building on the Raw Coast, long before the war. A horrific example of anti-imperial extremism. Macmiddan *could* have been responsible. She mouthed at Latebite, "Seriously?"

He offered an annoying enigmatic smile that Emi would've been proud of.

"All the more proof he knows what he's doing," Wish said, trying to make it sound like a joke herself. Deflecting again, she asked Unders, "How much further till your damn village?"

14

Ordinary people suddenly had extraordinary means of destruction at their fingertips. For every man who had a gun, another a bomb, and the next a cannon. We think of the fighting in terms of firearms, but forget just how increasingly explosive it all became.

***A Fine & Baffling War,* Flegherty, p. 5**

Macmiddan was sceptical about the Tarrish girl's specific plan from the outset, but the closer they got to the standing stones, the more confident he grew that a few well-placed explosives would gnarl up these woods anyway. The path was densely enclosed, and while he didn't have an intimate understanding of the Stranded, he doubted even the smallest Gonish waders could navigate the thorny vines. A couple of powerful tripwires would take out the nevolk forerunners and give ample warning of where the bastards were coming from, and they'd be funnelled down tight passages, easily covered. He was only surprised the Drail hadn't thought to do something similar already, but he guessed they were expecting to move through this area themselves, so why riddle it with defences. The Comity should've sent scouts in a lot sooner, to make life difficult for them. Then, the same was true of areas everywhere along the front line. You could do a lot with a few imaginative sappers, but such sappers were in short supply.

The company could've been better, though, trailing an unpleasant Stain sergeant who in peacetime Macmiddan might have drowned in a canal. They all kept their mouths shut – the Stains and Iggy, who was itching to talk, always. It took a bit under two hours to reach the Petitioner's Rocks. Seven miles or so, Macmiddan figured; far enough from the road that the others would have time to prepare if anything went wrong. Not too far that they couldn't get back in a rush themselves. And no sign of the Stranded so far. But seeing the rocks brought a fresh dose of doubts: set in a clearing thirty metres wide, penned in by pointy trees, there were about a dozen stones varying from a metre to three metres high, in a rough cluster with one or two fallen at angles to lean against others. Macmiddan cocked his head to one side to take it in, fairly sure they had been deliberately placed, with their slopes resembling a children's play area: a ramp to the top of one, a short jump to another, a little tunnel under three close together.

"I don't see this projecting sound," Macmiddan said, but Iggy was beaming, hands on her hips.

"No, this is perfect," she said, unstrapping a pouch from her belt. She pointed about. "Good distance between these two. And see that angle, aiming west – we'll blow this shit like a trumpet."

The small woman ducked into the shadows of the rocks, starting to place explosives and unravel wire without waiting for help or orders. The rest of the group stared. She seemed to know what she was doing. Macmiddan threw a look to Grebe, the only person he halfway wanted to confide in, and found the recruit looking worried. He was barely out of school, like so many of them, but had a thick, square forehead and heavy brow that gave him a seriousness beyond his years. He spoke in an unfortunately high voice, calling out, "Do you need a hand?"

Iggy laughed. "Got it under control! Gimme five minutes!"

Bluefern's men spread out, watching the trees, rifles at the ready. Sergeant Hark came closer to Macmiddan as Iggy flitted between the rocks, unrolling a length of cable she'd had strapped to her. "She better know what she's doing."

"Or what?" Macmiddan said. He had a few inches on the Stain, and a lot more muscle, and Hark seemed to recognise that, retreating slightly but keeping his sneer.

"Or we all die, don't we? Crazy fucking flog. But I guess you should know, eh?"

Macmiddan didn't react. He'd met a thousand Harks. Faced down a million insults. He knew how to keep his emotions flat. That always tended to rile them more than responding.

Sure enough, Hark scowled with rising irritation. "What's a bunch of bloody Rawboys doing in the Stanish military anyway? Thought you hated our guts."

"We do. But the Drail are worse. Stains, we could handle alone."

Macmiddan watched Iggy scrambling up a rock with the wire trailing from her teeth, an explosive package of some sort in one hand. She twisted awkwardly around to secure it on the underside of the next slanted rock, Saints knew how. As he frowned at this positioning of a bomb near the tip of the rock, he grew certain she leaned more towards mad than genius.

"What'd you just say?" Hark said.

"Come again?"

"What the fuck did you just call us?"

"Oh brother." Macmiddan turned square to him, making it clear how much wider his shoulders were. He noticed Grebe nervously watching them, finger on his rifle. "Can you wait until we get this done?"

"Let you say whatever the fuck you want in the meantime?" Hark hissed, drawing his men closer. "Bluefern might turn a blind eye, and Command clearly have their heads up their arses, but *we* see what's going on. Fucking ringers and Rawboys, *women* with stripes. It's a bad joke."

"Oughta do it!" Iggy announced cheerily, hopping off a rock to land a few feet away with a flourish. No one looked, all eyes on Macmiddan and Hark, and she let out a long, "Oooh. Not sure this is the best time for measuring dicks, guys."

"Watch your damn Tarrish mouth," Hark snapped. "You are talking to a superior officer and you will address me as *sir.*"

"Sorry, sir, didn't mean to hurt your feelings," Iggy replied, raising her hands innocently. Hark's face reddened. Yeah, Macmiddan knew this man: a petty tyrant who'd never fit in at home. Never had respect so tried for power instead. He was itching to take it out on someone.

"This man talk for all you?" Macmiddan asked, glancing around the half dozen other soldiers. A couple of them appeared tough enough, but they all looked as uncertain as Grebe.

"Don't address them," Hark barked. "This is *my* operation. And –"

"And you wanna keep your voice down," Macmiddan said. "Considering where we are."

"Are you trying to give me orders?"

"Fuck it, go on then." Macmiddan spread his arms. "You want a fight, first blow's free. Make it count. And make it quick. We need to go."

He kept his arms out, motionless, and red-faced Hark looked him up and down, almost trembling with rage. Looking foolish. He clenched a fist, considering it, readying himself.

"Cocky fucking Rawboy," Hark snarled. To his men, he said, "If he tries anything –"

Macmiddan punched him in the gut. The idiot crumpled with a wheeze, the air knocked out of him, and knelt gasping as Macmiddan scanned the other soldiers.

"Anyone else think we got time to waste?" he asked.

They had their rifles but zero confidence, to a man. Not the best advance team, but not blindly loyal to their sergeant either.

"Alright." He held a hand out to Hark. "Done?"

Hark looked into his face with wretched hate. This was a moment where a man could recognise his failings, take the hand and move on. Swallow the humility and grow. He chose the other option, slapping the hand away and spitting into the ground. Hark struggled unsteadily up, almost falling over and snapping at a soldier who moved to help him. He glared furiously at Macmiddan but didn't make another move. He'd probably try and stab him in the back later.

"All good?" Macmiddan asked Iggy, and she nodded, face alight with wonder at his punch. "So how are we doing it?"

"There's a timer good for an hour. But we should probably lay a few surprises on the northern and western paths before committing to that – what do you think?"

A call came through the trees and the group collectively turned towards it.

Bluefern's men shuffled together protectively, guns rattling, as Macmiddan tried to follow the piercing cry to its source. West or north? It was growing, like earlier, into a distant mess of screeches and screams. Hard to believe that was anything civilised.

"Fuck's sake, look what you've done," Hark said, no logic in it, wrestling to ready his rifle but tangling the strap in his haste. "Set the timer – we'll go back the way we came."

"That'll draw the bastards after us," Macmiddan warned.

"If they're not already coming! Wait to find out and we're screwed." Hark paused as the sounds drew closer. It only got harder to tell where they were coming from. Whooping, sinister, malevolent. Pounding feet – a mounted approach. "Second thoughts, we need a trigger. Can't risk them disarming this."

Macmiddan considered the three paths out of the clearing. West or north, if not back the way they'd come . . . which was most likely to bring the Stranded? Either way, objectionable as the man was, Hark had a point. He asked Iggy, "How much cable have you got?"

"As much as you need," she said, lifting a considerable spool.

"We retreat, run it back after us," Hark said. "We've got more wire – can piggy-back a switch as far as possible before setting it off." It wasn't a question, but he did offer a deferring look to Macmiddan. The screams were getting too close to risk anything else.

"Okay, okay," Iggy said, racing back to the rocks and attaching her wire and a trigger box. She squeaked as a particularly fierce shriek split the trees – then she tied things off and skipped back to Macmiddan, unravelling wire away from the rocks. She paused. "I should check all the connections, make sure it's –"

"No time. Go, the lot of you – I have the rear," Macmiddan said, grabbing the trigger box from her hands, the cable from the other. "Run."

"But –"

"Move!" Hark all but shouted and Macmiddan cringed. Hard to tell if the Stranded's mad warbling answered his call, but it sounded like there was a shift. The men ran, back along the tight path they'd come by, tripping over roots and making frightened sounds as their guns hit branches and the hunters got closer. Macmiddan rushed behind them, unravelling the cable from the trigger box, careful to lay it out but barely slowing. Grebe jogged at his side, throwing looks behind them with his rifle up to defend the rear. Absolutely terrified.

"Push on lad," Macmiddan said. "Keep the –"

There was a gunshot ahead and the soldiers started shouting. Macmiddan froze, unable to see far up the winding path, only the shapes of the nearest couple of men scrambling. More gunfire and the sounds of branches snapping, a creature's snarl.

"Contact!" Hark roared, all hope of stealth gone. "Open fire!"

The hunters' screams were still far away – they should've had more time. Macmiddan spun back towards the sound.

A shape was blocking the path, twenty metres away, almost black in the shadow of the trees, angular, unreal. A barely humanoid rider on a fearsome dog, hunched as it paused from stalking closer. They'd approached silently. Surrounded them.

He should've known. As he locked onto the horrific silhouette ahead, the sounds of battle escalated. The soldiers were screaming. Iggy shrieked and Grebe shouted in panic. More gunshots, animal snarls. Hark's yell was cut off with a brutal squelch.

Should've known better. The very basics of light-feet tactics. A big noise was great for distracting your enemy.

The Stranded rider before him shuddered with intention, readying to pounce as Macmiddan stared it down with only the trigger box in hand, his gun on his back. Only one trick available. As the bandit dog sprang forward, kicking through the dirt, he flipped the trigger, and the explosion tore the woodland apart.

15

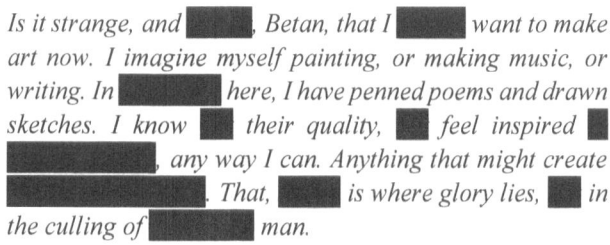

Is it strange, and ▓▓▓, *Betan, that I* ▓▓▓ *want to make art now. I imagine myself painting, or making music, or writing. In* ▓▓▓▓ *here, I have penned poems and drawn sketches. I know* ▓ *their quality,* ▓ *feel inspired* ▓ ▓▓▓▓▓▓, *any way I can. Anything that might create* ▓▓▓▓▓▓▓▓. *That,* ▓▓▓ *is where glory lies,* ▓ *in the culling of* ▓▓▓▓ *man.*

Extract from the Letters of
Corporal T. Sander, Balnia, 719

On his return trip to Haven, Pitt was greeted with the same deferential salutes and politeness from the guards, but with heightened nerves, Sergeant Kether clearly feared he would bring more unpleasant orders. He told them not to worry, they were just here for a walk this time, enjoying the fresh air, and the man slumped with relief.

Chiara had already continued towards the clock tower, and he tried not to watch. He'd wondered the whole way here if he'd see a shift in her again, and tried to make his peace with it. Let her go, see what happens. To Kether, he asked, "Was it bad? Meeting with the Stranded?"

"Ha!" Kether responded brightly. "I expect it would be. We didn't meet them directly – I left orders on the mile-marker back at the main road. I haven't heard them come this way since, so it may be they've not even seen it yet, or maybe it's duly noted. I had an earful from Captain Brender though, sir – apparently some confusion in the orders."

"Ah. Yes, things are so busy in town not everything is being clearly communicated. He, uh, didn't rescind the orders?"

Kether gave him a lingering look, surely aware by now Pitt had acted on his own (or rather Chiara's) initiative. He let the pretence lie there between them, though, and said, "No, sir. I expect he appreciated the confusion of the situation himself."

And if the captain was anything like these men stationed here, he would be secretly happy the Stranded were pushed away, whatever he had to say to maintain an appearance of command.

"Okay. Well, that should be the last of it."

The soldier nodded hopefully. It would be the last orders they got from him, anyway, after Terrifold's scolding, even if this had worked out. No, he was just here to enjoy the break, as instructed. But he saw Chiara hadn't gone into the tower alone as before, and was waiting by the door, expectantly. He gave her an uncertain look and she beckoned with a hand.

"Are you coming or not?"

With a farewell to Kethers, Pitt rushed around the barricades to join her, inwardly cursing himself for so quickly jumping at her command but with a little thrill that this wouldn't be like last time.

She opened the door and led him into a cluttered office space, and on to a set of steep stairs. As they climbed she said, "He's a little particular, our Erol, but I think you'll like him."

"I'm sure I will," Pitt said.

He shouldn't be here, technically, he knew – hiking out of town with a girl, getting to meet her family, was the opposite of the nature-fuelled meditation Terrifold had in mind. But it was worth it for the view of Chiara climbing the stairs alone.

They reached the top, Pitt somehow more out of breath than her, and she twisted back, catching him looking at the last moment. He smiled sheepishly, and was rewarded with her sly smirk. As she went into the tower's loft, did she maybe swing her hips a little more deliberately, just for him? That stole what little breath he had left. But a distraction came from the space they entered: the room was a world apart from the administrative office below, with every inch of the tight space covered by painted canvas panels, stacked against each other, hanging from beams, alive with vibrant landscapes. Pitt stared open-mouthed as he took it in – there were common themes of trees and lakes, cloudy skies, evoking the

Harmonial area, but all rendered in unnatural colours. Lively, with dashes of vivid pink or bright orange, highlights in white and yellow. As if the artist was revealing an energy only he could see.

"Pitt," Chiara said, gently. "This is my brother, Erol. Erol, this is Pitt – remember I told you about him?"

Pitt saw they weren't alone in this incredible gallery. In a corner of easels and scattered painting equipment hunched a man in a robe-like smock, stained all over like a butcher. He was big, blocky, and would have appeared fearsome in the half-light, if not for the paintings and Chiara's smiling presence. He glowered darkly and spoke Lomish in a deep rumble.

"That's right," Chiara replied. "Now come on, you can manage Drail for our guest."

"Welcome," Erol huffed, sitting up straighter, appearing even bigger. His paintbrush appeared tiny in his large mitt. "Thank you. It has been easier without the noise."

"My pleasure," Pitt said. "Wouldn't want our troops disrupting this work. It's wonderful." He nodded to a bright green image of a wall of trees wound with red vines, birds overhead.

"Yes," Erol agreed. "Would you like tea?" His low voice fit his ogreish appearance but he spoke Drail well. More eloquently than Pitt.

"I'd love some."

They settled on stools while Erol delicately produced a set of paint-splattered mugs and warmed the tea over a small fireplace. Pitt watched him with wonder, such a big man but so graceful. He didn't say much, nor look at Pitt, but made agreeable noises as Chiara explained that his work was in growing demand, and had been hung in cities as far apart as Tyne, Pace and Voralla. There were plans for an exhibition in Farne's Sunset City, at one of Boldarow's most exclusive galleries, but Chiara's mood got a little darker as she added that the war had got in the way. That gallery might not exist anymore, with Sunset City potentially in ruins.

"But we keep on, don't we?" she said, patting Erol's leg, and the big man nodded. "By the time the war's done, he'll have quite the collection to tour. And without Sober Sound's usual tourist trade, the war's given Erol a lot more time to himself. Away from our father . . ."

Pitt didn't have to ask to know that Rotus didn't approve of this. Most likely, Erol was destined for a place in the family businesses of real estate and hospitality, to which he plainly wasn't suited.

"So there's one benefit to the fighting, at least." Chiara smiled sadly. It was the most raw emotion Pitt had seen from her yet: vulnerable, dearly caring for her brother.

"And friends," Erol murmured. "Brought friends, too."

"Yes, that's right." Chiara looked at Pitt. He smiled, but she explained, "Erol gets on well with the soldiers. They join him for tea up here, playing cards and keeping a lookout. They're that much simpler, and kinder, than the sorts of friends Father tries to impose on us."

"Fun," Erol said. "They enjoy life."

Pitt found himself warming in Chiara's gaze, aware that she might knowingly think the same of him. He said, "So how else do you enjoy life up here, other than through painting?"

Erol met his eye properly for the first time, with the same slyness as Chaira. Quiet and gentle as he seemed, he was not slow, Pitt sensed. Erol said, "Have you tried Lomian rock vodka?"

It was getting dark as they staggered up the path to Sober Sound, and Pitt slurred his words as he spoke. He did not care that he was bumping into Chiara, nor that he had lost so many hands of cards to Erol and the soldiers who had joined them in the loft. There was too much laughter and lightness. He didn't know what he was saying to Chiara on their return walk, but she was laughing. Possibly something to do with the contrasts between Lomian rock vodka and Necostrian ice wine, and the happy coincidence of him encountering two such drinks in one day. That was a recurring point for him, as Chiara responded drily, "You might have mentioned it."

She was careful to hush him as they got within hearing distance of the town, a finger on his lips, whispering they needed to part ways. It was too risky to continue together, when they were both likely to draw attention. He protested, but agreed, and they kissed. It might have lasted an hour, he wasn't sure, but it wasn't long enough. She broke away, breathing heavily, and promised, "Tomorrow. *Tomorrow.*"

Then she was gone and Pitt was focusing hard on keeping himself upright, winding through the little alleys to the inn. Or should he go to the town hall, get some food? His merriment could continue there, accepted, *normal.* All of this, he realised, a welcome distraction from the magic, and the perhaps too-close attentions of Terrifold, which he quite resolutely was not wanting to unpack. He turned towards the hall, realising that he needed to relieve himself, too. But as he stepped through the dark, a hand up to support himself against a building, he was hit hard from the side.

His thought he'd caught his ankle, tripped, but as his shoulder smacked the wall, he was pulled forcibly around and struck again, in his chest, pinned as cold metal touched his neck. Pressed in. He looked into the narrow eyes of a man with only his crinkled brow visible, cloth covering his mouth and the rest of his head. Pitt went stiff, mind slow – had this man caught him as he tripped?

"Hear me, mage," the man said, roughly, and gave him a shake, knocking his head into the wall. That brought the reality into sharp focus, and Pitt's pulse spiked. He tried to resist at last, but his attacker pressed the knife in harder. Knife! Pitt felt it nick his throat. "Stay still, you don't want to get gutted."

"I'm still," Pitt insisted. "What do you want, money –"

"Want you to stay away. Your filthy Drail hands don't belong on our girls." Another harsh shake, banging Pitt's head again. "Definitely don't belong on *that* girl. Go near her again and I'll fucking skin you, understand? Nod."

Pitt nodded, throat tense against the knife.

"We don't *want* you here, Drail," the man spat. "Plenty of us waiting for an excuse . . ." His eyes twitched, rapidly, like he was considering gutting Pitt anyway. He stepped back, releasing the knife. "You understand. You stay safe."

Pitt nodded again, and the man turned to stride into the shadows.

His heavy footfalls continued rapidly away, and Pitt trembled with the will to chase after him. Use his power, call for help, run to Terrifold. He was a mage of the Drail army, destined for great things. He was from the mean streets of Arrow – he'd been in a few scrapes. But by the time the thoughts had swept through him, the man was long gone and he realised he was too exhausted, afraid, and ashamed. He wouldn't dare explain what had happened to the soldiers, let alone to Terrifold. Shaking, he stepped away from the wall, all hint of inebriation gone.

Just needed to get home.

16

In the blink of an eye
The world ends
With the flash of a gun
All that could have been
Is done.

"Goodbye Markon", *The Collected*
***War Poems,* Trekallen, 723**

For an abandoned village in the middle of a monster-patrolled front-line woods, Haven was surprisingly intact. It wasn't untouched by war, with a scattering of barbed wire, sandbags and miscellaneous crates, as well as a broken wagon painted Drail green and at least one burnt-out building that Wish could see, but past those details it could as easily have been a few miles behind the line than on it. There was a cluster of low stone huts with only one slightly larger central building and a clock tower. The windows had glass in them and only a couple of buildings had been boarded up. The rest looked like they were patiently waiting for this rabble to move on through.

The soldiers, however, were set to stay. They had a cosy camp in the centre, where there was a bit of space below the clock tower – a three-sided barricade with a fire burning in a barrel and a machine-gun mounted at the front. A sheet hung on a metal frame to keep out the rain, with some hints of foliage for camouflage, bless them. Yet they clearly weren't expecting company, as they sat chatting over hot drinks, not watching the road. Three men. Another was ambling between the buildings, stretching his legs and inattentive – bored, from the way he hung his head.

Wish had a reasonable vantage point at the curve of the road, lying prone by a tree, vines twisting overhead, rifle propped on a branch and scope powerful enough to pick out the spots on one young man's nose. She could hit them without the scope from here.

A gentle scuffling of leaves behind her announced Quickness's arrival, whispering as she hunkered down, "Dalliance says total six soldiers visible from his side of the road. No way round, unless we wanna spend half the day hacking through thorns."

Wish glanced sideways. Couldn't see her fellow marksman from this angle, but she suspected he'd got the better spot.

"Two in that building closest to us here," Quickness explained, guessing who she couldn't see. The squat stone cottage with a thatched roof marked the entrance to the village, about thirty metres ahead, barely big enough for a latrine, with no windows on this side. "Latebite reckons there'll be at least two more watching the other side of town."

"There's windows in the clock tower," Wish said. "They'd be mad not to have at least one person up there."

"Think they could've seen us already?"

"Could've," Wish said, though she'd taken every precaution, slowing to a crawl as soon as Unders announced they were getting close. When the tip of that tower came into view, she'd kept an eye on it every step closer. "They didn't, though. No one raised an alarm."

"So how do we do it, boss?"

Wish checked the village again, the little portion she could see. There was plenty of cover amongst the buildings. She said, "We've got maybe two hours of daylight left. Major Bluefern might catch up in that time, so we'd better handle this before then. Still, the lower the light the better. Tell everyone to wait for my lead. We'll keep watching, be sure we've learnt all we can."

A thump like thunder split the air, as if the sky disagreed with her plan, and Wish frowned as it echoed lightly through the trees. To the east of the village, a flock of birds took flight squawking angrily, and two of the guards at the central barricade stood, looking in the direction of the sound. Quickness swore.

"Guess that was Iggy," Wish murmured, unhappy with both the timing and the result: that explosion plainly did not sound very far west. A green-coat burst out of the closest hut, looking worriedly at his friends at the barricade, then out to the forest. "Shit."

The man shouted in Drail, likely *what was that?* His friends called back, equally concerned, and started a short argument: one of them was probably blaming the Stranded while the other two thought it was something they needed to check out.

"Boss," Quickness muttered. The nearest man was turning towards them. "What should we do?"

"Hold on," Wish said. "If they send word to Sober Sound, we're done."

The arguing got more heated, and the soldier in the road shouted something offensive. Behind the machine gun, Wish saw another man turn heel to jog the other way. Past the clock tower, towards the north road – to Sober Sound and potential reinforcements.

"Fuck. We need to take them out. Can't let anyone go – everyone to follow my lead."

"You mean –"

The jogging soldier was about to turn a corner, a second from slipping from sight, when Wish's survival instinct took over. She pulled the trigger and he jerked through the air, down, then she aimed to the left, where the nearest man was a big target ducking in the road. She fired again, square in the chest, throwing him into the wall. The blasts of her rifle sent Quickness scurrying, relaying her orders in yelps, as the two soldiers behind the barricade ducked. Dalliance's rifle fired from across the road and the glass of the nearest hut shattered, a man inside screaming. It was a bad sign: he wasn't dead. Another shot from Dalliance, and another, tearing into the stonework. He had the man pinned, but couldn't hit him.

Wild Wish rose to a crouching run, charging the hut, and made the distance just as she saw movement behind the barricade, another soldier bolting. She slid into the cover of the wall and leant out, sighting the machine gun through her scope. No one there yet – the men might've fled. But she kept her scope on the position.

Dalliance stopped firing and she heard the man in the hut whimpering in Drail, praying: Wish knew the words even in his language, having heard them often enough: *"Saints save me."*

Rapid footsteps brought company. She recognised Quickness's

light breath as she slid in behind her, along with two men. Wish calmed her own breathing as she instructed, "We need to get through to the other side, catch anyone leaving."

The man in the hut shouted to his companions. Someone replied from between the buildings. Then another shout, at least two men trying to coordinate.

"Someone roll a grenade in," Wish suggested, and Latebite replied, "On it."

She didn't take her eye from the machine gun as he moved past and tossed his grenade. The soldier shrieked and dashed to get out, footsteps hitting the dirt just before the bomb exploded. It blew out what was left of the window and a few chunks of stone, but was contained. The soldier cursed in fear, having escaped, but a gunshot from Latebite silenced him.

Another soldier screamed a long, accusing word that was probably his dead friend's name, then a hand finally shot up to grab the machine gun, squeezing the trigger blind. The weapon opened up in a barrage of heavy fire, bullets shredding through branches and hitting walls. The shots spread wide, tearing into the sky, as the man raked the weapon back and forth, screaming. Wish glimpsed more movement in her periphery, another man running under the barrage's cover, but she had to leave him. Another moment . . .

At last, the shooter's head poked up to aim, and she fired, ripping his head back and ending the salvo. There was a moment's stillness before the remaining soldiers started yelling in panic and Wish ordered, "Advance! No one gets out alive!"

She sprinted from the hut into the cover of the next nearest building, followed closely by her troops. There were shouts down the road, a few gunshots aimed at the clock tower or into the road to warn off anyone waiting. Wish raced on, confident with her cover – the little paths between buildings left limited visibility for anyone further out. She leant around a corner and saw a distant green-coat disappearing behind a cottage. No chance to hit him. She ran on, towards a roofless house with the walls half broken, mossy and in disrepair rather than damaged. She slid down to shelter in what little wall there was, and Quickness pressed in just behind her.

As they stopped, gunfire blasted from high above, and a brick next to them erupted. More rifle shots followed, peppering their position and making Wish and Quickness flinch.

"Shooter in the tower!" Wish shouted, as another gun joined in, two rifles in the tower, covering both directions. And more – rifle fire from ground level. She gritted her teeth, glancing ahead. It was a couple of metres in the open to the next building and better cover, or a couple of metres to retreat. From the sounds of the gunfire from both sides, no one was in a better position to hit the tower.

Shit shit shit. The Drail didn't need a good sniper to cover the whole village from up there. She looked back to her support: Latebite and, surprisingly, Gaussica, both crouched at the next building ready to follow, with Lieutenant Jonus and a few of his men in tow.

"We're pinned down!" Wish shouted. "Has anyone got a shot on this fucking guy?"

"Want me to shake them out?" Emi offered loudly, unseen.

"Absolutely not! We can't let Sober Sound know we're here!"

"Might be a bit late for that," Latebite said, and Wish shot him a fierce look. It wasn't, she told herself. The gunfire wouldn't travel that far; they might've heard Iggy's blast, but without confirmation from here there was a chance they wouldn't appreciate the threat.

"I can get up there," Gaussica said, barely raising his calm voice.

Wish scowled, disbelieving, at his blank expression. "Not sure we can get closer than this," she said, as the rifle fire continued erratically. She held his gaze and found it coldly certain; he was waiting for an order, that was all. He *was* supposed to be capable of great things. Well, screw it – she nodded. He did not retreat to find another route, as she expected. He ran past her, without waiting for a break in the gunfire.

Latebite cursed with surprise and Quickness gasped as the Azirian passed with a nearly casual gait, bullets slamming into the walls around him. The Drail were shouting again, equally startled by his movement, panicked by their failure to hit him. He cleared the opening, pressed his back against the wall of the next building, and took a breath. From his still-blank expression, it was just a pause for air, not to settle any nerves. He pushed off and continued, jogging around the corner. A barrage of rifle fire erupted at ground level, in his direction, then stopped. No more movement or shouts. Had they got him?

"Did he even have a gun?" Latebite asked incredulously, and Wish realised she hadn't seen one. He was either a brilliant maniac or already dead.

"We can fall back, Captain," Jonus called out as the gunmen in the tower resumed their random shots. "Take cover and keep them busy until Bluefern arrives. We've got plenty of ordinance that can take down a tower."

"Not quickly or quietly enough," Wish replied. "We don't have *time!*"

"I'll go," Quickness volunteered, with a sharp breath. Wish spun to lock eyes with her, to tell her no, but the woman was already up, inspired by Gaussica's example. She was the fastest they had, after all.

Quickness ran past before Wish could complain or pull her back, a leaping step taking her into the opening. Immediately, a rifle fired above and she was thrown to the side, gun flying as she hit the ground. Wish shouted, rising to follow her, but a strong hand caught her shoulder.

"Hold, boss!" Latebite shouted in her ear, as the shooter fired on their position again, stone shattering where Wish's head had been an instant before. She tried to squirm free, eyes fixed on Quickness as the woman lay on her back, mouth gasping. Her chest was torn open, blood pooling. "Angry won't make you bulletproof!"

Wish shook Latebite's hand off and twisted to him baring her teeth, but his frightened eyes stilled her. He must've made a dash himself to stop her, now crouching where Ness had been.

Wish looked to her soldier lying on the ground again. Her friend. Dying.

The gunfire continued and she couldn't move. Could only stare as Quickness's head rolled her way. Eyes wide as they found Wish's, lips moving in a silent question. Why? How? *No.* Wish shuddered as a voice came back to her: Loose, beautiful Loose, the moment before she was thrown from a cliff. *No.* A scream. Fixit's terrible scream as she was cut down by a grekkel. Newk, down and bloody, just like this. Wish hunched down, tensing all over, and it was all she could do to keep hold of her gun and not explode.

Then the gunfire cut off with another horrible scream, a man's, descending, with a cascade of shattering glass. Wish rose unthinkingly to look as Latebite warned her *stop.* His grip was weak this time, though, as he looked too.

A big, heavy shape hit the barricade at the base of the clock tower, breaking over it with a squelch. Wish glanced up to the top window, smashed and empty. There were only a couple of scattered Drail voices left now, shouting as they ran, followed by rifle shots not far behind.

"He got them," Jonus announced, running around the corner, towards the village centre. He raised his voice. "It's clear! Secure the road ahead!"

Wish glanced from him and her platoon racing out of cover to the final retreating soldiers, down to Quickness, unmoving. Eyes glass. She yelled, "Medic! Medic over here!" Men's voices echoed hers, spreading the word as she ran to Quickness, knelt by her. She took her hand, fully limp. She held her other hand just off the open wound, startled by how wide the hole was, how thick with blood. To put pressure on it could cave in her chest.

Heavy footsteps brought Graveguard next to her and he shoved her aside, swearing as he tore at his medical packs. He took Ness in, similarly pausing in shock.

"Ah fuck," he said gruffly as Wish stared at Quickness's face, like a broken doll's, already pale. Wish felt her pulse peaking, her face hot, and she squeezed her rifle tighter. She turned towards the centre of the village, her men and Jonus's spreading out through it, and strode towards the crumpled heap on the barricades.

Wish shouldered Jonus out of the way as he stepped into her path to speak. She stomped around the barricades, past the bodies of two men missing parts of their heads, and up to the fallen body. He was a heap of dark rags, a monstrously big man broken into unnatural angles. Wish lifted her rifle, the barrel an inch from his forehead, eyes locked on his as they stared up. She clenched her teeth, making sure he saw her, this bastard, this animal who'd taken her friend. But what was left of his bloody face stared back with a horror that equalled Quickness's own. The same big eyes and mouth open in pleading. The same fear.

The same emptiness of death.

17

*Much is recorded about the rise of the battle mages with
near-mythical impacts on the war, while similarly effective
elites are often ignored or erroneously consigned to that
same "magic" group. General Potexous, in particular,
championed unconventional fighting units who explicitly
did not rely on magic, including Ardent Daggermen,
Weagalian Sky Spears and, most feared of all, Lock Cavern
Ghosts.*

Dueley's Comprehensive: The One War in
10 Volumes (Vol. 4), p. 139

"Well what the fuck is all this?" Wish demanded, striding into the
clock tower loft and receiving a strange look from Gaussica. There
were paintings everywhere of landscapes with fantastical colours,
decorated by swathes of blood. The furniture was scattered and
broken, and a green-coat lay half-shredded on the floor, as if he'd
been killed by a grekkel. He was even more dead than the man
broken on the barricades, not a trace of Drail left for revenge.

"They put up a fight," Gaussica said flatly. "I'm not normally so . . .
imprecise."

Wish eyed him, recalling the chaotic violence of the troll house
and the bloody state he'd come out in then. Not unlike his
appearance now. The ruined heap of bones on the barricades might
also disagree. Then again, the soldier she'd found outside the tower
door had been cut down with a single cut to his neck.

She looked out of the window, north. Lots of trees, and a
glimmer, the distant suggestion of water. The lake. No other
buildings beyond the village, with the road eaten by branches only
a short distance off. However far off Sober Sound was, there was
no line of sight between them.

"We've taken the village?" Gaussica asked, wiping his hands on a rag.

"Yes. And . . ." She waited, still watching out the window as a man ran back into the village. Dalliance? He drew up to Ohno and the ogre pointed up. Wish waved. He raised a hand, thumbs up. They'd got whoever had fled. As far as they were aware. She said, quietly, "We should be safe. Except for Quickness. She died, following you."

Gaussica placed down his bloody rag. "I'm sorry. I did not intend for anyone to follow me."

"No," Wish replied. *No, you're not sorry. No, that's not enough. No, just no . . .* Was it his fault? Bitingly, she spoke without knowing where the words came from: "Do you *see* more now? Are you close, here? Is the barrier between life and death thin enough for you?"

Gaussica considered the questions seriously, not reacting to her tone, studying the mess. "For a moment, there was something. But there was no choice involved. Only, that which –"

"Save it," Wish huffed, no interest in more distracting bullshit. "It's done, it doesn't matter." She took in the butchery again and let out a big sigh. *Just another image that I will have for the rest of my life.* The worst of it was that he'd obviously not needed help. Quickness's sacrifice was meaningless. Not expecting an answer, she said, "Why did they get her and not you."

"Because they were expecting you," he said, simple as that. He offered no more, and she understood. He wasn't in uniform, just a strange civilian with archaic weapons and too casual an attitude to make sense. If she'd seen him jogging about on a battlefield, she might've hesitated to shoot too.

"Well shit," Wish said. "If there's nothing useful up here, come down. I'm going to address the platoon."

She left and he came down the stairs behind her, saying nothing more. She wanted to twist back and cut his ankles open. To toss him down the steps. She knew it wasn't rational, but dammit. He'd cost her a friend. He'd cost her any chance of justice for Quickness's killers. However much he'd hurt them himself.

Wish exited the tower, into the fading light of the village centre, to find most of the platoon were already gathered. Emi was with Graveguard, arms folded and looking upset, the pair standing vigil over Quickness's body, covered by a sheet. There was a mix of sombre looks and a few slightly elated, coming down from the adrenaline of winning the day and struggling to hide it. Wish supposed that was the real reason Quickness was dead. She'd got caught up in it, thought she was invincible . . . wanted to make up for disappointing Wish about not volunteering earlier? By Bly, let it not be that.

"We'll bury her before we go on," Wish said quietly. "I don't think she was a part of any particular church." There were some murmurs of agreement. She was too young to care about such things. Younger even than Wish. Not even old enough to sign up? How *had* she got here? So much Wish didn't know, and never would. "That's the last of the Drail, right?"

"Yeah," Dalliance said. "Caught one runner. No sign of another."

"No sign of reinforcements," Ptrangus added, "but we've got a couple boys keeping watch."

Wish scanned the crowd, not sure who he meant, seeing as everyone seemed to be there. Jonus's men, she supposed. Good; she needed all her people here. Clasping her hands together, she said, "Right. So. From now on, I want to be extremely clear on something. No one else is allowed to die. This is an order. Absolutely non-negotiable. No one else dies under my command."

There were a couple of uncertain smiles, taking this as a dark joke, which disappeared when she held her serious expression. Then they were looking to each other, everyone waiting for someone else to say something. Emi muttered, "Well, that's what I've always been doing," The mage shook her head as if in disappointment at the others, but she was alone in her ability to make light, so went quiet again.

"I've had enough of it, alright?" Wish said, doing a good job of keeping perfectly calm. It was, after all, a reasonable request. "So, there we are. No one else is *allowed* to die." That sounded less reasonable, a touch aggressive.

The uncomfortable silence stretched out, before Ptrangus managed a response, much more hesitant than usual. "But . . . we're gonna."

"What?"

"We're gonna die. You can't stop that. It's war. That's just –"

"I wasn't asking for opinions," Wish said. "I've said what I said. Are we clear?"

She eyed them firmly, her men and Jonus's alike, and no one else spoke. Graveguard looked more severe and concerned than the others, definitely had something to say, but he held it in for now.

"Alright, no one dies," Ptrangus said, finally, and a few others murmured agreement.

She then turned to Gaussica in particular. "Understood?"

"No one here," he said, an easy answer for once. But he frowned and twisted quickly to look up, to the clock tower, or beyond it. He then spotted Emi and pointed. "This. Doesn't *this* remind you of the ball?"

Emi's eyes were huge as she stared back, and for a moment Wish thought she might finally snap, attack the Azirian – but a soldier interrupted, running up the road from the south, shouting, "Captain Wild! Captain! Word from the rear. We've got two of yours. Badly injured."

The first thing Macmiddan was aware of, coming to, was a crackling. A lively popping that he realised was fire. Lots of it. Then there was the pain, his chest flaring. He winced and made it worse, couldn't move as it clamped him in place. It radiated out, with stabbing agonies up and down his body. A harsh throb in his temple.

Then came the smell – smoke, thick and harsh. He coughed, triggering a new wave of pain. His eyes shot open, and stung. He coughed again, more carefully, and blinked to clear his eyes. The firelight danced brightly above. It cast flickering shadows, his body cross-sectioned with black branches that looked like they'd impaled him. But only one had gone through. One gnarled stick, protruding from his chest. He rolled his head back and braced himself, then tried to shift and couldn't. His legs were caught in thorns, his torso spread on a bed of them.

"Saints dammit." He threw his head about, checking the area. Couldn't make out the path. But he saw movement. A dark shape. Human. "Here! Over here!"

The man beyond the trees froze like a deer ready to run.

"I'm stuck!"

The man checked over a shoulder, considering fleeing, before scanning ahead and seeing Macmiddan. He started thwacking his way through the thorns, a short blade in hand.

"Sergeant Macmiddan, sir!" Grebe's voice. "You're alive!"

"Barely. Got a fucking tree stuck through my shoulder. Anyone else left?"

"No, sir, just me," Grebe said, pulling closer with little winces as he snagged thorns. A tree cracked from the spreading fire, making the young man double his pace. He paused on arrival, to consider Macmiddan's tangle, no doubt asking the same *how the hell did you get here* before tugging at the branches to free him. More pain exploded in Macmiddan's chest. "Sorry, sir! Sorry." Grebe paused, hands on a branch, voice wavering. His eyes were watering, not just from the smoke. "I'm so sorry. I . . . I ran."

"Good on you," Macmiddan growled. "Means you can help me out."

"But . . . I couldn't do it. When the fighting started –"

"If you stayed, you'd be dead," Macmiddan cut in, no time for this pity. "And you'd be no use to anyone. Got any vodka, whisky? You need to pull me off this tree."

"Yes, sir, I think so," Grebe said, patting at his pouches. "How did you . . ."

"Iggy set a hell of a bomb. Threw me halfway back to Rae. How did *you* get away?"

"Um. In the trees. I crawled in. I'm . . ." Grebe slowed down. He was cut all over too, Macmiddan saw, his uniform torn and his face bloody. He cleared his throat. "They got Iggy."

"Figures," Macmiddan sighed. The poor young lass. "We didn't stand a chance –"

"I mean they took her," Grebe said. "She was alive. They reacted weirdly when they saw her. Like she smelt different. They dragged her away. I couldn't do anything. But. We need to go after her?"

Macmiddan almost laughed. "Only get ourselves killed. We need to get back to the others." He shifted again with a shout, as Grebe tugged at another branch and a thorn dug in. "Fuck." He checked their surroundings again, wary of how loud they were being. "The Stranded. They left?"

"Yes, sir. There weren't many of them. I think the explosion drove them off. And maybe the smoke?"

"Yeah. There's nought alive's not scared of fire. Now where's that damn whisky?"

Wish's blood turned to ice at Grebe and Macmiddan's account of their disaster in the woods. She had just ordered everyone not to die and they give her this fucking mess. They had entered Haven in a flood of soldiers, the company having caught up since the fighting, though their big guns were lagging behind. Bluefern's medic had done a quick job of patching up Macmiddan's wounds, enough to get him to the village, but Graveguard was attending to him more thoroughly. Wish stared at his chest with dread, a bloody mirror to Quickness's wound. But Graveguard insisted he'd be okay. Yes, the man had been impaled on a spike, but it had gone through his shoulder, missing anything vital. Besides, Macmiddan was too stubborn to die.

They gathered in a cottage on the periphery of Haven, as many people as could fit inside while Graveguard stitched Macmiddan up on a table: Major Bluefern and his permanent aides, Pillson and Crash, along with Gaussica, Jonus and Emi with more soldiers behind, spilling out the door, all listening for their tale of surviving the Stranded. When someone asked how Grebe got away, Macmiddan boomed through pained huffs that the boy had dived after him and got tangled too, shielding them both from the fleeing Stranded.

Bluefern said, "Tell me exactly what it was like. You've no idea how rare accounts of fighting the Stranded are."

"It was horrible," Grebe answered as if that was a profound, all-encompassing insight.

"Details, lad, from what they looked like to how they fought."

Grebe was plainly reluctant to relive it, but he met Wish's eye and she gave him an encouraging nod. That rallied him somehow, and he said, "Well. They were on dogs, as you thought. But not like any dogs I've seen. Big as hunting hounds, maybe wolves, long and dark, with jaws like a grekkel. Skinny, but powerful. They came at us quickly – we saw them far ahead and the next second they were on us. A couple of them –" The words caught in his throat. "The dogs did for some of the men straight away. Ripped their . . . throats out. We started shooting – someone got a dog, and another a Stranded, blew him apart." He searched for Gaussica in the audience. "They do break, like you said. Shattered like dry wood. But that might've been the only one we hit. They're thin, and not tall. Shorter than a mattick, I think? No thicker than your arm, I'd say, sir."

"Go on," Bluefern instructed. "What'd they look like?"

"Roughly human-shaped," Grebe said. "I mean, they're not unlike the pictures – that Sinister character in the papers, you know?"

"Simister," Graveguard corrected, through his focus on Macmiddan's stitching.

"Right. But they don't have goofy flat teeth or glasses. They're sharp, man. Sharp all over. Claws, narrow eyes, jagged heads. They moved so fast, made horrible noises. And they used spears, knives, stabbing at us. Some had old rifles, like muskets, and I heard a couple of shots, but they weren't using them. I saw Sergeant Hark, sir, I'm sorry . . . He knocked one off its dog, but another came at him. Put a –" Grebe gestured loosely at his neck, not finishing the explanation. He finished, barely audible, "Almost took his head off."

That *almost* somehow made it worse.

"And they took Iggy," Wish confirmed. "They didn't kill her?"

"Yeah. I don't know why."

"We have to go after them. We'll get her back."

"Out of the question," Bluefern said and she almost leapt across the room to punch him. The table with a wounded soldier was in the way, and Graveguard offered her a very serious warning look.

"Respectfully, sir, that's one of mine captured by the worst creatures the enemy has at their disposal. I already lost one soldier today." And at least Quickness hadn't suffered. Who knew what the Stranded might do?

"Equally respectfully," Bluefern rumbled back, "we're not jeopardising this mission for one soldier. We've no idea how much time we have, but chances are they heard that blast in Sober Sound, if not the fighting here, and they will send someone out here when they don't get a report."

"That's fine – it's better if only a few of us go anyway."

"You're not hearing me, Captain. The request is denied." Bluefern held her gaze, hinting at that first forceful anger she'd heard approaching his tent. She struggled to hold in her protest. Or just an insult. In her silence, his expression softened, and he said, "We can have this finished within a day, *if* we keep our heads. First, we need to make sure no one's coming to catch us on the road – and that this place is fully secure. We want daylight to survey the town properly, but we're out of time today, so, assuming we're not already busted, you'll get eyes on Sober Sound at dawn while we get into position. Once we're satisfied observing, we fire the barrage by lunchtime and pull back. Then you're free to chase down the Stranded."

"If we're waiting until morning there's time tonight for me to –"

"Denied, Captain," Bluefern said, that warning tone returning. With a breath, he said, "I am not risking you or any more of our troops on a distraction until the main job's done."

"But the Stranded know we're here now," she countered. "Iggy aside, we *have* to deal with them."

"Perhaps," Bluefern said, "but the message I'm hearing, though we have some regrettable losses, is that the Stranded uncovered our soldiers' position and have *not* pursued us. In fact, it seems they fully retreated after the skirmish. I expect the fire helped. Now we control Haven, we can defend ourselves from the Stranded for a day – if they come back. And maybe we can revisit the idea of having your mage seal off the paths."

"Maybe they got enough to keep themselves amused for the time being," Crash said, and this time Wish did surge forward, shouting, "You miserable shit, that's my soldier –"

She hit the wall of Graveguard, who easily bounced her back, a lot bigger than her, and the medic shouted louder than her, "Trying to fucking work here!" A bloody hand print on her chest reminded everyone he was still stitching Macmiddan.

Crash sneered, "I mean generally, woman. They're out hooting up a storm, running mad – probably don't give a shit about this war. And if we've set the woods on fire, well . . ."

"Woman?" Wish said, and he made an exasperated sound. Hadn't they already had enough of this bullshit from Sergeant Hark? But the logic of what he'd said settled between them. It was hopeful for the mission, but not for Iggy.

"About that," Macmiddan said, through a pained grimace. "Something you need to know. The Stranded can move quietly. These ones got around us. That war chant is no guarantee."

And there was the discomfort again. The very thing Wish had worried about herself and never got round to revisiting. Things were going wrong because they'd trusted claims made by people who didn't know better. Iggy with her crazy plan, Quickness recklessly making a run for it, Unders assuring them he knew how things worked out here. The major bringing his damn animals. But Wish wasn't much better – she hadn't acted on these instincts, and those she *was* acting on were dangerous. She wanted to hunt the Stranded? She would've run out after Quickness. She steadied herself, tried to slow down. She was better than this. She said, "Alright. We'll take a moment. Secure the mission before anything else."

"Glad you agree," Bluefern said, then, to the room in general,

"Pass the word on – at the moment, the Stranded are a secondary concern. You won't want to hear this, Captain, but this has, so far, been a successful day. We gained a strategic location and cost them, what, a dozen men? And we've disrupted the Stranded, despite our own losses."

"Yeah. Can't say I do want to hear it, thanks."

"My point being," Bluefern continued, testily, "this is no time to feel sorry for ourselves. Take the rest you've earned, and tomorrow we get this damn well done. Understood?"

Wish held his gaze, indignant but resisting fighting back. He was, after all, in charge.

18

*Around the third or fourth month of it, we stopped caring.
Stopped worrying about burials or pyres, though the fire
boys pestered us like gnats to keep the flames high. They
only cared about the sickness. We'd all seen too much by
then to fuss over our dead friends. Their troubles were
over. Ours kept coming.*
   ***All This Aflame: Memoirs of a Soldier**, Lindon, p. 67*

Into the evening, while the small village of Haven filled with
upwards of two hundred men, the area remained quiet and tense.
Sentries were rushed into the clock tower and sent up and down the
main roads to watch for reprisals, while everyone else readied
defences. After the initial activity, what remained for most was to
sit and wait and hope the enemy did not come. It was a busy and
tightly packed operation, but with the minimum of noise, like when
she'd first reached their camp. For soldiers not typically given to
missions of stealth, Bluefern had produced a surprisingly effective
company.

   Between setting up defences, the men cleared the Drail bodies
out of the village, tossing them aside, while Ohno and Lugger dug
a grave for Quickness. Wish watched, staring into the hole in the
dirt that would forever hold her potential friend. It had been a long
time since she'd seen a burial. Almost everyone she'd seen die
recently had been burnt or abandoned. Many of them in pieces.
They could do better for Quickness. Even if it was just a group of
eight people who barely knew her watching Ohno lower her
shrouded body into the ground. They were absent Graveguard,
Macmiddan, Grebe and Iggy. And Emi and Gaussica weren't
paying attention, distanced from the group as usual, but this time,
worryingly, *together.* Emi was whispering at him with squinted

accusation. If they caused trouble at this wake, Wish would kill them both. But she tried to ignore it, for Quickness's sake.

They shared Latebite's latest pilfered bottle of whisky, and Wish offered the best eulogy she could. "She was a good girl. She deserved better. But I guess she's at peace now."

It was cold and simple, and Wish found she was too tired to feel any more emotion. It wouldn't help anyway, she supposed, to be sad.

"Get some food, a hot drink," she went on, "and turn in. You all deserve a break."

They offered thanks and good nights and filtered away with companionable pats and nods. She headed towards a cottage that had been reserved for her, trying to go unnoticed through the crowded village as men watched her pass. Emi appeared alongside her and said, "You know, Bluefern gave you permission to send me out there."

"To block the paths?" Wish said, wearily.

"I could do more than that."

Always wary that the slightest wrong word could have severe consequences with Emi, Wish said nothing. The mage's eyebrows were raised suggestively, like she'd love a chance at taking on the Stranded. She was powerful and might even succeed. Wish said, "Is that what you were talking to Gaussica about? You two finally bonding over monster hunting?"

Emi replied scathingly, *"Bonding?* Yuck. No."

Wish frowned, recalling their last exchange. "He touched a nerve talking about that ball, right? What was that?"

The mage's eyes momentarily startled, the same way they had when Gaussica first hit her with his cryptic comments. She said, "Sigh. Since we're basically best friends, I suppose I can share. You might not believe it, but there were one or two times in my life that *I* made mistakes. It was nothing much really. A school dance, before I knew better."

"So why did he mention it?"

"Oh, a few people died."

Nothing much really. Emi said it so blithely, with her leer, but her eyes looked glassily ahead, towards the memory. She must've lost friends then, too. Wish wondered if she should offer some comfort, but the mage went on.

"Kind of my fault. The other kids were egging me on, I tried to make a table dance, it got out of hand and there were candles, lanterns smashing, bla bla." Emi rolled a hand. "The hall caught fire, bits of it collapsed, you know how it goes."

"I'm sorry. But what's that got to do with anything out here? Or with Gaussica?"

Emi's eyebrow arched wickedly. "There *were* similarities and he tuned in to that. In a way that's not natural. It's not even exactly what he said but how . . . Look, I don't need to approve of him to wonder a little about what the hell they do in the Lock Gate Cavern."

"Seems to me his mind's all over the place."

"Yeah but *which* places?" Emi asked. "I'll see what I can find out. Though I would still rip open his mage-killing rib cage." She was doing a bad job of hiding her reduced aggression. She was always so blunt, Wish imagined she had little practice with lying, and was tempted to press exactly what she thought of Gaussica, but she was tired and as long as they weren't going to kill each other, that was all that mattered. Besides, Emi went on, *"Anyway.* In the meantime, how about I get to work with these nevolk already?"

"I'm not sending you after the Stranded, Emi. Last time we went off half-cocked, you almost got killed. I don't like it, but Major Bluefern's right. We stick to the plan and worry about Iggy afterwards."

"Go back for her later, you mean? Like the others?"

That stung Wish into taking a step away, brow folding. Emi's expression was serious, tone flat. Accusing? Was she actually upset by today's loss? Emi had always done her own thing, without evident care for the rest of the Blood Scouts, beyond dramatic expressions of violence mid-fight. Wish had never considered her especially connected to anyone they'd lost. She asked, "Do you think there's more we could've done? That I could've done? Before now?"

Emi scrunched up her mouth. "Maybe. Maybe not, I don't know. But experience is starting to suggest when we delay certain things they never get done."

"We *will* do something, Emi, I promise. For Iggy and the others. A day, that's all. We need a day to take care of Sober Sound, then we'll get her back. We'll get everyone back."

Emi read her eyes, and a twinkle returned to her own. Her froggy grin stretched wide. "Everyone?"

"Yes."

"And these woods? You see how worried everyone is about the damn Stranded? I don't need to come further, when I could be, you know . . ."

"No, leave it for now. We might need those paths. And if there's any chance of avoiding a fight, we need to take it."

Emi considered this, then nodded, for once accepting orders without comment. "Sleep well, then." Then she twirled away with a flourish of her coat.

"Wait. Emi."

The mage leered over a shoulder.

"About Gaussica . . ."

"I'm not going to hurt him, Wild. Yet." Emi winked, and Wish accepted that was about as much as she'd get. She smiled by way of dismissal.

Wish continued into her home for the night and gave a huge, private sigh. The single-room cottage had stone walls and an actual bed, which she sat on and hung her head between her legs. A light patter of rain started on the thatched roof and she listened as it grew. It quickly became a downpour. Thank Bly they had got Quickness in the ground already. And that she had a room indoors for once, not a tent, or worse. She hadn't slept properly for days. Maybe months, maybe a year. No, that wasn't fair. She'd slept well in Rock Stable, before the Mire. After that, she had a bed in the priories. In Midpeak, where she'd woken in the night to speak with Havikare.

Before she realised what the woman was capable of.

Yet the thought of her face brought Wish comfort now, even knowing what she'd done. What she might still be doing. Havik's touch. Her smile. Their kiss. Wrong, brief and coming only after Havikare had punched and kicked her, thrown her down some stairs. Their lips had touched by the Well of All Remains, before Havik blew that damned horn and raised a demon horde of giant crabs. Hurting from more loss, shaken, Wish wanted to be in her arms, to be held by her, however crazy she was. The others weren't enough. They were coming and going too quickly. Her irreverent Rawboys, her ogre, her young men and even younger women, all ready to follow her and die. For nothing.

There was a knock at the door and Wish smeared a sleeve across her face, wiping away tears. Before she could respond, the door opened and Graveguard entered, followed by Ohno, both dripping from the rain. Ohno had to stoop low to fit in the small space, hair in dark strands down her face, so imposing Wish almost didn't see Scraper slip in behind them. Wish frowned as the slighter woman slunk into a shady corner, wondering if the other two realised she'd followed.

"A moment, boss?" Graveguard said.

Wish drew her eyes from Scraper to the blood all over her medic's wet uniform. With a pulse of her heart, she said, "What is it? Is Macmiddan okay?"

"He's fine. Relatively. Fine as anyone impaled by a tree is likely to be. Admittedly, though it, er, might be the end for him. Militarily. Lucky sod should get to go home."

Wish's pang of worry shifted, then. Great that he would live, but she was still going to lose him? She'd been coming to rely on Macmiddan, someone who actually had experience steering a ship like this.

"The rest of us aren't going anywhere," Graveguard added, apparently reading her worry. "Between me and the lads, we can muster a fraction of Macmiddan's wits to keep us afloat."

Wish tried to smile, unsuccessfully. "Thank you. But . . ." She looked up at Ohno. "What do you need, then?"

"Wanted to check on you," Ohno said. "To make sure you're alright."

"I just saw you a few minutes ago," Wish said. "Why wouldn't

I be –" She stopped, noticing Graveguard glance at her rifle bag, leaning against a wall. "What? You think I'm going to go off on a rampage?"

"Wouldn't be the first time," he said.

"I said I wouldn't. I've just told Emi to keep cool. We'll get Iggy when the time's right."

"Even if it might be too late by then?" The medic stared, hard, and she stared back.

"Why would you say that?"

"Because it's the truth and you know it. And much as we all took a liking to the young lass, we'd rather you didn't die on her account."

"Why would I *die?*" Wish almost laughed, cut short by their combined expressions. There was little more intimidating than a disapproving ogre, but it was possible that the disapproving look from her grizzled medic rivalled it. The dying tinkle of her laugh settled unpleasantly as she appreciated her reaction was telling in itself. It wasn't unthinkable that she might trek out into the woods, and she didn't expect to die doing it, but now they were questioning it . . . She assured them, "I am not going to do anything stupid. Not tonight, anyway. But we will do all we can for Iggy. With or without Bluefern's support."

"Against fifty or more Stranded?" Ohno said.

"We've faced worse. And I'm not scared of the Stranded. You heard what Grebe said: they break up like wood."

The severe looks returned.

"Okay, yes, they're terrifying, but all the more reason to get Iggy back. When we can." Wish looked to Ohno again. "Is that enough, or were you planning to block the door to keep me here?"

"Hold you down, if necessary."

"Yeah?" Wish couldn't help another laugh. "All night?"

"We aren't just here for that," Graveguard said, popping her out of imagining the ogre pinning her down. "We know it's a blow to lose Macmiddan. We need you to understand you still have us. You need to talk, you need to delegate, you need something handled, we're not going anywhere."

Wish resisted the urge to dismiss the offer flippantly. He was talking about them, specifically – these two volunteering as potential lieutenants. Probably not Scraper – *did* he know she was there? It made her heart swell slightly. She thought of Macmiddan, with a hole in his chest, and Captain Brade, and all they'd done together. Sergeant Caracker, the formidable ogre who'd died under her command. Now these two, offering themselves up. Scraper keeping watch. The warmth cooled slightly as she questioned, "Why?"

It was their turns to look uncertain. Ohno said, "Why what?"

"Why this? Why me? I'm a bloody . . . I'm just an idiot from Swelig and you're a great ogre and you" – to Graveguard – "were fighting wars with Macmiddan before I was even born. Why come here, why tell me this, why follow me? You weren't even sure I could keep from running off into the woods."

"Because you might do something like that," Graveguard said readily. "Most of us are here to fight, not make plans or take responsibility. I'm just trying to stitch people up where I can. You, you're ready to lead."

Wish stared silently, not sure if that was true. Who of them wouldn't want to go save one of their own? She had taken on responsibilities merely by accepting them, mostly unwittingly. Captain Tate had told her to take charge when Sarge died; generals had developed ideas of her as a leader she'd never encouraged herself. And it *was* easier on the other side, awaiting orders. Not fretting over whether she'd made the right choices or how she was going to keep anyone alive.

Graveguard and Ohno were now watching her too earnestly, though. She couldn't tell them it wasn't really her. She wasn't anyone special.

"Sorry about where it puts you," Graveguard said, understanding anyway, "but that's how the bones roll. We *are* here to help. We just need you to keep leading."

Wish nodded slightly. "Okay. I mean, like I have a choice? But thank you. And don't worry about me. Dismissed, I guess?"

The medic touched a finger to his forehead, more an

acknowledgement than a salute. "Good night, boss." He passed Ohno, giving her a farewell nod. The door closed and she remained, filling up the room, with Scraper behind her. Wish waited, hoping for something slightly more encouraging from the ogre.

Ohno said, "Do you want some company tonight?"

Wish's eyes bulged. Not expecting that and, absurdly, wondering, would that *work* –

"Just about enough space on the floor," Ohno went on, and Wish flushed with the realisation that it was not a proposition. The ogre glanced back, involving Scraper at last, and the smaller woman nodded. So they did know she was there. "Don't need to talk, but . . . if I got to be an officer, Saints forbid, I'm not sure I'd always enjoy private digs. Maybe that's an ogre thing. When it's lonely, and hard, especially at the worst times, it's good to have your clan nearby."

Wish considered that maybe it was improper, or that she would sleep better, could sob privately, dwell on her dark thoughts, alone. But maybe their presence would distract her enough *not* to dwell. And maybe Ohno needed it, too. Maybe even Scraper did.

"Thank you. I'd like that."

The rain continued into the morning, creating enough chaos that Wish had no time or space to reflect on her stirring emotions. It was mostly just guilt anyway, for sleeping so well, and for waking with the happy realisation she wasn't alone in the stone cottage, letting whole minutes pass before she recalled Quickness being shot.

The good news was that there was no trouble overnight, with the lookouts reporting no patrols from the Stranded or Sober Sound, but the rain turned the road to mud, slowing their progress. Soldiers squelched back and forth, working together to get the artillery moving. Ohno lent her strength to weaving the guns between buildings, hefting their wheels out of muddy ruts. They stowed most of their equipment in the village, freeing up scores of men to manoeuvre the weapons, which Captain Crash organised with

barked commands, but it still took hours in the dark winter morning
to get moving.

It was almost midday when the company reached the clearing
they'd earmarked to set up the guns, which Wish and her team had
scouted ahead to secure. It was a small plateau of grass, on a ridge
that overlooked the lake, alive with the patter of rain below. The
trees blocked off the view in most directions, and it was far enough
around a bend that there was no direct line of sight to Sober Sound
itself, but the map showed they should be in shooting distance of
the town. They just needed Wish and her team to get a closer view
to confirm the location and bearing. And to spot the enemy mage.

Bluefern insisted they wait until he was satisfied the artillery was
in position, particularly after he saw how much use Ohno was, and
when at last the time came, the clouds broke, slightly, and the rain
reduced to a drizzle. It gave Wish a chance to look properly at the
weapons they had been escorting. Their barrels were longer than
she was tall, maybe wide enough to crawl inside, with carriages the
size of market carts, if those carts were panelled with metal and
layered with cogs and levers. They had shields with vertical slits for
the barrels and long braces sticking out the rear, all snugly fit
between two chest-high wheels with studded treads. They were
caked in mud from the journey, but that did little to detract from
their hulking, mechanical nature, painted matte grey all over
without decoration. If they were Wish's guns, she'd give them
ornate flourishes, a touch of colour, floral patterns maybe – or
better, if you could find a talented artist in the company, a landscape
or tableaux of their exploits, like the old tapestries hanging in
museums that told stories of great battles.

Or you could give the barrels teeth or put eyes on the shields.
Anything to hide the fact these great feats of engineering had one
monstrous purpose. Maybe that was the point, though. Was it taboo
to make light of their darkest tools?

"Six months ago," a gravelly voice said, and Wish jerked around
to see the scar-faced misery of Captain Crash approaching, "these
were some of the best guns in the Empire."

Wish tensed, sure that he'd waited to find her alone for a threat or at least some snide commentary that he'd been bottling up.

"This model, I mean – the IA RI-82 Herald," he went on. "We had a hundred or more of them across the army back then. Highest calibre field gun in the world. Things have moved along fast, but these are still army-beating weapons."

"I was thinking they could be brightened up a bit," Wish replied, honestly.

Crash looked unimpressed. He was probably the least likely person to appreciate such a comment. He said, "The men take pride in keeping them clean. You won't find Heralds in any finer condition across the Empire. Especially since our hiatus."

Wish gave him a pinched-mouthed look that she hoped she equally conveyed *I don't care* and *why are you talking to me.* His grim facade didn't shift.

"I'll be coming with you to the lookout," he announced and she huffed.

"I don't need a minder."

"And I don't intend to mind you. We need to be a hundred per cent on our targeting coordinates, which I will be personally relaying to the guns here."

"My girls can mark crosses on maps as well as you, I'm sure."

"It's not a pissing contest. We're doing this right, that's all that matters."

They held each other's gaze, the captain waiting for her to look away, to prove some pathetic prideful point that she was not going to cede. She considered sticking her tongue out, but was more tempted to kick him between the legs.

"I have nothing against you, personally, Captain," Crash said, though, breaking first. He considered the big gun next to them rather than look at her. "I would just rather you weren't here."

Wish stifled a bitter laugh and he shot her another look.

"This is an ugly business. The war. We have far too many men mixed up in it and I consider it a moral failing that we've allowed women to get involved, too."

That stalled Wish. Not exactly the flavour of hostility she expected from him. For lack of anything better, she fell back on a common response, "I can do my bit, as well as anyone."

"Not the point, is it?" Crash's lip partly rose in a grimace, tangled by a mess of menacing scarring. "Before we had these things, I lost a team using an RI-76. The breech cracked, caught three men in an explosion that didn't leave enough to bury. I could feel my own skin dripping off my chin." He indicated the particular scar. "During a *training* exercise. No one should see that, let alone endure it – and you. Look at you. I've got a daughter your age. You shouldn't even have to hear about such things."

Wish was silent. Thrown by how earnest he sounded. As his words sank in, she recalled Reeve Abbey, where flames had licked at Rue. She'd seen her best friend's skin burnt off. She'd left her there. Barely thought of that horror since, because there had been so many others that got in the way. Still she heard Loose cry, *no*, and now saw Quickness thrown aside like a rag doll. Those vacant eyes. She'd seen so much more than Crash might imagine. When at last she spoke, it was a whisper, *"Should* doesn't really matter anymore, does it?"

Crash sighed unhappily. "Doesn't mean I have to like it."

"Fair. But you also don't have to worry about me doing a good job."

"I'm not. You wouldn't choose one of my men to scout for you, so why would I discharge our duty to you?"

Fair as well. She let her eyes rest on the massive guns again. Best, she decided, to move on: "You can really hit a target from seven miles away?"

"Up to seven kilometres," Crash corrected. "With the trail dug in. About two-thirds that without. Each shell will decimate a four-metre circle, completely destroy a house with a direct hit."

"Why even have us on in the field with rifles?" Wish said. "We could all just be sitting behind the lines firing these."

"My sentiments exactly," Crash replied. "Except who's going to defend us when someone like you gets close enough to start shooting the men behind the big guns?"

Wish supposed when you started defending artillerymen with soldiers, and needed more men to attack those soldiers, and more to defend, that was how you got a war . . . She let the thought drop. Rays of sunlight were cutting through the clouds to hit the lake in patches, and the air smelt fresh with life. Never mind these weapons and the task ahead, Wish couldn't help feeling someone was smiling down on them. Was Quickness watching from wherever the dead went? The sunlight and revelation that Crash wasn't a total arse were auspicious signs. Just a little further, and this would be over, and they could get Iggy and return for Relight. Things could still go as planned.

Minus a few people.

All that remained was to check on the Drail's defences, leaving these men and their long-distance guns to destroy the enemy without ever really seeing them. The Stranded weren't coming and the Drail would not mount an attack over that lake. Positives all around, if Wish could ignore her usual niggles. She said, "You really think the Stranded have just ducked out of this fight? That they're not up to something else?"

"The men have been watching since we took Haven," Crash said. "There's been no movement. They're the myriad, stationed in a nowhere post – I doubt they had any loyalty to the Drail to begin with."

"Yeah," Wish said, fearing that was too simple. But hoping this time she was wrong.

19

*Some practitioners insist that a mastery of emotion in
magic means containing your feelings. It is true that you
cannot conjure well under the shadow of heavy emotions.
However, ignoring or avoiding emotion is not the answer.
A true witlacer must fully understand their feelings, and
learn to accept, rather than resist, what comes.*
Essential Witlacing Theory, Kilmack, p. 20

Pitt gave up channelling his energy with a loud curse, sending a pulse
out through the fish barn. The floor and walls shook and men shouted
in surprise below. He stood up, glaring at his hands as if they'd
betrayed him – his fingers were oozing blood around the nails again,
enough that when he flicked his wrists it sprayed the floorboards.

"Everything okay up there, sir?" Droll called from below, and he
snapped back *of course.* Fast movement drew his attention out the
open doors to the road, though, the flapping coat of Terrifold
approaching. Pitt cursed again. He'd had a frustrating morning,
barely able to conjure a shield wide as the loft, and he could do
without another lecture.

Pitt hurried to scrub the blood off his hands with a rag as
Terrifold rattled up the ladder, reassuring the soldiers below. The
moment he pulled himself into the loft, Terrifold lowered his voice
to a harsh whisper, "What's the matter with you, man? You're
scaring people."

"How?" Pitt laughed, raising his hands. "I'm not *doing* anything
– that's the problem."

"You just made an unclean break!" Terrifold warned, stepping
into his space, face as fierce as Pitt had seen it. "You could've
knocked people over. You could've shaken up that very *big* pile of
ammunition."

Pitt froze, coming out of himself to appreciate what he had heard. He'd sent out a vibration when his shield broke. Terrifold had warned him about this – hell, it was witlacing basics. Fear of the cost of magic was drilled into children as early as possible, and especially into those training to use it. Though the truth was often less dramatic than popular belief, he'd seen for himself that a misuse *could* send out a pulse. Pitt held up his hands again, as Terrifold kept glaring at him. His fingers were still streaked with blood.

"I just can't . . ." Pitt said, and it was so pitiful that Terrifold couldn't maintain his anger.

The mage grabbed one of Pitt's hands in both of his, turning it over. "Oh my – by Bly, you've pushed too hard. How many times has this happened?"

Pitt was thrown by the question: should he have been counting? Wasn't this just part of the process? Terrifold rubbed his hands over Pitt's and warmth ran between them. Another little charge, like he'd felt in Terrifold's room. The sting in his fingers started to subside. The mage took his other hand, repeating the process. "You're . . . healing it?"

"I have very rudimentary skills in flesh magic," Terrifold said. "Enough for this. There." He stepped back and Pitt looked at his fingers, red but no longer oozing, or hurting. Terrifold chuckled. "Well, at least now we match."

Pitt saw the mage's own hands were blood-smeared. That was his blood, dirtying the Empire's finest. "Oh, Saints, I'm so sorry –"

"It's nothing." Terrifold waved him off. "But clearly we need to talk. This isn't right, Pitt – I appreciate you are pushing yourself hard but you're better than this. These faults come from too much distraction. What is it, the pressure?"

"No, I . . ." Pitt hesitated, looking away, out to town, because he knew he couldn't give an honest answer. How could he tell Terrifold that he had been attacked? That he was distracted almost in equal parts by the threat in the dark and fear of having to cut things off from an incredible woman. The attacker was no rankled, drunk local, but a serious danger that would not go away. The more he thought about it, the more convinced Pitt was that Chiara's father was behind it – and how could he cross Rotus Axefell without compromising the entire military operation? But at the same time, how could he focus on creating shields when all the hope this power brought him, of a better life, seemed trivial if he couldn't even see Chiara?

"It's this place," Terrifold grumbled, and Pitt met his eye with surprise. There was understanding and a hint of anger. "I should've known better than to keep you in town. We should've done your training elsewhere, before coming here." He moved to the loft's open doors, considering the town centre, more martial than ever with its barricades and crowded roads of men in uniform, the scant Relight decorations barely noticeable. "It's too late now. I suppose you've found a woman. Or a man?" He kept his back turned, clasping his hands behind his waist, so he didn't see Pitt's glower.

"No, sir, I haven't," Pitt said, bitterly, because it was true. She wasn't his. Couldn't be his.

Terrifold looked over his shoulder, distrusting. Did he know? Of course he did. He could probably smell Chiara's perfume from two days earlier. "You're quite sure? You're focused?"

"I am. This is just hard!" Pitt said, sounding like a child.

"Slow down, then. Clear your mind, not just of the task but of whatever has you upset. Remember, Pitt, that this is a stepping stone for you. For us. You will be here only briefly, and the time we have must be used well, if you are to move on to greater things. This town and its baubles must *not* get in your way."

Pitt held his tongue, sure that Terrifold knew exactly what was distracting him. And also sure, in that moment, that the disappointment was more than professional. Was Terrifold being protective or *jealous?* That sent a jolt of different concern through Pitt – that this man, supposed to be a mentor, wanted something more from him that he definitely did not want to give. *A steeping stone for* us? Pitt wanted to tell him to go to hell, with his attentions and attitude. It was the man who'd attacked him, and the loss of Chiara, that was troubling him, not meeting her in the first place. And it was none of his business.

"We do have a war to win," Terrifold reminded him, and Pitt's defiance caved.

He heard his own thoughts. The pettiness of it all, with a war out there.

"I'm sorry," Pitt said. "I'll do better. I won't . . . I won't let anything else distract me."

Terrifold held his gaze a moment longer, making sure he was telling the truth. He patted his arm. "Good man. Now, do you want company? I can provide guidance. Would it help if –"

"No, thank you," Pitt quickly cut in. He definitely didn't need Terrifold breathing over his shoulder. They'd spent little time together since the touch in his room had made things strange, and Pitt preferred to keep a distance now. "I'd like to meditate alone. I'll take it easy. I'll keep myself focused, I promise."

Terrifold hesitated, plainly hoping to stay, but he produced a false smile. He repeated, "Good man. We'll make a master out of you yet."

The rest of the day passed with Pitt first straining against and later actively looking for distractions. When he tried to clear his mind, he thought of Chiara, and when he blocked out the noises from outside, he found every sound niggled at him for more attention. He gave up trying not to think, and moved to the loft edge to watch the soldiers. He realised that a trundling engine had particularly invaded his thoughts, and its source rolled into view.

A tank. The army had sent a tank into Sober Sound, creeping through the amassed soldiers to settle in the square, on show alongside the Relight tree. He'd heard of such vehicles, but suspected few people had seen them – almost everyone in town was vying for a look. It was the size of the trams they had back in Arrow City, but sat lower, wider, and fully encased in metal. There were a couple of slits on the front to see out from, while the only entrance was a hatch on top, thick and round like a furnace door. Left of the hatch was a turret just tall enough to squeeze someone in squatting, with two wide gun barrels sticking out, connected to large boxes by chains of ammunition.

Here was another marvel, as special in its way as being able to enjoy Sober Sound itself. To see Chiara. A reminder of the opportunity at hand, and the privilege of being here. He would be on the front line when the Drail swept into the Comity and knocked them aside. Pitt felt fresh lightness in his breath, exhaling his worries. The war needed his focus, he reminded himself. First would come victory, then the rest – the proof was right there in that tank, a weapon so advanced it would take a mage like himself to damage. And if a mage rode inside it, imagine how powerful it could be. Perhaps he would propose that to Terrifold, for later, when they pressed on into the Comity cities, following the enemy's surrender.

Though it wouldn't hurt if they improved its appearance in the meantime. Why did it have to look so dull and lifeless? A feat of engineering like that, with all its potential, like him, should be celebrated.

Night had fallen by the time Pitt was done for the day.

Some of the shielding had come back to him, the magic growing. He stretched his power out, holding it steady, with enough strength to cover the front of the barn. Focused and relaxed at last.

With his energy waning, he needed to get some food and rest, but was concerned that his night-time walks regularly produced unwanted attention. He watched the quietening streets for any sign of Chiara, or the man who'd threatened him, but saw neither. There were too many soldiers around for the town to fully empty, anyway, so he imagined he could go unnoticed. At last, he mustered the nerve to climb down the ladder, and there at the bottom, sitting on a gun crate, was the woman he intended to avoid.

In the glancing light of a gas lantern, Chiara had a devilish tint as she pounced off the crate and approached him. "Finally. I didn't want to disturb you –" She reached for his hand and Pitt stepped back.

"You shouldn't be here," he whispered, glancing at the door, closed. No one else here.

Chiara laughed. "It's okay, I made sure I wasn't seen. Though you ought to tell your lieutenant to secure that rear window, it's –" She went to take Pitt's hand again and again he jerked away. This time she frowned. "What the hell, Pitt?"

"It's not – it's just –" He glanced from her to the door again. He was hit by the irrational fear that the man with the knife would burst in at any moment. Or worse. Terrifold might be listening. He needed to be strong and clear. He took in a breath, looked her in the eye and said, "I can't see you. We need to stop this."

"What the hell?" she repeated, weaker, hurt.

The pain he saw in her eyes hit him with a flash of emotion, which came out in anger. "There's a damn war on, Chiara! For the sake of the Body, I need to focus. I can't be distracted by some – some tryst."

"Tryst?" She laughed again, this time bitterly. "Are you serious?" He held her eyes. "By Bly. You are serious. Let me guess, your crusty old mentor said it's not allowed?"

"No, it's not that," Pitt replied defensively, hearing how feeble it sounded. "Though yes, I can't do what I'm here to, can I, if you're distracting me."

"I've been waiting here for almost an hour!" Chiara spat, pointing to the crate where she'd been sitting. "You know how careful I was *not* to distract you? You fucking animal. You child." She turned away, crossing her arms, but not quickly enough to hide the tears in her eyes. "No. No, I should've known better. Why *would* you be any different to the rest?"

"I am!" Pitt squeaked, before he could stop himself, and she shot him a chilling look. "I'm sorry. I just . . . can't do this. Not now."

Her eyes narrowed like she was ready to strike him. But something stalled her. The same pitiful energy that had stalled Terrifold earlier. That's what Pitt was, after all, something to be pitied. She said, "This was no tryst. You don't believe that."

He wanted to deny it. To tell her it was all a mistake, just a fling. Break her heart and push her away. But the words didn't come out.

He only said, "No."

"Then why? I'll go, Pitt. You'd better believe I will leave you here and never look back. But you tell me why."

"Because there's a war on, and I'm needed," Pitt muttered.

"Why?"

"Someone threatened me!" he blurted. "We can't get mixed up in –"

"Who threatened you?"

"I don't know, a man with a knife. In truth, I suspect your father –"

The crack of a slap rang through the barn, the sound piercing Pitt's ears before he registered the pain, his head snapped to the side. Wide-eyed, he drew his head back to Chiara, and she waited for him to fully focus before snarling, "Don't you fucking dare. You must be stupid as well as a coward."

"Chiara –" He reached for her, and this time Chiara recoiled, hands high.

"Don't touch me. You're pathetic. My father has done nothing. Do you really think he would hide behind someone else's threats? If he had a problem with you, he would face you like a man." She stabbed a finger at him, and Pitt flinched. "But you know what makes me certain?"

Pitt swallowed, shame and worry flooding over him.

"Because I told him about you this morning. I asked for his blessing and do you know what he said? *'As long as he makes you happy.'* He said I should invite you for dinner!"

Pitt cringed as her voice rose, her tears now streaming, emotion overtaking her. He didn't dare speak. She wiped a hand over her mouth and nose, sniffing loudly.

"Well. Maybe I am the real idiot." Chiara shook her head. "One threat and this is the man I find underneath? Forget it."

Pitt itched to say it wasn't that simple. The man had a knife – could've been a killer. And he'd thought . . . But he'd thought it was her father, and he might have the whole town to contend with. If she was right, if it wasn't Rotus, then was it truly just an upset local? Or something else? His mind drifted towards his own camp. Terrifold's concerns that very morning.

"Wait," Pitt said, quietly, holding up a limp hand. "Please."

"It's too late." Chiara sniffed again. "You think I'm not scared too? We have a tank here. So many guns. Explosives that could destroy the world." She gestured to the crates around them. "I did not *want* to –" She shook her head again, deciding he wasn't worth the explanation, then strode past him, aiming for the door.

Pitt moved after her, hit by panic that she might walk away forever. He caught her wrist and pulled her back. She shrieked and pulled free, Pitt's own actions surprising him into throwing up his hands in innocence. "Sorry, I didn't mean to – but wait! I can protect you –"

Her bark of a laugh cut through him. "You can't even protect yourself. Do you even *know* what's happening out there?" She pointed to some unseen distance. "They laugh at the explosions – the violence we can hear in our own woods! As if those unhinged Stranded animals are a joke at our expense. To think I was going to ask *you,* of all people, for help. But I shouldn't have waited and I shouldn't still be here now."

"Stop stop stop!" Pitt cried as she went to leave again. "What's happened in the woods? I didn't hear – I've been up here all day."

"Thinking how best to get rid of me, yes?" Chiara sneered, and he faltered, because there was truth in it. She saw that. "Goodbye Pitt. Good luck."

He called for her to stop again, but didn't move as she opened the door and marched out of his life. It was raining. He hadn't noticed before. A heavy downpour, banging at the roof, forming a curtain for her to disappear into.

20

The noise and disruption of front-line barrages and increased industrial activity, as well as the emergence of aerial assaults, meant soldiers and the general populace became increasingly adept at ignoring all but the closest sounds. Life went on against a background of explosions and gunfire, such that stealth required little in the way of silence.

***Light-feet: How Hiding Changed History,* Prodder, p. 31**

There was shouting in the road ahead, and Wish recognised Ptrangus' voice. She waved at her platoon to take cover as she called for the nearest couple of soldiers to join her in racing forward. After an hour of cautious walking, Wish had started to worry they were taking things unnecessarily slow, hiding at the sides of the road, always two or three scouts ahead of the main squad. But no, they'd made contact, and there was going to be a fight, and the whole mission was fucked.

Captain Crash moved to come with her and despite their chat she instinctively snapped at him to stay back, "You have the command!"

His scarred face was moodier than ever, but he didn't argue and she ran on. The voices grew louder, then cut off, shouts turning to grunts. Wish sprinted, rifle in both hands, to turn the curve in the road and take the bastards –

She skidded through mud and leaves, gun up, but the scene ahead was calm. Ptrangus was crouched over a body and looked up sheepishly. Scraper stood a few paces to the side, one of her butcher's knives dripping in her hand, equally guilty. Two more bodies lay at her feet, one twitching his last, neck cut wide open.

All three wore green Drail overcoats.

Ptrangus stood, one hand spread as the other lowered his knife, like he didn't want to startle a frightened animal. "We checked ahead, boss – just the three of them."

From their stillness, the way everyone was waiting, Wish realised her gun was raised at them and lowered it. She wanted to do something, run on, fight, but slowly accepted it was already done. Their big fear of the day, of hitting a patrol, had come and been handled. She opened and closed her mouth before saying, "No other . . . problems?"

"Textbook." Ptrangus shrugged, like he murdered armed men in silence every day. "Pulled the old *help a confused, lost Rae boy, would you?* routine to get close and Scraper came at them from behind."

Wish goggled, fascinated that his easy charm could've stopped these men from getting off even a single shot. But the Rawboy accent was disarming, despite what she knew of these men, and in his black kit he didn't immediately resemble a soldier. Not a Stanish one, anyway. She came closer, checking the bodies, all three having bled profusely but from only a couple of stab wounds. As she met Scraper's dark eyes, Ptrangus said, in a stage whisper, "You know, whatever doubts I have about you Stains, *she's* worth having around."

Wish gave him a scolding look, not sure Scraper appreciated his humour, if anyone did. She checked over her shoulder. Lugger, Crag and one of Jonus's men had come with her, and she said, "Can you guys shift these bodies to the side? Ptrangus and Scraper, keep on ahead. We should almost be at the path now." She checked the lifeless young men again. The one with his throat cut had lush blonde hair, looking especially young and more confused than pained. Like Quickness. *Why.* His uniform was clean besides the blood and mud from this scuffle. No creases – had it ever seen battle?

Wish cleared her throat, and, for something more to say, said, "Really good work, guys."

Good.

That was one word for it.

***

The path to Serenity Overlook was encased in doming vines like a hallway, letting sunlight through while also providing complete privacy, so Wish could lead her platoon without much care for being seen. When they reached the overlook itself, she found it similarly sheltered by trees, with hedges cropped low along the cliff edge, parted for a quaint bench. Wish crawled up to the edge on her belly, instructing Dalliance and Gaussica to creep to the hedge on the other side of the bench. Captain Crash joined her with Lieutenant Jonus, neither invited, to survey the view below. She was quite sure there had never been quite so picturesque a spot as this. The world was created for this view: a sweeping, beautiful lake, lined with rocky ridges and trees, dusted white with frost. To the left, sunk in a pretty inlet, sat a gingerbread town straight out of a fairy tale, with painted walls, tiled peaks and turrets. She could have reached out and grabbed a piece to eat, if she was lying next to anyone other than Crash. He was too serious for fantasy, and immediately set to scribbling notes in a tiny pad, offering Jonus occasional whispers as they checked their maps and tools.

But once Wish got over the beautiful view, she recognised the threat within quaint Sober Sound, and appreciated for the first time how serious this mission was. She whispered, "There's a whole invasion force down there."

Crash said, "Key targets are the main thoroughfare and those two big buildings by the lake's edge. We'll keep a barrage going, ten minutes on, fifteen off, thereabouts, until they're gone. We'll await your flare to confirm that. Withdraw immediately when it's done."

Wish was barely listening as she was drawn to the sight of a big Relight tree in the town square, then the ugly tank next to it. Scores of men in green coats were milling about there, and lounging at the lake's edge, dipping their toes in the icy water and laughing. A platoon was drilling in tight lines, marching. A group of important uniformed men were talking with important suited locals. Their exchange made her notice others out of uniform. Colourful coats and hats, fishermen's garbs, *dresses*. White and blue frills, flirty smiles from civilian *women*.

"The town's still occupied," Wish said.

"Huh?" Crash's grunt had a little uncertainty to it.

"There's civilians. Look, between the bloody green-coats, there are *lots* of civilians. There's –" She swept her scope back and forth, every angle now picking out more civilian clothing. Pretty young ladies, pipe-smoking older men, older women knitting on balconies – children. A group of children playfully running from a boy swinging a stick. Men gathered around a ladder trying to hoist a Relight garland. "The town's full. It hasn't been evacuated."

She looked to Crash. He stared intently through his binoculars, motionless.

"Wasn't the town supposed to be evacuated?" Wish said, a ball of panic stirring in her gut. She looked over Crash's shoulder to Dalliance, prone on the other side of the bench, rifle propped through the hedge base. He returned a concerned expression. Even Gaussica, crouched with a small telescope in hand, was frowning. Wish raised her eyebrows, inviting some input here. Why was no one saying anything?

"Unders mentioned some locals had stayed," Jonus said, at last.

"That's not *some!*" Wish exclaimed, shocked at his callous response, but equally at herself now, because Unders *had* said that. And Bluefern had mentioned the town had kept functioning after the war started – had they all assumed the civilians had left when the military came in, or not cared? She'd never stopped to think about it. It had never registered with her that this wasn't just an attack on a strategic enemy location – they intended to wipe out a whole town. Because why *would* they bomb a town if the civilians were still there? She said, "There's too many. We can't shell civilians."

"We're not," Crash said. Thank Bly, a rational response. But he went on, slowly, "We're shelling a Drail military outpost. Any civilians who chose to stay there did so willingly."

"The fuck? They couldn't have known we were planning on bombing them to hell!"

"With the town in no man's land?" Crash lowered his binoculars. His voice was unemotional. "They invited the Drail in."

"We *can't* bomb that town," Wish said, that ball of panic swelling into her chest, filling her. "They're still civilians. They might have had no choice. There has to be another way. We can shell the lake when it freezes."

"With Haven compromised and their latest patrol not coming back?" Crash countered. "We're on borrowed time, Captain. It has to happen now. You said it, that's an invasion force – if they realise we're here, they'll push through the woods before we can mount a proper defence."

"There's a hundred innocent people. Women and children."

Crash took another look. His mouth formed a grim line. "I don't like it. I agree, it's regrettable. But it's what we have to do."

"Indiscriminately killing anyone in our way? There are *women* and *children*," Wish repeated firmly. How quickly he seemed to have forgotten his concerns for defending her gender.

Crash eyed her again. Unapologetic, but not hostile. Just empty, dispassionate, to tell her yes. That is what it meant to run an artillery outfit. She checked the others' faces again and found no solace in Dalliance's unhappy expression, deferring to her. Gaussica didn't appear to be listening, eye on his telescope, and Jonus was looking ahead, blankly obedient.

"You guys got nothing to say?" she snapped.

"I support whatever you decide, boss," Dalliance murmured quickly, ready for that. Damn Graveguard, the thought came to Wish, as his miserable pep talk came to mind. No one wanted to take responsibility.

"I see him," Gaussica said.

"What?" Wish demanded.

"Terrifold." The Azirian pointed, as if that would help. "Towards the centre. The tall man in a crimson coat."

Though reluctant to drop this argument, Wish checked through her rifle scope, running over dozens of relaxing soldiers. There it was, a crimson coat, on a stiffly self-assured man striding between the ranks, skin lined from age and seriousness. She didn't ask how

Gaussica recognised him – she could've guessed herself that he was a mage. He gestured at some soldiers, gave orders, then turned off between the buildings, out of sight. Their target clearly wasn't worried about being seen. None of them were, these clueless soldiers enjoying their fairy-tale town. The jovial civilians were equally oblivious.

"Could you hit him from here?" Crash asked.

"Easily," Wish answered without thinking. Then she shook her head. "No, we have to stop and rethink this."

"You'd prefer to get closer?" Crash said.

"That's not what I mean! You can't be okay with this. That's an entire town of people."

"It's a threat to our entire front line," the captain replied. "We need to disable this outpost or risk a breach that our army cannot handle. The order has been made, Captain, and I see no reason that Command would accept for not following through."

Wish was locked with disbelief. No reason. There were hundreds of reasons down there. People's lives. But Command had disregarded many thousands of innocent lives spread along the front line, hadn't they? She heard Havik's voice whispering of times it had been done before. Names she knew only as tragedies, sneered at her by a goblin: Havik's hometown of Kopice. Hartland. Purnjay. And *Wick*. The city of Wick she had inadvertently helped decimate herself. How many civilians were caught up in that?

In her hesitation, Crash sat back. Getting serious. He was here to keep her in line with his natural grimace and ingrained disapproval of her presence. But his voice remained flat as he said, "If you think it's unsafe to remain here, you can withdraw your platoon. Wash your hands of it." He glanced aside. "Mr Gaussica, if you would remain?"

"It's busy down there," Gaussica said. "I could get in and out without a problem."

"In ninety minutes?"

The Azirian nodded and Crash turned back to Wish.

"It would be beneficial if you could confirm that those buildings and the thoroughfares are destroyed, so we can withdraw with confidence that it's done. Likewise, if the mage survives and we can't break through, we'd need to withdraw quickly. But if you don't believe this is a secure position for your men . . . I'm sure Lieutenant Jonus can keep watch."

The suggestion, a blatant lie as it was, wasn't said to goad her, but offered as a way out. She could have nothing to do with this, if she only said the word. He would get his wish and at least protect the Stanish women from the horrors they might see. Never mind what the Lomian women would endure. Those people would still die. Somehow his reasonableness was even worse than hostility. If he was prepared to fight her, it would be easier to resist. She said, "Or I could stop you. Call the whole thing off."

"You can withdraw your platoon, that's all," Crash clarified. Not blinking. "Do any more than that and you'll be committing treason."

Wish didn't blink either. They understood each other. She had taken things into her own hands multiple times in the past, when she disagreed with Captain Brade, but that was only when her own platoon was at stake. When the difference was pulling a trigger or not. Major Bluefern was in charge here and had orders from Command. If she wanted to stop this, it would mean breaking rank against him, and there would be no coming back.

"It is regrettable," Crash said, again, with the slightest crack of emotion, "but this has to happen. Put your feelings aside, Captain, and you will see it."

Wish glanced at the pretty town packed with its pretty people and soldiers in repose, unready for the violence that might soon come. She wanted to tell him she would *not* put her feelings aside, with no intention of stopping feeling, or caring, but a little part of her already warned this wasn't new. This wasn't different to gunning down hundreds on Green Rise or exploding a chunk of Wick. Her actions had cost countless lives in the tribes and priories of the Saints Mire. But they never looked quite so innocent as here. Her targets had never looked quite so much like somewhere she might think of as peaceful. Where she might live. She swallowed as she saw the locals finish successfully hanging their garland, clapping and cheering at an achievement so mundane it made her heart ache.

"It's almost Relight," she whispered.

"And when it comes, I'd like our troops to be safe," Crash said. "Our boys will have enough trouble surviving the cold. We need to plug this hole."

"But . . ." But it wasn't fair. It wasn't right. It wasn't in any way good.

"Captain Wild Wish," Crash tried again, gravely. "You lost one of yours yesterday. This is to prevent that happening again. For all of us, from here back to Stanclif. That town and the people in it is the price of a winter's mercy for our whole front line – because they won't show us any. It isn't our choice, but a necessity. *They* put those civilians in the firing line."

Wish said nothing. There was nothing else – never a choice, really, since the fighting had started. But mercy was a cruel word, there.

"He's back," Gaussica interrupted, and Dalliance confirmed, "Got him."

Wish scowled at them. Were they even listening? Didn't they care? But watching their dead focus on the task, pointedly *not* looking at her, she understood. It was better not to think about it. Crash was right, again, and still staring at her, waiting for it to set in.

She couldn't say anything. She wanted a solution, wanted to race for an innovative answer, but her mind was going blank. Numb.

"I can make it back to Bluefern in fifty minutes at a run," Crash said, as if her silence had confirmed it. "I've got what I need. We can call it an even ninety minutes: take your shot on the hour, if you have one. Get close if you need to, but only if you can get clear in time. Take your shot sooner if you think it's necessary. Jonus, leave them your flares and monitor the road. We'll be watching for a signal either way – yellow when the mage is down, red if he succeeds in shielding the town, green if the job's complete. If you can't get to him, retreat without delay. Understood?"

"Wait," Wish said, swept up in the rapid flow of practical orders.

She wanted to talk more. To put it off. But by his icy stare, it had all been said. She took another breath, and replied, shakily, "Let's check our watches."

21

Naysayers like to dwell on finicky points of collateral damage, but it was a remarkable advancement, by anyone's measure, that in the space of mere decades our cannons supplanted magic users as the greatest thing to be feared [on a battlefield].

History of the Imperial Artillery,
Sir Ebwin Darnfale, p. 79

Wish had endured countless miserable hours on the front, and behind the lines, and in the nights when she relived horrors both in and out of sleep. She wasn't sure any were quite as maudlin as sitting waiting for the destruction of Sober Sound. A small part of her continued frantically straining for another solution. What if they sneaked in and assassinated Terrifold and planted bombs around the warehouses as she'd first suggested? Somehow evaded thousands of men in uniform. But within minutes of Crash leaving, too much time had already passed for that to be possible before the artillery opened fire. And besides, he *was* right. It was only a matter of time before alarms started sounding over Haven and the missing patrol. The Stranded were sure to come around eventually. And Iggy needed saving. It all demanded a quick end to this nightmare.

But Wish had to do *something*. She scouted the streets through her scope, following women as they carried baskets, cleaned windows, and straightened out decorations. A woman in a postal uniform was delivering a sack of mail and there was a woman in overalls with a toolbox – taking up the jobs of their absent men. Another woman was pushing a pram, comforting her crying baby. What if Wish fired a few warning shots and got them to retreat? Shouted at them to evacuate? Impossible without giving their position away and alerting that mage.

Terrifold was a distraction, at least, as he strutted about town on show. She got the impression he enjoyed being seen. There was little question that when the time came she would be able to neutralise the man, and she said, "Sorry to have brought you all this way for nothing, Gaussica, but I'll handle the mage myself."

Gaussica made a noise that could've been dismissal or surprise. He had volunteered to go into the town, but she had told him to wait while she assessed the situation.

"I've got him at six hundred yards. Dalliance?"

"Yeah, roughly."

"We'll give it a five-minute window before the hour. If he looks like he's about to step out of view within those five minutes, I'll drop him."

"He's a parser, remember," Gaussica said. "At his level, he might conjure a shield as a reflex, without even seeing the danger coming."

"Faster than a bullet?"

"Faster than a bullet. He *is* the best of them."

"And that reflex shield would save him?" Wish asked. She wasn't overly familiar with how strong such magic was against bullets, because the trick to killing mages was to never let them know what was coming.

Gaussica considered the question carefully. "Maybe. It might still knock him down."

"Then I'll be ready with another bullet," Wish said.

"Me too, boss," Dalliance put in.

The Azirian hummed, baiting her with a little unspoken doubt. She tried to resist biting, sure Gaussica would prefer to glide into Sober Sound to duel the man head-on. Probably reciting bad philosophical quandaries and apocalyptic poems as he went. She huffed, "Alright. You have some sinister prediction to go with that look?"

"No. My preferred method is to cut off a mage's head, to be sure. I have a hammer that can break their shields, but you need to be close."

"You've got a hammer for everything, don't you? Where do you carry them all?"

"There's still time. It would be the surest option. I've seen the fire. I will look into his dead eyes, but it might not touch you, yet."

There it was, the nonsense that had been missing all morning, in his focused quiet. Wish said, "Those visions of a dark burning future include children screaming? It doesn't bother you?"

"It's not their flesh," he said, a response so sure it gave her a shudder. He added no more, staring intensely into the doomed town.

"Hey, Gaussica," Dalliance ventured, "You got any useful tips for us shooting him?"

He didn't reply.

"Did the orders in your black envelope say you needed to do it yourself?" Dalliance pressed, clearly vying for any response. "Some reason you can't just help us out?"

"She refused it," Gaussica replied distantly, making Dalliance look Wish's way.

"Who?" Wish asked, but the Azirian shook his head, like he was shaking himself from an unwelcome thought. He didn't answer, trying to refocus on the town below, so she whispered, "Dick."

Secretly, she made up her mind that there was no way any of hers were going into that town, with what was about to happen, including Gaussica, even if he was frighteningly odd. If she could shoulder this kill herself, all the better. Maybe she could balance out her complicity in the attack by personally removing a fearsome battle mage. Though Terrifold, strong as he appeared, with his dignified poise and general amiability, hardly looked fearsome.

The way he held his head high and looked down at people, he had a clear arrogance about him. But the people he talked to and passed were animated by his presence. They looked happy to see him, confident in his presence. Soldiers and civilians – everyone looked happy.

Wish strained to find someone who didn't, zipping her scope about, until she spotted her. A woman lingering near what had to be a tavern (infinitely charming), arms folded. She was beautiful, in an expensive fur coat with silken raven hair, but with a face like thunder as she watched people passing by. Wish hovered over her.

This was even worse. A woman who resented the Drail presence. Didn't want them in her home and didn't deserve to be punished for having it forced on her. A man came to her, moustached, older, and put an arm around her in a paternal way. She relaxed into it, and they shared words. She nodded, partly consoled, then went indoors. The man took her place, arms folded and scowling at the invaders in the same way.

"Captain Wild," Lieutenant Jonus whispered, crawling up behind her. She gave him a glance, but put her eye back to her scope. "Private Unders has requested that he be relieved, now everything's in position."

Wish frowned, having forgotten the nervous local was even here. He knew those people down there. No doubt cared for some of them. He should've been screaming and crying and trying to kill them for what was coming. She never should have brought him this far to begin with. "Absolutely. Anyone who doesn't want to be here can withdraw."

"I appreciate that, Captain, but it's only the lad asking."

At his dismissive tone, Wish pinned her eye on Jonus again. "I'm serious."

That got a worried look and she reconsidered how her suggestion sounded. Accusatory, challenging, sarcastic? Soldiers weren't supposed to withdraw at a whim. But they didn't all need to be here. Involved. She said, "Do you really think we'll have any trouble on the road, Lieutenant? The Drail will be running for their lives."

"Yes, Captain," he said, "and they might run this way."

Wish hesitated, wanting to push the point. What if the Drail got around the attack and sent an army to meet them? What if the bombs went astray and hit their own people? Never mind the innocents, what if things went wrong? She'd already lost Quickness. Wish said, "How safe are we from the barrage here?"

"Oh, totally," Jonus said, face relaxing at something he could handle. "Those guns are accurate to within a forty-yard radius. Targeting the centre, there's little room for deviation outside the town limits." He went quiet again, then said, "Did Captain Crash explain how the barrage works?"

"Ninety minutes until everything goes boom," Wish replied simply. "As long as one of us clips that Drail mage before then." She checked her watch. "Twenty-eight minutes to go. Still got him, Dalliance?"

"Yes, boss. East of the tank, twenty paces."

"With a full team, the 82 Herald can safely fire four shots a minute," Jonus said, filling her in anyway. Maybe as a distraction, or maybe he really thought she should know. "With three guns, we stagger the shots so you have twelve shells a minute, roughly every five seconds, which is effectively continuous if you're on the ground. Once they start, they'll have about a hundred shells hit that town in eight minutes. They'll give it ten to fifteen minutes for the enemy to think its over and start coming out of hiding, adjusting the aim slightly to cover a different area, then they'll repeat. The timing's rough and changing, so it's not predictable, but you're looking at two to three barrages an hour. Major Bluefern will keep going for three hours unless we signal the job's done, probably eight barrages."

"Three hours," Wish echoed. "Is there going to be anything left after the first bombing?"

"You'd be surprised. Once we've created a few craters and knocked down some buildings, it'll create natural shields limiting the blasts that follow. After four barrages, though, the destruction will hopefully be complete. We're unlikely to need the full eight."

They were quiet, letting that hang in the air, watching the cheery little town below, hard to imagine it would be gone by nightfall. Or the horrors it would suffer in the meantime. At least they were happy for now, though. They didn't know, not like Wish. She said, "Thanks, Lieutenant. I suppose we're in for quite a show."

"I'm sorry, Captain," he replied, impressively taking that as she intended. "Do you have any further instructions?"

"Nope. Time's coming fast now. Tell everyone to keep their heads down and boorah, I guess."

He gave an *mmhmm* that was suitably unenthusiastic and crawled backwards on his belly, out of the clearing. They stayed in silence after that, waiting.

Wish grew aware of a noise from near the lake, voices carrying from town. A commotion almost loud enough to hear. She scanned towards it as Dalliance announced, "He's moving towards the lakefront, to whatever's going on there."

Wish found the mage before the trouble, Terrifold walking swiftly past some distracted soldiers, having to shoulder his way through and making a burly man stumble. The soldier almost took a swing at him before realising it was the mage. Terrifold broke through a circle of men to reach a young couple arguing. A man in a tatty great coat, with a good head of dark hair, and that sad woman from by the inn. She had dropped a basket, scattering food. The man was gesticulating, pleading, as Terrifold broke between them, angry. He made some fierce demand of the young man, who stepped back with surprise, and the woman said something equally fierce, then all three were having a go. It looked personal, the mage bizarrely wrapped up in some domestic dispute. Was the younger man his charge? A father-son, or master-student, relationship. Terrifold was telling him off but the man didn't back down. Good for him, standing up for the woman, now, it seemed: he cared about her, more than he cared about the old mage.

"Two minutes," Dalliance announced and Wish seized up. She wanted to see this play out, but the unfolding drama was a perfect opportunity, at exactly the right time.

"Six hundred twenty yards," Wish said, checking the viewfinder and adjusting her sights.

"Six hundred twenty," Dalliance confirmed.

She rested her cross hairs over Terrifold's face, the man frozen in shock at something that had been said. Thanks, angry young couple, for holding him in place.

She said, "Taking the shot."

And did.

22

The newspapers were instructed to report numbers roundly, even where precise records were available. This is because 10,000 dead is a soulless statistic, while recording the loss of a town of 9,937 invites you to consider that number represents a great many individuals.
Atrocities Through the Ages, Buckman, p. 158

It was about more than just Chiara.

Pitt had spent a cold morning in the Tin Pot, nursing a black coffee behind a crowd of loud men clinking mugs and plates. The cafe had been co-opted by their occupation's rougher soldiers, making it the ideal place to avoid both Terrifold and her. He couldn't return to the fish barn, to sit cross-legged with bleeding fingers, failing to conjure magic. What was the use, when he knew there was no chance of success this morning? He had barely slept, fretting over how to make things right with Chiara, trying to avoid thinking about Terrifold.

However he tried to unravel this, the threads pointed back to Terrifold. The man with the knife had been very clear, and cogent – not a drunk or irrationally angry individual. And if Rotus didn't disapprove of Pitt, then it was unlikely any rational local would interfere in his daughter's affairs. Meanwhile, Terrifold had hinted clearly enough that he knew about Pitt's distractions. His latest frustration made more sense if he was expecting Pitt to perform better after being warned off Chiara. And the old, miserable fool had made advances . . .

Pitt rethought their relationship over the past weeks and saw how frequently the man sidled closer to him. How Terrifold watched him, not with the fondness of a teacher, but with something more like longing. How Terrifold spoke to him as an old friend, someone to confide in. What lengths might the mage go to to secure this fantasy?

Pitt had been a fool. Should have known this was all too good to be true, and that Terrifold wanted more from him, something which he couldn't get from the countless higher-class mages he might have chosen. No, he *had* known, and chosen to ignore it. His inexperience, and willingness to play along, he expected, was the point, and he clutched his mug almost to the point of breaking it with anger. Because of course a poor pipeman from the streets would do anything to get ahead. That wasn't him, though. That had never been him.

He could've been happy here, in this remote little town, even without finding this incredible woman. He could've been happy anywhere, never so much as thinking about the war or pushing himself beyond being a simple plumber. There was no part of him now, he told himself, that was tempted to go begging for scraps of learning and advancement, not from a man who might have had him threatened.

Pitt had to confront him, though he doubted it would do any good for fixing things with Chiara. You only got one chance with a woman like that. But he had his pride to think of, and the question of doing what was right. Even if Terrifold was hiding immense, frightening power under that skin-deep friendly facade.

Yet somehow time rushed past Pitt, with the cafe filling and emptying. More coffee. No food. He couldn't eat. He barely registered the sounds of soldiers talking or the touch of them bumping into him. Told the waitress yes, he was absolutely fine, when she came to check.

He needed to act. Couldn't bring himself to.

Until Chiara's dark coat drifted past the foggy window.

It fired him into action, out of his seat and through upset soldiers to burst out the door. She was turning onto the main street and he slid on the icy cobbles, shouting, "Chiara, wait!"

She stopped, and her moment's curiosity turned to malice when she saw him. Scrunching her nose, she shook her head and walked on. Pitt ran after her. She picked up her pace, walking into the square, but did not run, so he slowed his approach, calling out, "Can I talk to you just for a second?"

"No," she snapped without looking back.

People were pausing to watch, conversations dying and whispers starting, but Pitt blocked them out as he jogged alongside her. "Just a second, please? Let me say one thing and you can never speak to me again."

"We said all we needed to," she said, not stopping. She had a stuffed basket under one arm, he realised: far more supplies than she'd taken her brother before. Was she leaving? Pitt tried to take her elbow.

"Will you just stop, at least look at me!"

"I said *no!*" She pulled free, so hard the basket came loose. He let go, stepping back as it hit the road, bread and fruit rolling.

"Shit, I didn't mean –"

"I don't care!" Chiara's voice bounced off the walls, silencing whatever other noise was left in the town centre. "Get away from me!"

"I will!" Pitt cried back. "If you just hear me out –"

"Here, pal, the lady said leave her alone," a man interrupted and Pitt turned to a soldier twice his size, flanked by similarly mean-looking men in uniform.

"I'm the fucking mage second here!" Pitt told them. "Back the hell off."

The men's eyes widened, their heroism shattered. When he turned back to Chiara, her expression was thick with disgust. She said, "I'm going to Haven and you're *not* to follow, damn you Pitt. I do not wish to see or speak to you."

"Let me walk you," he said, trying desperately to calm down but shaking. Scores of people were suddenly watching. "I know I was wrong – it was him, and I'm going to –"

"What the hell is going on!" Terrifold's voice boomed, as though he had been summoned, and people quickly parted to let him through with hushes of fear and scandal sweeping out. The mage was veiny with anger and it took all Pitt's nerve not to back off. "Pitt. What do you call this? I've been looking for you all morning."

"You can have him," Chiara sneered. *"Please,* take him."

"Contain yourself," Terrifold warned her, brow heavy as he observed their audience. "And explain to me how with a thousand enlisted troops in this town it's the mayor's daughter and my protege who are causing a scene."

"Because of fucking *you!"* Pitt shouted, all the nerves and uncertainty exploding against the accusation. "Admit it, you hired some – some thug! You couldn't stand my attentions straying to someone who deserved them!"

Terrifold was, for once, wrong-footed, so pompous he hadn't even conceived that Pitt might guess what he'd done. As Pitt breathed heavily, daring him to deny it, the entire town held its breath. Chiara, he realised, was motionless.

At last, Terrifold said, "Have you lost your mind?"

"I'm more aware than I've been in weeks," Pitt said. "And you know what? I was at my best when *she* helped me relax. Not thanks to anything *you* did. But you're a bitter old man, aren't you? You couldn't let me have it."

"What is this damned schoolyard drama?" Terrifold replied, regaining his composure, his air of authority. "With the fate of the Empire at stake, you're worked up over a bloody woman? Weaving imaginary –"

"You sent a man to attack me!"

"Why would I do such a thing?"

"I don't know, maybe because you couldn't have me for yourself, you damned queer!"

That hit the mage like a punch and Pitt immediately regretted it. His chest heaved from the shout and the pain he saw in Terrifold's eyes. But he saw power stirring there, too. Fear twirled in his stomach, fear he felt mirrored in the countless people watching.

Terrifold's upper lip curled back and he said, "You ungrateful bastard."

Pitt's mouth was dry. He couldn't move. With Chiara so close and staring, though, he didn't even want to take it back. He might be ruining everything, risking his life, but dammit. She was worth it. His pride was worth it. And how long since anyone had dared –

Terrifold's head jerked back with an explosion of blood and for a moment Pitt thought he'd pushed the man back with his growing anger. But it wasn't magic. A crack of rifle fire followed, ringing through the town like a hammer blow. The mage fell against the cobbles as part of his head dropped away, eyes wide in lifeless shock. It took a moment for the first woman to scream, but when she did, total panic followed.

"Sniper!" someone roared, as Pitt was knocked aside by an eruption of people moving. He kept upright to stare numbly at Terrifold. Waiting for him to get up. "Sniper on the ridge! Take cover, get a squad –"

A great whoosh fell from the sky, barely time for anyone to register it before the corner of the Cherin Bank exploded, stone and tile punched out in a black cloud, men and women tossed aside. Pitt ducked, far too late, and spun to see another blast tearing through the roof of the town hall.

"Artillery! Retreat!"

Pitt was moving too slowly, with everyone darting about, knocking each other down. There was too much screaming to hear the more coherent soldiers' orders, and Pitt looked numbly to the lake. His eyes were drawn skyward to another shape screaming below the clouds. Beyond it, a puff of yellow colour hung unnaturally in the air. A flare?

The third shell struck the narrow street to Pitt's right, where he'd spent the morning in the Tin Pot. The tightly packed explosion funnelled out into the square, catching a handful of running soldiers. A man flew past, spinning into a lamppost which snapped him in half.

"The barn!" a voice screamed in Pitt's ear, a hand clamping on his arm. "Protect the barn!"

Pitt snapped out of the daze and was running before he recognised Lieutenant Droll at his side. They jumped at the sound of another explosion, but shoved their way towards the lakefront. Pitt dug into his feelings, his power, before the fish barn came into view. He surged out into the open and threw his energy forward, spreading a force to the large building ahead. Men were running around it, mostly away, and the wave of energy smacked them down, made one soldier collapse grasping his chest. Pitt ignored them, focusing only on the building, spreading the shield. He could see it pulsing over the structure, a shimmering blanket – and just as it covered the barn another shell hit, right at the top.

Pitt gasped and staggered to the side, the shield faltering as the bomb exploded above them. The ball of fire and smoke spread into the air, a terribly loud concussion that hadn't gone through. He caught his breath, staring at the barn in disbelief, expecting that it might still collapse. But it stood. It barely even shook from the blast. And he was still holding the shield. He'd done it.

Another explosion made him spin to a nearby house, stonework tearing through people nearby. He set his feet, gritted his teeth and strained to hold onto the barn shield as he tried to split his attention to the rest of the town.

"Can you do it?" Droll shouted, straining to be heard. "Is Terrifold gone?"

Pitt nodded. It was up to him. He pushed at the shield, as another shell hit the centre of the main road, flinging cobbles into walls and windows. With a roar, Pitt pushed at the shield and it spread, his energy flowing out, an umbrella not just for the barn but the street around it. He *could* do this. He tried to move, stepping towards the barn itself – needed to get in the loft, to his vantage point. He was almost knocked down as an impact came directly overhead, a shell exploding high above the rooftops. Pitt took a blow hard as a slap, feeling it through every inch of his body. But again, the shield held. Gasping for breath, he righted himself, with Droll's help.

A scream drew him quickly around, a woman kneeling over a crater, painted by blood and ash, amidst splattered gore that might've belonged to her or someone else. Pitt gagged, and in the same instant saw Chiara's dark coat, flitting towards an alley. Another shell whizzed overhead, and he sensed it coming directly for her.

"No!" Pitt shouted, spinning his energy, throwing it across the town. Men were knocked down as if by an invisible carriage, and the shield reached her just as the shell did. A whoomph of fire and smoke engulfed her, smashing through the surrounding walls. Pitt screamed, firing all his energy into the shield, sprinting towards her.

"Wait!" Droll yelled, trying to grab his arm.

Another impact struck behind them and Pitt's legs were thrown up and to the side, so he crashed hard on his face. His ears chimed, shouts and screams muffled now, eyes stinging. He rolled over and coughed on smoke, flapped a hand to clear it. In the road where he'd been standing there was now a crater, three feet deep, rubble scorched black and smeared with blood. A hand lay severed beside it. Probably Droll's. Then Pitt was up, swaying on his unsteady feet as he tried to pick his way through the thickening smoke. His shield had broken. His street, the barn, they were unprotected.

But Chiara. Where was Chiara?

As he staggered, weary, barely able to hear, Pitt saw the town square through the smoke, where people lay dead and dying, trampled or in pieces. There were craters and holes in charred buildings. Fire lanced out of the windows of the town hall. Soldiers ran in blind fear, though one man had made it on top of the tank and was gesturing around, roaring commands. An officer, a good man doing his best – until he was hit by shrapnel or a bullet and flung off the tank out of sight.

Pitt continued through the square, hitting a man running the other way, trying hazily to reconnect to his energy, to bring back the shield. He wasn't sure he could. He needed to sleep. His right leg was warm and wet with urine or blood. Couldn't stop to check. He staggered past more panicked soldiers, wondering if it had stopped, or if it was just that he'd gone deaf. But he heard shouts, noises that sounded roughly human . . .

Pitt stopped at Chiara's alley and waved his hands through the smoke, coughing on it. She was there. She lay crumpled, legs and arms at odd angles, coat spread out like a burst skin. Tears filled his stinging eyes as he stared at her, saying her name but unable to hear his own voice. She was *there,* so he'd saved her, hadn't he? His shield had worked. It had to have.

Movement drew his eye up, the building next to her quaking, and he saw half of its bottom floor was missing, a bed frame hanging over a burnt pile of rubble. The house shuddered, about to fall. Pitt quickly crouched and took Chiara by the arms, dragging her from the alley. He gasped in pain and stumbled, body not quite working, but doubled his efforts at another creak and rain of debris. Then there was a man at his side, someone in uniform helping drag her, and together they sped out of the alley, pulled Chiara into the road, as the building came down. Pitt rolled to avoid the cascade of stone and tile that crashed past them. As the dust settled, he sat up, panting, as the soldier knelt by Chiara, checking her neck for a pulse. The man, caked in dust and blood, uniform torn, shouted enthusiastically at Pitt – she was alive.

The soldier stood shakily, scanning about, and barked a few more words at Pitt that he tried to read on his lips. It seemed the barrage *had* ended, and the man was looking for shelter, or others to help. He pointed to something, and as he did the ground shook. Pitt flinched at a nearby explosion and a large flat object flew past. A broken bit of something large. He caught his breath again, startled by the near miss, and looked up to the soldier to share this relief. The man was still standing, upright and steady, but his head was gone.

He remained there for an impossible minute before crumpling.

Quaking in horror, Pitt bent over Chiara again and dragged her away from the body in a writhing crawl, unable to lift his own weight, let alone hers. More explosions followed. He bent over her screaming in mad, terrified defiance, giving up moving, flooding out his energy, whatever power he had, to encase them. A tiny shell, the only protection he could offer. They shuddered together, one blast after another, as Sober Sound crumbled around him and Pitt didn't dare look up again. He clung on hard to the unconscious woman and his waning shield, straining with everything he had to stay conscious, to keep protecting them.

If he could just hold on. The world could fall if he could just keep this pocket alive. But his energy was fading and the sky was black with smoke. It might never stop. This was everything now and he couldn't keep going.

He whispered an apology to Chiara, knowing before it came that the next blast would break him. And he was flying again, into the smoke and the fire, and she was gone. When he crashed into the cobbles, he barely felt a thing.

23

There were too many massacres to count. Too many crimes to punish. No one ever answered for the bombings of a hundred Lomian, Farnish and Garter towns, to say the least. No investigations were conducted. The hearings that did follow were performative and symbolic, because too much was done by too many for any punishment to ever mean anything.

Atrocities Through the Ages, Buckman, p. 213

It got easier once Wish started firing. Fighting was mechanical, and this was a fight, even if they were far removed from the action and no one was strictly fighting back. She instructed Dalliance coldly to pick out anyone who looked important and she did the same, watching for officers and those few men who managed to keep calm in the rain of explosions. After the first few blasts, though, Gaussica said, "One didn't get through."

"One what?"

"A shell. It exploded above that roof."

Wish saw plenty of roofs and lots of smoke, bits of buildings crumbling. Distracted from firing, it was all she could do not to flinch at the next barrage, every terrible shudder met by fearful screams. She had no idea what roof he was referring to. "Maybe it was a dud."

"No – it exploded but didn't go through. Is Terrifold alive?"

Wish ran her scope back to the main road, hard to see between the frantic bodies and the growing smoke and debris. But no, that was him, wasn't it? Where she'd left him, coat spread flatly around him as people ran past. "He's definitely dead."

There was another blast and Gaussica said with surprise, "Another one. Definitely a shield. There must be a second mage."

Wish searched with her scope but failed to pick out anyone who looked like they knew what they were doing. But there was the young man who'd been arguing with Terrifold, almost crouching in the road as if in fear. Another mage.

"It's him, isn't it?" Wish asked, as if Gaussica knew who she was looking at. As she trained her sights on his frightened and confused face, the man twisted around and screamed something. The road exploded behind him and smoke filled her lens. She scanned about to pick him out again. "Think he just got hit."

Another cluster of explosions followed, thickening the confusion, and Gaussica said, "I'm not seeing a shield now."

"Guy on the tank," Dalliance said, and fired. He tutted – a miss. "Is that a colonel?"

Wish moved from the fallen mage to the tank, where a man was trying to organise the panicked people under the shade of the wobbling Relight tree. *Not today,* she silently told him, and fired.

She roved the town, distanced from the reality by her scope, little vignettes popping in and out of visibility, most of it obscured as the town was torn apart. Soon, there was more smoke and rubble than space between the buildings, and she lowered her gun to stare at the whole, watching the explosions thumping in with increasingly little effect, blasts absorbed in craters or blowing out the remains of already ruined buildings. As Jonus had promised. In the space of minutes – half an hour? It hadn't been an hour yet, surely – the barrage had turned Sober Sound into a killing field as bloody and brutal as if a hundred men with machine guns and grenades had penned all the people in. But half the buildings, perhaps, still stood, as if protected by some higher force, somehow left outside the pattern of the guns. Among them was the large warehouse Crash had wanted destroyed. Good for them. Maybe they could rebuild. Maybe they would cancel the invasion without *total* destruction.

Her prayer was answered by a shell bursting through that very barn as Wish watched, and quicker than she could say *oh well,* a much greater explosion followed. The force of it pushed her back and made Dalliance swear as the cliff shook under them. The lake lit up with the biggest ball of fire and fury Wish had seen since

Wick. She held an arm over her head as tiny bits of rubble scattered around them.

Dalliance looked up in wonder, whispering, "Wow . . ."

"Watch out," she warned, moving under the trees as larger chunks fell. A slab of cobble thunked down by the bench, embedding itself in the mud. She peered out at the town and saw fire flaring up around the big building as smaller explosions followed, a cascade of blasts that ripped through anything left standing nearby. A quarter of Sober Sound had disappeared in the smoke.

"Guess we hit the ammo dump," Dalliance said, with a giddy laugh, more nervous than amused. Wish watched as another artillery blast hit the road, right by the tank, the barrage uninterrupted by that massive blow. The Relight tree was thrown back and shredded, igniting in little puffs of fire.

"Send up the flare," Wish said. "That's enough. Tell them it's done."

Dalliance nodded, getting the flare gun loose again. He fired into the sky, a green plume of smoke gliding above them, as another pair of shells hit the town. Wish stared emptily as the explosions slowed, then stopped. The smoke hung there, not wanting to clear, like it owned the town now.

What people remained near the lake weren't moving, scattered through the ruins. The ones further back kept fleeing, anyone close to the north side of town sprinting away, like sheep out a paddock. Plenty more were twitching in the mess, partially buried by debris. She willed herself to remember this. She deserved to live with this forever.

"I'm going down there," Gaussica announced, standing from the rear, dusting off his coat. "I need to check those mages."

"They're dead, Gaussica," Wish told him. "And there are still plenty of soldiers to worry about."

"You don't have to come," he replied.

"Fuck you," Wish said, standing too. Of course she had to come. If he was going to see it up close, so was she. "Wait ten minutes. We need to make sure Bluefern got the message."

***

They passed more bodies on the way, soldiers cut down fleeing through the forest. Jonus had mounted an able defence, stopping anyone from escaping south without incident. It wasn't just merciless killing, though – by the time Wish reached them, escorting Gaussica towards town, Jonus had over twenty people on their knees with their hands raised – soldiers and civilians alike. They looked thankful to be captured, such was the horror she had unleashed on them.

"Are we taking prisoners?" Wish asked.

"We'll turn the civilians and conscripts loose," Jonus said. "Keep the officers. For now."

Wish realised that many of her own people were watching her warily, a heavy atmosphere hanging over them. She gave Graveguard a questioning look, and he indicated the prisoners, one in particular – a young woman in a torn frilled dress. As plainly a non-combatant as possible, meaning everyone here understood what she might otherwise have kept from them. Ptrangus cleared his throat, not voicing the question that everyone had but didn't want to ask.

"Yeah," she said. "There were civilian casualties. Unavoidable." She hesitated, hating this, wanting to scream about it – she hadn't *wanted* this to happen. But if she was on breaking point, they all would be too, knowing the full extent of it. She couldn't prevent it, and she couldn't make up for it, but she could, at least, protect her people from the worst of it. She added, "There was nothing we could do; our targets were military. The civilians shouldn't have been there, and had the best chance of anyone to get clear. Just . . . all of you wait here while we check on the mage situation."

"*All* of us?" Latebite said. "The place could still be crawling with soldiers."

Wish eyed him grimly, willing him to just shut up, because she knew what lay ahead well enough. No one in that carnage was rallying to fight back. But he had a point: it wasn't safe. She just had to consider very carefully who would be able to handle the bare truth of it.

"Graveguard," she croaked, "you and Ohno, with me. Emi . . . I guess you'd best come." The other two Rawboys were glowering hard, daring her to leave them behind. She supposed they knew war better than anyone. Crag and Scraper looked barely less insistent, though Lugger and Dalliance at least weren't putting themselves forward. Damn, Dalliance had already seen enough. "Okay. Bite and Ptrangus, too. Crag, Scraper, no – get ready to fall back."

No one protested. Her group marched quickly but attentively into the devastated town, echoing now with moans and groans, people pleading in Lomian and Drail, as weak and wounded as if they were already ghosts. The first buildings they reached were half standing, with arms and legs sticking out of the collapsed stone. They stepped over severed limbs and chunks of flesh, charred enough to almost blend in with the ruins. The pervading smell was smoke, but there was a tinge of cooked meat, as fires burnt low, all around. Well done on the fortune, Gaussica. Easily predicted.

Someone shouted in Drail ahead and it spurred a fearful scrabble. Wish's team ducked in ready poses, guns up, as a group of soldiers ran out of cover, not towards them but away up the main road. If they had any weapons, they'd dropped them, and clearly feared a bigger Stanish force was coming to secure the town.

"Let them go," Wish said, watching the last of the men sprinting out of sight. "Take up defensive positions, but only engage if necessary. We just need to find these mages."

The platoon spread out, picking spots behind fallen walls to peer out through the smoke while Gaussica moved ahead, sniffing the air like an animal searching for prey. Emi climbed onto a small pile of broken stone with her hands in her pockets, looking back and forth with the most serious expression Wish had ever seen her wear. They met eyes and Emi looked down, nothing to say. Wish got more unhappy looks from the others as they collectively took in the extent of the damage. The death. The civilian decorations and clothing. Even the Rawboys looked like they might be sick. Latebite whispered a plaintive, "Boss . . ."

"Them or us," Wish said. "Nothing else we could do."

No one said a word, but Graveguard offered a nod. One that said she was handling it right, somehow. She wanted to tell him to piss off, but instead went to join Gaussica, walking into the town square, if it could be called that anymore. It was uneven and scattered with the same piles of broken buildings as elsewhere, but punctuated by the tank, untouched within the mess save a hefty black smear from the blast that had killed the tree.

"They hit the whole town and failed to take out the single most obvious military asset," Wish said, and Gaussica hummed, not listening. He focused on something ahead, and she spotted a sliver of coat herself, between the rubble. Terrifold. She watched as the Azirian pulled chunks of brick and road aside before standing over the man's body, staring hard to fully assess how dead he was. She already knew, of course. That was one corpse in this graveyard that belonged without question to her.

She heard movement to the left and turned, leaving Gaussica. Someone was pleading, struggling with something. There was half a tavern ahead, its sign swaying with a light squeak over part of a wall with exposed flooring, a fragment of building that defied gravity by still standing. She cautiously moved around it and found a man leaning over a body. He was moving back and forth, making promises or begging as he patted at the person, trying to provide medical aid. As Wish got closer, treading carefully not to disturb him, she saw that it was a woman on the ground. Ash-coated and bloody, her coat was ripped and scorched, but Wish recognised it as well as she did Terrifold's. The fur coat. That sad woman. Her upturned face was deathly pale, eyes closed, and as Wish got closer she saw that there was nothing where her right leg should be, and only half an arm on the left.

She wasn't bleeding. For a moment, Wish thought a blast must've knocked the blood clean out of her, or instantly cauterised the wounds – before she saw the man move his hands down, and the stump arm bunched up, puckering unnaturally. A force closed on it, squeezing as though the stump had been wrapped in an invisible bandage. She took in a breath with surprise, and the man looked up. Wish's rifle was already aimed from her hip to his head.

He spoke quickly in Drail, desperately, voice breaking as he tossed his head from side to side. He couldn't see her. One eye was blackened shut and the other crusted with a thick smear of blood. He was pleading for help.

The rubble crunched alongside Wish to announce Gaussica's arrival.

"He says she is alive," he translated. *"Please help."*

"It's the other mage," Wish replied.

The man went quiet, hearing their voices. Fresh fear crept over his face. "Comity?" In stilted Stanish. "Where do – where do you come from? What is your name? Excuse me?"

Wish was silent, gripped by the mad contrast of his phrasing, that of a schoolchild barely learning the language, against this horrific backdrop. She hoped Gaussica saw it too.

"Please. Do you help me?"

"He used his magic to heal her wounds. Maybe not a parser?"

"He's a parser," Gaussica said, certain of it. Then he asked something in Drail. The man hesitated, scared to reply, so he added something more, almost sounding sympathetic. The mage replied and Gaussica translated, "A pipeman. He . . . fixes pipes."

Wish grimaced at the painfully mundane detail. A plumber. The mage they'd come to kill was a damn plumber, blocking the leaks of a woman with half her body missing. "For fuck's sake. Gaussica . . ."

"My orders were for Terrifold," the Azirian said. "This is your choice."

She didn't need telling twice, and let the measured calm she'd been carrying break. She shouted through the town, "Listen up, scouts! We're clearing out fast, but if you can help anyone on the way, damn well help them. Graveguard, get your arse over here!"

24

JUDGE WATT: And the numbers of dead –
GENERAL DIAMOND: The numbers, the numbers! All I
hear from you eggshells is about the numbers, as if you can
tally this and tally that, to count your way to a justifiable
opinion. It is all war, understand? It is not about how things
balance – the numbers do not matter, only the final result.
Who won? Ask me that, Justice, if you dare. Who won?
JUDGE WATT: Again, if the general would let me finish
my question. A simple yes or no. The numbers of dead
reported by the grave-diggers and pyre burners, while not
precise, nonetheless far exceed the number of combatants
in the area, which are recorded precisely. Is there any way
such numbers were possible without significant civilian
casualties? Yes or no?
GENERAL DIAMOND: [Extended silence]
Transcript from the Hingbarman Trials, 734

Wish led a funereal procession back to Haven. Those who had
walked through the ruins carried a silence so heavy that the rest
understood without words. They marched in pairs, the prisoners in
the middle of the group, without looking at each other or speaking,
only the sound of their scuffing boots, Wish imagined everyone felt
as alone as her. She tried to lodge the images of Sober Sound in her
mind, to recall all the details, not to shy away from what she'd done.

   She hadn't seen any children, she realised. Women, men in
civilian clothes, severed limbs, even the scorched fur of dogs, damn
it all. No children. Part of her wanted to believe there was the
slightest truth in the excuse she'd invented, that by some miracle
the greater part of the civilians had managed to escape with the
bombardment focused on the military. Had all the children been

carried away, blessed by the Flesh or Castor or the Saints looking over them?

She had seen a pram, though. At least, the burnt, twisted wreck of a pram frame and half a wheel. Nothing in it or near it. She imagined the contents had been eviscerated. The *contents,* she cursed her own thoughts. The baby. There *had been a baby.* She knew for sure that if she asked one of the others, they would've seen children. They had all observed their own horrors which, put together, would be too much for any one person to bear. They couldn't talk about it, wouldn't talk about it, and that truth hung over the entire platoon in a cloud you could almost touch.

They heard Bluefern's men before catching up to them, shouting as they tried to manoeuvre the field guns in the road, making slow progress. As Wish's troop approached, they gradually quietened, reading the atmosphere and sharing it. A couple took off their caps and helmets in respect, nodding at the scouts as they passed. The guns themselves were surrounded by dozens of soldiers taking turns to drag them, a wheel of one sunk in the mud. Ohno looked a silent question Wish's way, but with a subtle shake of the head she instructed the ogre not to help. Ohno didn't seem about to anyway. The platoon continued past ranks of ambling artillerymen who all gradually got much quieter, all the way into Haven, where they found the village itself, and the bulk of the remaining company, weren't much livelier anyway.

Major Bluefern was organising his men into general retreat, packing up whatever they'd left in the town. They were darting around with the same quiet efficiency as before, heads low, serious, and Wish wondered how the reality of Sober Sound's destruction had reached everyone here. Was it an act so monstrous that it could simply be felt at a distance?

But Captain Crash came out from the ranks to greet them, grimly explaining, "Our men heard the Stranded about forty minutes ago. Somewhere to the south, but not anything the lookouts in the tower could spot."

"You said –" Wish stopped herself as she realised what a daft response she was about to make. He had said the Stranded didn't even want to fight for the Drail; they weren't supposed to come back. Of course, he couldn't know. They might've just been taking their time. Instead, she said, "Shouldn't we be establishing defences, then? Looks like you're heading for the road?"

"They didn't come close," Crash replied. "With no other reports of movement, Bluefern wants us moving out. Wait here – he'll want to talk to you."

The captain strode off, searching for the major, as Wish tensed her jaw. It was typical. Right, even, that more trouble lay ahead. They deserved trouble, if there was any sense of balance in the world. She looked back to her platoon.

"Someone ought to let those freaks know the fight's over," Latebite commented, to a few nods and murmurs of agreement, the group as a whole tired out.

"No, it's good they haven't left," Wish replied, but caught herself from voicing her first thoughts. There was another chance for redemption in this, she realised: "We've still got to get Iggy back." Their concerned and pitying looks said not everyone was hopeful for their fellow soldier. That only firmed her resolve, and she picked out Gaussica. "Surprised you're not already on the case, Gaussica. Now we're done with the mage you're free to follow up with the myriad."

He narrowed his eyes like she'd somehow insulted him.

"What? You waded in against those trolls for defection."

"Not for defection." Gaussica shook his head. "For death. They came towards my side, on the path of death – that's how I track threats. How the barrier shifts around us."

"You mean like with all the bombing and bloody gunfire?"

"It's not the same. It's not about killing, or life in the physical sense. Some people, creatures, situations, create worse risks. With this, and the Stranded, I don't feel . . ." Whatever he didn't feel he kept to himself. Distractedly glancing towards the woods, he added, "You have to choose. *You* . . ."

Wish blew out an irritated breath, looking to the village rather than wasting more time with him. Bluefern's men were filtering towards the south road, forming up ready to march. Didn't feel right or sensible. She said, "Dalliance, can you and Crag get up the clock tower and see if you can't get a better view than whoever Bluefern has up there?" She addressed Ohno. "And if you can take everyone else someplace secure, take a minute while I talk to him."

The ogre nodded and instructed the platoon away: "With me, scouts."

As they dispersed, watching Wish protectively, Gaussica remained, still staring at the trees, at nothing a normal person might see. Emi was also there, in turn watching him. Wish scanned from them back to the clock tower, recalling Gaussica's attack the day before. The dead man at its base. Quickness's killer. Past the busy soldiers, at the broken barricades, the blood stains were still visible where the man had fallen, even after the rain. Wish's brow knotted as a detail hit her.

"That man," she said. "The one you threw out the window. He wasn't in uniform."

Gaussica slowly focused on her, not seeming to understand.

"There were civilians in Sober Sound. Was he a soldier?"

No answer, just a dead stare.

"I thought . . ." Wish had to hold it down, the disquiet balling in her again. Thought he was responsible – the very one who'd shot Quickness. Thought he got what he deserved, even if she hadn't been able to do it herself. But – "Was he even armed?"

"He attacked me," Gaussica replied. "As I dispatched the others. He held a fury."

"Because you hurt his friends? Or ruined his paintings?"

"Or maybe he just didn't like you?" Emi added.

There was no apology in Gaussica's expression, nor any hint he considered he'd done anything wrong. Damn, when he focused, those eyes were chilling. At once both dead and deadly. He had gone into that clock tower in a state of ruthless attack. And on a day when they had bombed hundreds, this somehow stung harder. Couldn't that man, painting in his tower, at least, have been spared?

Was she really that naive, though, thinking that anyone or anything could be saved after all this? She wondered if at the end of it all, when there was peace, would there be any way to tally it that made any kind of sense? All these little disasters that stacked upon each other and made some twisted sense at the time, put together, measured against all that was lost and what precious little there might be left . . . How could it make sense?

"Captain Wild!" Major Bluefern interrupted her thoughts as he stomped through the soldiers, flanked by Captain Crash. "Let's hear what you've got. We're satisfied the destruction was complete?"

Wish bristled at his tone, not exactly happy, but brisk enough to feel inappropriate all the same. Trying to put Gaussica out of mind, she said, "I'm not sure I'd say *satisfied.* But the job's done."

"Splendid. And the mage –"

"Terrifold's dead. We put both of them out of action."

"Both?" Bluefern exclaimed like he'd just won a prize. "Well there's something. Excellent work." He seemed to hear himself then, and corrected his expression. "That is to say, a successful operation, exceeding expectations, despite regrettable circumstances."

Regrettable, that word again. Like unavoidable, the word she'd used herself. Bollocks.

"You're to be heavily commended, Captain. I see why your platoon's in such demand. You shot the mage yourself, I understand? I'll admit I wasn't sure exactly of your credentials, but my faith in Command has been rewarded. And I suppose we brought this lunatic monster hunter for nothing, huh?"

Wish rankled again, at Bluefern's doubts over her and his now apparent distrust of Gaussica, who perhaps should *not* be trusted, throwing civilians out of windows. It made her defensive, and she said, in part to convince herself, "He helped us secure Haven."

"From what I hear, you would've coped," the major replied.

"That *is* true," Emi said.

"Anyway, we're about ready for a quick exodus. We'll all be back on friendly soil before you know it. Are you planning on taking leave, Captain? I can help get you home for a spell. Long journey all the way to Stanclif but it's important to check in. Reminds everyone what we're fighting for."

Wish found herself scowling, this rapid chatter feeling even more inappropriate and deliberate. Like he was trying to distract her, either from thoughts of what they'd done, or from thoughts of what she still needed to do. Yet she couldn't help picturing the trip home, days on trains and the boat, to get back to Swelig, with its warm fires and cosy cottages. Modest decorations, nothing as lavish as Sober Sound's, but heartfelt. She'd been hopeful of a peaceful campfire, and friends to laugh with, and hadn't even considered she might actually go *home* for Relight. It'd been so long.

But they weren't even over the line yet.

Snapping herself out of it, she said, "Just a moment, Major. I understand your men heard the Stranded's Blood Call? Should we be moving right now? Your company would be safer remaining here while we scouted out the situation, and found Private Iggy, don't you think?"

Bluefern gave her a confused look, before fixing his expression. "We're confident the road is safe. We'll push hard and make a long night of it if needed, but we'll be over the line before any of us gets some sleep."

"But the Stranded can't be far off. We need to –"

"I've given my orders. We've already sent a vanguard out, and as soon as the guns catch up the rest of the company will follow. Everyone wakes tomorrow on solid Stanish soil, job well done. You can start hanging your Relight decorations."

There was that attempt at distraction again, but Wish only saw a garland burning. The tree in Sober Sound eviscerated. She said, "We're a long way from Stanish soil."

"Ah, anywhere clear of the damn Drail is home! Captain Wild, let's not invite trouble where there is none, what do you say?"

Indignation flushed through Wish. She never expected him to help with Iggy, but to suggest she drop it, while wilfully rushing out into danger . . . Clamping down her anger, she said, "Sir, if you're really set on moving, then we've done all you needed from us, and perhaps we can part ways. I'm not leaving Iggy behind."

Bluefern glared, considering turning her down. "You realise that whatever major action we've curbed here, this territory is likely to become very volatile in the next few days, even the next few hours? They may be organising a counter-attack as we speak."

"I very much doubt that, sir," Wish said. If the Drail had any resources left nearby, after all that destruction, they'd be using them to salvage whatever lives and supplies they could from the wreckage. "And if that were the case, all the more reason to Iggy fast."

Again, Bluefern looked like he wanted to complain, to order her off this crazy idea, and he glanced at Captain Crash, seeking a second opinion. Crash's face didn't twitch, but in that stoicism the major somehow got an answer. He said, "I suppose that's why you're out there killing mages while I'm just sitting on my laurels tossing bombs over the wall. Far be it from me to suggest what else you might be capable of. If you join us as far as the final path west, you'll –"

"Drail in the road! Drail in the road!" A desperate shout came outside the village and the gathered soldiers started scattering back towards the buildings. Another shout followed – Dalliance, calling from the clock tower: "Stranded!"

Wish swung her rifle off her shoulder as Major Bluefern blundered off to one side, drawing a pistol, and Captain Crash yelled for everyone to take cover. In a panic, men threw down their packs and dove into doorways or behind walls, wrestling to get guns ready. Rather than hide, Wish ran towards the road, shoving past men, and she saw Ohno's head lumbering over others, emerging with the rest of her scouts.

"Get a view on the road!" Wish shouted. "Take up –"

"They're calling for parley!" A frantic soldier cut her off, running into the village. "Got a flag! They want to talk to the women!"

25

*The generals knew no mercy. The commanders, officers,
and admins behind the lines wanted to push, push, push,
and leave nothing behind. They saw only lines on maps and
numbers alive or dead. We on the ground, whether Stanish
or Drail, Khib or Slane . . . It was hard, I think, for any true
soldier to maintain the belief that anyone dead or dying
was truly our enemy.*
All This Aflame: Memoirs of a Soldier, Lindon, p. 98

Wish had to get clear of the village and its supposed safety to reach
the Stranded. Most of the company had fled into the cottages but
some braver, or more diligent, soldiers remained on the road, lying
by the thorns with guns ready as she and her scouts passed. At the
front, some hundred metres out of the village, a soldier hiding
behind a tree trunk flagged her down and held up three fingers,
pointing ahead. She saw it for herself anyway. Three dark shapes in
the empty road, mounted. She lifted her rifle to scope them out, Emi
skidding up alongside her on one side and Latebite taking a knee at
the other, rifle up. The creature caught her breath, as Latebite said,
"There's an ugly little bastard."

Real, living Stranded, less than another hundred metres ahead.
They were shadow black with jagged, oblong torsos, riding savage-
jawed dogs, almost as dark. Two were further back, with the closest,
in the middle, pacing side to side at the front, the dog itching to
move. The leader had a tall pole tied to their saddle, a dirty white
rag hanging from the top.

"Peace!" the Stranded shouted in Stanish. "We seek to talk."

Its voice alone caused shudders among the soldiers close enough
to hear, the words clear but in a timbre unlike any sound a human
throat could produce. It had a faltering wheeze, scratchy and

clipped, as if the creature was whistling through a broken flute.

"Send us the Woman General. We seek to talk."

"I think he means you," Emi said.

Wish glanced aside, finding her other scouts looking thoroughly concerned on her behalf. Near the treeline, Ptrangus managed a smirk, like it was typical of her to draw the attention of horrible little creatures.

Bluefern swore fiercely from a little way back as he followed, and she saw him and Captain Crash at the trees' edge, around a curve in the road so they'd not be in the Stranded's eyeline. The major's glower seemed to include her: angry at both the enemy's presence and their wanting to talk to *her*. She said, "I have *never* called myself a general."

"Where's the rest of them?" Bluefern demanded. The question carried a troubling implication: *probably not far off.* They were trapped in this canal of trees, an easy target if the enemy were anywhere nearby – and with the fading daylight, the woodland shadows offered a lot of hiding places. But if the Stranded could get this close without being seen, Wish somehow doubted the village itself was much safer. They might be completely surrounded already. She had her scouts, though: they were spread out like a firing squad, ready to hold the road. If anyone came from that direction, at least.

"Only one of them has a gun," Crash pointed out, venturing a little further forward than the major. The rider on the right had a monstrously large musket, the sort that had gone out of fashion a century ago, not least because it was twice the size of a modern rifle with about a quarter of the firepower. The other two were carrying blades almost as big as their bodies, wide and curved with bonus circular blades under the hilts. The leader twirled his with a practised flair to punctuate his words. From his swaggering posture, Wish had a feeling it was a *he.*

"The Woman General!" he called out again, swaying slightly as he struggled to keep his dog steady. The mount snapped nastily, not a natural riding creature. They might as well have been riding crocodiles or fenstarts. "We will speak."

"Your army's withdrawn!" Bluefern shouted, standing as tall as his short body allowed, which was made doubly unimpressive by how he remained in cover. "If you're offering terms of surrender, I'll hear them."

Wish watched the Stranded through her scope, trying to make out what in its dark, woody form constituted its mouth. Some feature there stretched unevenly, slanted, vaguely resembling a smile. They reminded her of the barkmen, the inexplicable living tree creatures of Eardung, but where those eerie people were creepily unassuming, these ones exuded danger, their every edge sharp and at odds with nature.

"We offer an exchange," the Stranded shouted. "The woman bomber. The happy soldier."

Happy? Iggy must've been anything but happy in their capture. Had they been watching them before?

"We will return her. We seek to talk to the Woman General."

"Don't like this one bit," Crash said, as if anyone could be thinking differently.

"So talk!" Wish shouted. "If it's me you want, I'm right here." She spread her arms, on show at the centre of the road. A lunatic move, with danger possible from any angle, but screw it.

"Not here. You come with us. Make camp. Alone. We guarantee safety and return the happy soldier."

"I can handle them," Gaussica's soft voice came in. He was just behind her line of scouts, but stood taller than the others, no weapon in hand, all the more formidable for how brashly visible he was. "Will you allow me?"

"No ghost!" the Stranded leader shouted, apparently understanding Gaussica's suggestion from afar. Well aware of who he was. "No closer."

Was that something passing for fear? He was certainly capable of fighting them, somehow, and was apparently finally ready to do it, when they had come in peace. But he wanted her go-ahead. He somehow needed it, in whatever twisted logic passed for a chain of command in his head. She said, "There might be dozens of them in the trees. Maybe we try not to provoke them, and hear what they want to say?"

"It's you or me now, Captain," Gaussica said. "Do this and you will suffer. They're incapable of changing me."

She gave his weird wording the usual silence. But whatever he was prophesying, after all his hints at her needing to choose, and burnt flesh and suffering, she realised he'd never suggested it would kill her. If she took the lead here she might be hurt, but if he was unleashed a lot of people would die. Not least Iggy.

Emi said, "Do you want *me* to handle them?", hardly helping.

"Will you come, Woman General?" the Stranded leader prompted. "We do not fight."

"Fucking suicide to go with them," Bluefern growled. "What the hell do you have to talk to these freaks about? At best, you're a hostage. We can cut them down and retreat fast into the village. Everyone ready, Crash?"

"Haven is secure," Crash reported.

"The hell it is," Wish said. "Your guards didn't spot these guys coming. Your men in the tower haven't seen shit of what's going on in those woods."

"There's no choice," Bluefern snapped.

"I can go with them," Wish said, finding that the thought didn't entirely horrify her. She was tired and she didn't want to fight and if she could save Iggy without anyone else getting hurt, why not. If only *she* got hurt, wasn't it about time?

"And I'm going to tell Command I let an asset like you walk into enemy hands, am I?" Bluefern said. "We don't even know your soldier is alive."

"But if she is, I can save her." Wish looked at Gaussica. "I've got a better chance of saving her than you, don't I?"

He returned her look impassively. Slightly sadly. There was her answer. She checked the rest of her platoon: where the artillery company's reflex had been to hide, her soldiers had stood firm and had her back. Emi looked unpleasantly keen on trouble, with Ohno braced for a fight on her other side. The Rawboys were stiffly determined. And Scraper – shit – was by Captain Crash, a knife in her hand. Okay, she looked a little more ready to resist Bluefern's command than the Stranded, but it was still support. Graveguard met Wish's eye and gave his understanding nod again, this one saying she had their full support. But she had an opportunity to keep them all safe. If they were ready to die on her command, she had to be ready to suffer for them.

To the waiting Stranded, she shouted, "Return my soldier and I'll talk to you!"

"You come," the Stranded replied. "We take you to her. Guarantee safety."

"How far?"

"Not far. Meet the Path Writer."

"To hell with that!" Bluefern shouted. "Your Path Writer can talk here in the bloody road. No one's going with you. Return our soldier or we'll send them your heads."

The Stranded's mount turned again, angry breath puffing out in clouds. The rider appeared to be smiling again, and his voice took a lighter edge, almost like amusement. "We are not interested in you, Angry Lord. You do not want us to be interested in you."

The major growled like a poked animal. Out of sight, with the company supposedly safe in their village, he appeared more concerned about the blow to his pride than the actual danger: a nearly perfect mission thwarted at the last moment. A little monster on a dog disrespecting him.

"Listen, Major," Wish said. "This is the best option. It might be the only chance Iggy's got."

"If there's any chance at all," Bluefern snarled. "They might attack us anyway. Except if you go, we have one less fighter to defend ourselves, understand? A valuable one."

"Gotta agree with the major, boss," Latebite said. "It's a bad idea."

"We can follow you," Graveguard suggested. "Be ready to help."

"Not a chance in hell you move around here unseen by them," Wish replied.

"Woman General!" The Stranded was losing patience. "You come. Talk."

"Get down," Bluefern told Wish. "On my command. We strike first and retreat."

"They're flying a white flag," Wish said.

"They're the fucking Stranded! You can't trust a damn thing they say!"

"They're not the ones who murdered civilians today!" Wish spat back, stunning him. Stunning everyone in earshot. She'd done it now. It wasn't real if no one said it out loud and she'd made it real. And in the moment it bought her, she walked away from the company. "I'm here. I'll talk if you release her. And you'll let the company pass. No more killing today."

"Captain, you will not!" Bluefern took a step into the road, but stopped, not daring go further. Gaussica did follow, though, and the Stranded wheeled on its mount with a caustic hiss.

"The ghost stays!" it cried, in a voice like a tree splitting, releasing steam. It was such an unreal, biting sound that Wish cringed. She raised a hand to Gaussica, meeting his eye.

"I will pass through these creatures, and these woods, without harm," he promised with such calm that she could believe it.

"It's not *you* I'm concerned about. Go back. Protect my platoon. Or better yet, do nothing."

"Captain. I can shield you."

"I don't *want* your shield," Wish snarled. "You're not fighting them. So *go back.*"

He hesitated a moment more, then nodded, face steeling. But there was more movement as Emi appeared at Wish's other side. "You heard her, mage-killer. We don't need you."

"Emi!" Wish said, feeling suddenly like she was herding lizards. The fucking madness of managing people and opinions bobbing up in all directions when there were literal monsters watching ahead. "You do not –"

"Ah!" Emi said, lifting a hand for silence, so confidently that Wish froze with alarm. The mage lifted her voice for the Stranded to hear. "The Woman General will come only if you allow her to come armed. And I am her greatest weapon."

The Stranded made a strangled, staccato sound, which Wish took for some kind of laughter. "Bring the weapon, but no ghost. We invite the mad magic woman. We like her. And the Urlian. They are worthy of the Path Writer. They keep you safe. Agreed?"

"Then they can take us, too," Ptrangus noted, and Wish clicked her tongue at him. Further back, she saw Bluefern watching fiercely, not liking this but no longer resisting. Her scouts' expressions weren't much more encouraging. Wish hesitated. These creatures definitely knew more about them than they should have. She had no desire to take Emi or Ohno into the wilderness after the Mire, where they'd both already come close to death thanks to her decisions.

"Ohno has the command," she instructed, finally. She continued, particularly addressing the three Rawboys in turn, "None of you follow me. That's an order. You're all going home for Relight, understand? I'll join you later." Then, to Emi, she said, "Stay, Emi. Be safe."

"I have *never* been safe," Emi replied, grinning in a way that killed further discussion.

"Captain," a quiet voice interrupted and she saw Scraper standing by Ohno, having slid subtly to the front of the group. A single word that said if anyone should come, it was her. And, after Gaussica, she suspected that unusual woman might be more ready than anyone to fight these Stranded. All the more reason to leave her behind.

Wish looked to Ohno again instead, and said, "Ohno. Get *everyone* home, okay? I'll be right behind you."

26

The darkest shadows hold the deepest answers.
Azirian Idiom

The darkest shadows hide intangible solutions.
Azirian Idiom [Alternative Translation]

The Stranded formed an honour guard with the leader riding ahead
and the other two falling behind, leading Wish and Emi off the main
road onto one of the narrow paths. It wasn't one Wish recalled from
their maps, not this close to Haven. But maybe she hadn't kept
proper track. For a time, they walked in silence, watching the first
creature on its dog while the others watched them. Emi whistled,
hands in her pockets as casually as ever, and smiled at Wish. At
Wish's questioning look, the mage said, "All that fuss over a damn
mage-killer. We're going to show them how *useless* he was."

"Yeah?" Wish said. "I thought you'd started to get along."

"He's still a mage-killer who never should've been sent with us.
It's the principal, Wild."

"So I guess your investigation hasn't gone so well there? No
sympathy for the madman?"

"Sympathy? Curiosity, at most. He's got peculiar tuning and I
don't like things that I don't understand."

"And you don't like that he knew something about you."

"It was never what he said, Wish – it's *when* he said it. Any two-
penny arbitrator could've learnt about the Standen Ball – they've
all got files on me. But remember? You were raving about dying. It
did remind me of that bloody night, and he knew that before I did."

"He . . . but that doesn't make sense?"

"That's the *point."* Emi rolled her eyes expansively. They kept
walking for a moment as the mage scanned the trees, thoughtfully,

and Wish didn't press the point. Then Emi came to some decision, continuing, "Let me tell you a story. I had a teacher, Mrs Puntsmith. She gave us a speech after the hall burnt down, when people were all freaking out and terrified, kids crying, parents angry. She was trying to calm them all down, and she insists, *'This place of learning is a safe space, and I promise you no one else will die.'* I was scared myself, and thinking, what a thing to say about a school – why *would* anyone die? Except obviously they just *had* and she couldn't, you know . . ."

The mage trailed off, as Wish struggled to parse the rare (predictably erratic) vignette of Emi's past. It hardly qualified as a story. But the question of Gaussica's input was what gave it weight. He had mentioned the memory to Emi twice – the first time long before Wish made her similarly unreasonable speech. She asked, "How did he know about it?"

"Because I told him later," Emi scoffed, that part apparently obvious, and Wish understood she meant during their chat when Quickness was buried. "The question is how did he know it *then?* He jumps around. He's responding to things that we haven't seen happen yet, but he has. When I told him he was right about the memory, *that* was when he learnt it."

"Emi, what the fuck?" Wish asked, exasperated. It didn't exactly add up, but left one damning thought: if Gaussica's ramblings could, in any way, be explained as real, then should she be more worried about the mad things he'd said to her? He'd said more than once that he wouldn't fight the Stranded if she chose to go herself, and she had, at last, left him behind. She quietly said, "He told me this journey would end in burnt flesh."

"Yeah, but don't most of them?" Emi agreed as merrily as if Wish had said they'd get a drink when this was done.

"So what . . . I mean . . ." Wish didn't know what else to ask. How to even process this information. She looked ahead, to the Stranded, and couldn't help wondering if a better understanding of their monster hunter might've got her through this more safely. Because however strange he was, the Stranded were stranger, and a much more present problem. But there was no going back now.

She forced herself to study the creature ahead. The movements of its body as it swayed in its saddle, whipping the reins to settle the dog, were jittery and mechanical, like a spider. How *could* they be of this world?

That feeling got worse as night crept in and the Stranded produced lanterns from their saddles, casting vivid shadows on and around them. Worse still as they drew at last to the Stranded camp, and the wretched calls of their clan came through the trees. Wish had kept a good semblance of calm telling herself it was the right thing to do and they *might* just want to talk, but those fox-like screeches and broken-tree laughs made her skin crawl. The lead rider twisted in his saddle, sensing her discomfort, and its suggestion of a reassuring smile was a nightmare in the flickering lantern light.

Under a crescendo of squawks and laughs, the path brought them into a camp every bit as macabre as Wish expected. The riders pulled to the sides, allowing her and Emi to take it in. In a circular clearing between the trees, with one giant oak at the centre, likely landscaped as a peaceful picnic stop for Sober Sound guests, a half dozen campfires revealed scores of the nevolk moving between bone-framed tents, decorated with skulls and chunks of broken metal. Dogs roamed between them, much larger than the nevolk, occasionally snapping, eyes flashing red in the firelight. A pair were fighting over a body, wrenching out strings of flesh that Wish hoped weren't human. The Stranded were squatting over cooking pots, tinkering with tools and sharpening blades. Even at rest, their movements were too sharp and fast. Their chatter came out in a blending mix of indecipherable whistles and hoots, and she realised what sounded like laughter might have been conversation, as they weren't exactly partying or rolling about in hysterics.

The noises quietened as the tribe slowly saw they had visitors.

Wish's heart pounded just looking at them all, the magnitude of this bad idea settling in. There were too many of them and they were too damn bizarre to even begin to fight. They were going to strip their flesh and she had an urge to run rather than step one foot closer. But as they got quieter, she heard a more natural noise under their chatter: something human. Her eyes went to the oak tree, and she saw a person at its base.

"Iggy!" Wish exclaimed, striding into the camp. It sent up a rush of garbled barks and hisses, the sound of a dozen kettles boiling, a chalkboard scratched. She cringed and held up her hands, slowing as the crowd flexed around her, widening before drawing closer.

"Back! Get back!" Emi snapped, waving a hand that made a half dozen nevolk scatter. They closed the gap again quickly as the mage bumped into Wish. "I should level this camp right now."

"Don't," Wish said, eyes on Iggy, approaching more slowly as the nevolk let her through.

"Boss, that you?" Iggy croaked, with a hint of her former cheer. She tried to stand but slipped, falling back against the tree and gasping. As Wish reached her, given limited space by the pressing nevolk, she saw her uniform was torn all over, skin filthy with dirt and blood, hair smeared flat against her face. Propping herself up with an elbow against the tree, gasping for breath, Iggy managed a cracked-lipped smile. "You came?"

"Yes!" Wish said, pushing forward. Almost treading on a Stranded who darted aside at the last second, she put her hands on Iggy's shoulders.

Emi joined her, squinting at the tree, where the bark was dripping with a viscous, dark liquid. "Well, this is something . . ."

Wish focused on Iggy, hard to see the wounds for the charred patches on her uniform, crusty with dried blood. She reeled on the Stranded. "What'd you do to her!" Using the anger to suppress mounting terror at the sea of sinister black shapes, she searched for the rider who'd brought them here. No idea how to tell them apart – they wore no clothes and their differences in shape and size were warped by their erratic movements and the flickering firelight.

"She is complete," a Stranded said. "Healing."

"Stings like a bugger is all," Iggy said, hazily, indicating her right forearm, bandaged with a natty, stained rag where the sleeve had been torn away. Wish met her eye questioningly, but Iggy's pupils were wide and unfocused. "They've got this great –" Iggy winced. "Actually helped me. These little pricks are alright. Just really fucking stings."

The Stranded spoke again, nearby, in their language, and a large nevolk, tall as Wish's chest, hobbled out. From the way the others gave it space, it had some greater authority.

"The Woman General," it said, studying her with a chicken-bob motion as the ranks of nevolk bounced about encouragingly behind.

"I'm no general," Wish snarled. "What have you done to my soldier?"

"Saved her," the creature hissed. "And welcomed her. She wears the mark."

"Zatty!" Iggy announced, with the happy familiarity of a drunkard, then reclined against the tree with a sharp, pained breath. Regrouping, she said, "It's cool, boss. These guys fed me, got this killer drink, and their *dancing* – phew. We've been talking about the sea."

"Iggy, they've drugged you," Wish told her. She looked to Emi, but the mage was still staring at the tree, wonderingly. A couple of Stranded chittered closer and Wish flinched, thrusting one of them out of the way. At the creature's cry, she raised her gun. The Stranded leader called out, arms forming sideways Vs in a pincer-like motion. A gesture for calm, as the crowd settled – something like holding up palms for peace.

"Be safe!" it said, maybe at the tribe, maybe at Wish. "We welcome you, as we welcomed her. I am Zatricule, the Path Writer. Please, allow her the salve."

Wish gave it a scathing look, distrusting its oddly reasonable cadence, as well-spoken as their inexplicable voices were capable of.

But she felt a light touch on her arm – Iggy, reaching up to her. "Hear Zatty out, boss. Let them do their thing."

"What thing?" Wish asked. "It looks like bloody torture."

"The salve." Iggy indicated the Stranded nearby, with bowls in their talons. "It's good." Under her encouraging gaze, Wish reluctantly let the creatures pass, and the nevolk lathered a thick, sticky salve around her bandage, similar to what was dripping off the tree. Iggy murmured, "There's the good stuff."

"They did this," Emi said, placing a hand on the bark between the streaks of liquid. Her eyes widened and she made a cooing noise. "How?"

"Shit, Emi, don't touch that!" Wish slapped her arm down and the mage gave her a look as vicious as a kicked cat's.

The Stranded were peeling back Iggy's uniform on her chest, where the skin was inflamed, almost black, knobbly. They were tending burn marks, the sort caused by an explosion. Probably her own.

"Woman General," Zatricule said, white eyes empty. "She is safe. And we welcome you. We have seen you and wish to see more. We wish for you to see us. Do you so wish, Woman General?"

"I am not a general!" Wish shouted, mixed up with fear and anger at the eeriness of everything around her, only made worse by that repeated *wish,* which felt deliberate. They knew her name. How long had they been watching her and what else had they seen?

She realised, then, how still and silent everything now was. Even the dogs were watching her. The Stranded were a forest of burnt, leafless tree trunks, with only their claws and lifeless white eyes setting them apart. The smell of dried blood and fat crackling in the fires got in her nose.

"Listen, all you," Wish said carefully. "I don't know what you're after, but we defeated your army today. They've been pushed back, lost this position. These aren't your woods anymore. We've got no reason left to fight with you. I'm here to *politely* suggest you hand over Iggy and leave while you can."

"They are not our army," Zatricule said. "And these are not our woods. We do not own anything nor belong anywhere – but own everything and belong everywhere. Will you let us explain?"

"Please do," Wish replied quietly, thrown by the riddle-like language.

"You call us Stranded, and Strayed, and it is what we are. But we have strayed from your world and its cages, not our own. What you call countries, and empires, remain cages for you. They force you to act with regret, for the sake of illusions, not for yourself. You are stranded too – you and all the lesser humanity."

Wish swallowed, sure that this unsettling creature was well aware of what they'd been through today. That word regret, again – and for an *illusion?* Wasn't the horror they'd unleashed today in aid of something that didn't even feel real? She focused on that last unusual phrase, though, and said, "What do you mean, lesser humanity?"

"Women," Emi suggested. "She's talking about women. I've heard the myriad think of us that way – as a separate race, given how we live. Or are treated."

"She?" Wish said, and the mage shrugged, just guessing.

"The soil mage understands. She has part of the connection. But words are not enough for us to embrace. We invite you to accept the mark, see yourself Stranded, so we can grow our path together. Do you accept?"

Wish frowned trying to follow all this, and asked Emi, *"Do* you understand this?"

"It worked for me, boss," Iggy answered first, sounding more lucid after her treatment. They'd wiped her face clean and there was some natural colour coming through. "They had this little ritual and I got a much better feel for them afterwards. Like, I know they're alright?"

"No offence, Iggy, but you were clearly caught in an explosion and I don't know what. I'm not sure if you're thinking clearly right now."

"But she *is* touched by them," Emi said, thoughtfully. "I can feel it, too. In the ground, in the air – and the energy they've put in this tree. It's almost earth-minding, but they've *changed* this tree, to produce whatever . . . this is. Their mark could be some kind of bridge, towards that energy?"

"How did it work?" Wish asked Iggy.

"Oh, fuck knows – you're right enough, boss, I *was* bloody out of it. It happened somewhere in all the fire and pain and that. I dunno. I just had this idea we were gonna get on?"

"Oh Iggy," Wish said, heart falling at whatever they might've done to this brave girl. She addressed the Stranded again, "I appreciate the offer but I think we're okay. If you're not interested in this place anyway, then that's all good – you can leave and we won't get in your way."

"Don't you wish for more?" Zatricule asked. "We do. We wish to see your hope and feel for the future. We wish you to share in ours."

"In your . . . what?" Wish frowned, her repeated name again sounding strange. Her head was getting fuzzy, in this light with the crowd appearing to move even as they stood still. "Look, I'm just an idiot with a gun – I'm not anyone special you need concern yourselves with. And we've all had a tough day. Whatever you think I can do for you –"

"You revived Bonesun's call. You are the Woman General who walked in Eardung and along the Devil's River. You walked in the Mire and spoke to the myriad beasts."

"Huh." She looked at Iggy, who shrugged apologetically, but she couldn't have told them all that, could she? It was one thing for them to have spied on her in these woods, but how would a tribe like this know details about her previous operations?

"You have burnt cities," Zatricule went on. "And fought giants and mages."

"One city," Wish said, holding up a finger. "One giant." Then she paused. "Okay, I suppose two cities, if you count today – but that was a town. Wait. How do you know any of this?"

"You are *Stranded,* just like the one they call Queen of the Goblins. You are capable of great and terrible things, and we wish to see you. We wish you to see us."

The Queen of the Goblins, again, dammit. Apparently the Vulgar Division weren't the only ones who'd been preoccupied with rumours of the mysterious rebellion in the east, and Wish couldn't get away from Havikare's spectre. Was all this coming from the propaganda she'd been spreading, including stories of the Blood Scouts? She said, "I don't know what you've been told, but I'm not . . . I *am* with Stanclif. We're fighting to protect our country and stop this world falling into Drail hands. If you want to join us, there's conversations to be had, but out in the east, that's not my business –"

"You are *not* your empire," Zatricule said, emphatically enough to make Wish jump. "You are better. Those who follow you are better, and have strayed, just like those who follow her. We wish to see what hope you bring for ourselves."

Wish hesitated, realising from the heavy attention they'd clearly given her that, at least as far as the Stranded threat had gone, their success in this mission had not been by chance. Iggy had been taken care of. Had Macmiddan and Grebe been spared, rather than just luckier than Bluefern's men? If the Stranded were looking out for the Blood Scouts, this would be a bad time to offend them. She said, "You just want me to take this mark and we can go? That's it?"

"An end and a beginning," Zatricule said. "We will part together."

"Bloody hell," Wish huffed, almost to herself, "just speak straight."

"It's *clearly* a bonding thing," Emi clarified.

The crowd moved in a strangely coordinated way, suddenly, splitting down the middle to form a path, two paces wide all the way out of the clearing. It was impressive – they were hopping about, gnashing and laughing at the fringes, but this channel of bodies was steady, despite how they moved around it. Zatricule said, "We wish for it. You need to wish it too. You can go, or you can stay. But you have to choose."

The Stranded started moving again, stirred by the coming decision, making noises, their wall-scratching voices shooting back and forth. A couple of dogs snapped at each other and the outer reaches of the tribe began circling. The chattering grew in high laughter and broken crackles.

Wish stared up the path, the way out open and safe. They *would* let her go. She couldn't move though, chilled at how Zatricule had echoed Gaussica's words in Haven, *you have to choose.* It wasn't about facing this tribe without him, but this. The Stranded were offering her a view to something different. She didn't know what, or why, only that it meant change. A step away from all that had brought her here, with its senseless, endless death. An admittance that she did feel stranded in all her lonely, terrible dread.

They were restless, growing excited. One of them gave a particularly shrill birdlike call, and others echoed it in varying patterns. Iggy called out, "Here we go again!"

"It's powerful," Emi said, touching the tree. "This is . . . different, Wild."

"Will you take the mark?" Zatricule hummed, a chant fitting the symphony of mad sounds. "Prove you are stranded, too."

With the escalating noise and movement, Wish felt her pulse racing. Hard to think as more cries went up, a bone drumbeat sounded somewhere. She saw the Mire again, the rise of the grescind and the energy Havik unleashed, a power she didn't understand. Here again, a power she didn't understand. And she saw Sober Sound obliterated, the deaths of hundreds or thousands, thanks to a war she understood all too well. Civilian clothes in the rubble. Us or them. That man broken at the base of the clock tower and Quickness's eyes staring up dead. Us or them. Loose as she fell from the cliff. *No –*

The clamour grew towards something not far from the Blood Call and Emi erupted in mindless laughter, bunching up with her hands in claws. Iggy was clapping. "She gets it!"

"What is it?" she cried. "What happens when I take the mark?"

When, she heard herself, not *if.*

They screeched louder and moved faster, taking her response as a confirmation, not a question. Yes. She needed to understand. She needed to connect with this energy. Hope, they'd said. There would be hope on the other side. She needed *some* kind of hope.

Wish noticed one of the nevolk drawing something from a campfire. The crowd weaved around it as it held up a sizzling metal rod. The wide end glowed bright with intense heat and the Stranded howled with delight. Emi cackled, as feral as the creatures screeching and hooting, dancing in sinister shadows. Blades were slicing the air and terrifying dogs gnashed as it pressed it on her closer, and Iggy shouted, "Here we go!"

"Shit," Wish said. Her rifle felt light and useless in her limp hands, the nevolk pressing in and bumping each other. She tried to pick out Zatricule but they all looked the same. "That doesn't seem –" Her voice trembled. She didn't want to fight, though. Didn't want to stop this. Quickness was dead. Everyone in Sober Sound was dead. Wish closed her eyes, struggling to recall them all now. Loose, Sarge, Small, Fixit, all dead. Rue and Newk and Dakoda and Oksy lost. And she was whole and healthy, unmarked after leaving so many dead. Too many gone, too many names. Who had been killed by the Gonish, that stupid, unnecessary death? Pound, poor Pound. It could have been her, if they'd chosen different doors. Should it have been her? Her breath came quicker. Eyes trembling. Could she burn the pain away?

"You have to choose!" The voice seemed to come from everywhere. The world felt alive in a fever of activity and noise, dragging Wish in. The brand sizzled, air steaming around it. The path out was open but Wish was caught, rapt at the possibility that existed *right here*. They wanted to connect with her. Needed to, somehow. There was a power Emi could physically feel – that *she* needed to, herself – a step forward and away.

How bad could it hurt? One moment of suffering to keep this strange dream going . . . She deserved it, after all. She deserved to be afraid. Gaussica knew it was coming, anyway – somewhere, somehow it was already done. This war was a hell the empires had created together and she was stranded in the middle of someone else's squabble, wanting to stray. For the sake of Sober Sound and everyone and everything else, why shouldn't she at least *try* . . .

She saw the rubble and the bodies and that legless woman and the burnt-out pram.

"Will you take the mark?" Zatricule asked one last time.

"Yes!" Wish shouted above the noise, pulling up the sleeve of her uniform. The Stranded held her arms in place with more strength than their little bodies looked capable of and the brand pressed in. Her flesh bubbled with a foul stench and a violent hiss as pain shot through her, so intense her mind exploded, the world a pinprick of fury, the camp and the woods and the entire war reduced to one horrific, earth-shattering scream.

All she knew was the stench and agony of burning flesh.

Everything was white.

27

Errant magic incidents involving mages: 109 (23 punished)
Errant magic incidents involving non-mages: 32,410
(28,781 cases punished)
Errant magic incidents classified: 28
(Estimated -24% deviation due to wartime)
Statistics from the Office of Arbitration (720-1)

When Wild Wish woke, the Stranded were gone.

She stirred with uncomfortable aches beside a dying fire, pushing herself up from the frosty ground, and winced as pain coursed through her forearm. She breathed into it, teeth gritted as she took in the heavy bandaging, the wound throbbing but bearable. Iggy was right about that soothing salve – whatever was under that bandage surely looked a lot worse than it felt. Wish blinked away her bleariness, sitting up and trying to recall how things had ended. The clearing was a mess of smouldering fires and discarded scraps of bone and tents, empty of creatures. Except for Emi, who groaned, spread out on the ground the other side of the fire, and Iggy, who crouched a little further back, gnawing on something.

"Ah great," Iggy said, "you're awake. Want some of this? It's good, whatever it is."

Wish unsteadily got up, accepted a skewer of barbecued meat, and tried not to overthink it. Hard to believe any ordinary animals had remained nearby for the Stranded to hunt. She asked, "When did they leave?"

"Somewhere in the mess of it all, I guess."

Wish nodded, not expecting more clarity than that. She recalled writhing about in agony, seeing frightening images of the Stranded coming in and out of focus, fires jumping, creatures howling, and things getting easier as she let go. There'd been more of this meat.

Drinking and dancing. Emi running with the creatures. Chaos.

The mage stirred too, and after a moment of muttering suddenly sat bolt upright. She fixed her eyes accusingly on Wish. *"And?"*

Wish gave her the wide eyes imploring for more, getting nothing, then said, "And what?"

"What do you feel? How is it" – Emi frantically waved at her own arm to indicate Wish's wound – "working?"

Wish frowned, considering her wounded arm again. It hurt, and she wasn't sure what else it was supposed to do, so was more concerned with their absent hosts. She asked Iggy, "Did you see what direction they took?"

"Nope," Iggy said. "If I'm honest, feels kind of like being left passed out drunk by your mates in a market square with your pants down and a dick on your face."

Branding them with a hot iron was a hell of a step further than a drunken prank, but Wish understood the feeling. Who was to say what passed for entertainment with the Stranded?

"Completely gone," Emi said, hands pressing into the grubby earth. She shook her head and looked to the ichor-stained oak tree, appearing put out. "They took it with them. The energy they'd been building here." Her head snapped back to Wish. "Don't you feel it?"

"No," Wish sighed, rolling her head back to look at the sky. Dull grey, another cold morning, and they were left out in the open. Thank Bly the fires hadn't died overnight or they might've frozen to death. Abandoned by the creatures after they'd made such a fuss . . . Wish felt let down, as though the Stranded had found her lacking and decided to immediately rescind their generous offer of making sense of everything. Had she screamed too much? Or was this what they intended all along, to hurt her and run for reasons that only made sense to four-foot dog-riding maniacs? It was an act of violence that made about as much sense as every other in this war. She considered the remnants of the wicked camp one last time, knowing they were gone for good. Hopefully they had gone north and not out to attack the company, as Bluefern had feared. She said, "Come on. Let's get back and check if this was worth it."

Iggy hopped up obediently, whilst chomping down the last of her meat. Emi followed more slowly, unhappy about leaving the site that had so clearly inspired her. She fell into step as Wish gathered her rifle and led the way towards the south path.

"You can't hear anything new?" Emi asked.

"I've got a throbbing headache, but – no, I'm pretty sure I'm not hearing things."

"Can you feel the world through your boots? Coming up in your feet?"

"No. That sounds disgusting."

"What about the wind? Does it sound different?"

"I don't hear the wind. It's not windy, Emi."

"It is, look at the branches up there."

"Well, I don't hear it. I'm telling you, nothing's changed. I'm the same me, I'm just in considerable pain and feel like it was all a mistake. A really painful one."

"Hmm. Maybe it'll come later. There was something there, their magic, it's . . . Interesting."

"And gone," Wish pointed out. "Bottom line, as you already said. They're gone."

The mage pushed her chin forward to walk in silence. Wish was disappointed too. This madness had apparently bought Iggy safety and, she hoped, seen the rest of the scouts and the Vulgar Division away without incident, but for a moment, before that brand burnt in, she'd thought it was going somewhere further. Instead, she was still here in the woods, and the memories of the day before were slowly coming back. Not just the chaotic Stranded but the violence before. Fire raining on Sober Sound as she watched.

After a trudging, quiet and shameful walk, they finally reached the edge of Harmonial Woods, and Wish pushed the doubts and weariness aside, finding a smile for the dazzling winter sunshine glittering off the dew of the field that separated them from a distant pill box. Not Unders' one, but similar. Sheltering behind a tree, she waved a once-white rag for attention, and when they were sure the guards weren't shooting, Emi went out, holding up her hands, shouting that they were Stanish. The soldiers shouted back excitedly that they'd been watching for them, and two young men came hopping through the field, innocent of the sheer idiocy such an act would be anywhere else on the front line. They helped Iggy and Wish walk back, a rather unnecessary shoulder under their arms, and she quite liked not having to use her legs so much.

The men invited them into the bunker for a coffee, but Wish wanted to carry on to the company. The men insisted on escorting them, and after a brief argument the boy with a fuzz of blond moustache was elected to go, as proud as a mayor. It wasn't long before they caught sight of Bluefern's camp, with his sturdy tents and the crude field guns – soldiers moving between them, at ease. It looked robust and full as the day they'd first found the company – they had made it out, apparently without trouble.

But an ominous figure stood in the road, some two hundred metres before the camp.

Ty Gaussia, motionless with his coat lightly flapping, had the same watchful pose that he'd held outside the house of trolls. Ready for a fight. They stared at him from a distance and Iggy said, "What's his problem? You had a falling out?"

"Better find out," Wish said.

"About time," Emi said quietly. "If you'll allow me –"

"Emi, no," Wish said, and strode ahead. "Something wrong, Gaussica?"

He was silent.

"Great." Wish swallowed. She considered readying her gun, but that was absurd. They were just outside the camp, and soldiers were starting to notice, turning to look. She continued towards him. "You're waiting for me?"

"You chose," he said.

She stopped twenty paces away, a hand self-consciously drifting over her bandaged forearm, as if she could hide the fact that she'd been branded by the nevolk. "You already know what happened, don't you? You knew before I went."

His posture shifted, eyes flitting down. "It doesn't work like that. The change wasn't certain. But you bear the mark. It's an honour. And an aberration. It's . . ."

Behind him, word was spreading through camp and men were starting to gather, but holding back. Ohno's head and shoulders appeared above the others, the rest of her platoon around her. They stalled, the tension of this tableaux on the road unmistakable. Gaussica lowered his head, seeming to confer internally, and she understood why he was here. He might have felt no duty to pursue the Stranded themselves, but a soldier tainted by them . . .

"They burnt my arm," Wish said. "Horrifically. It didn't feel like an honour. And say what you want, you *knew* they'd do this to me."

"No." He glanced back at their audience. Ohno embodied the hard promise of trouble, most obviously, but the line of men either side of her looked equally ready. It was unclear if Bluefern's men would lean more towards Ohno's loyalty or Gaussica's caution. Somehow, Wish didn't think their support would help anyway. Turning back to Wish, Gaussica asked, "What do you intend?"

"What's it look like?" she replied. "I'm going to walk into that camp, debrief with the major and leave this mess behind me. Take a break."

He stared at her, checking for a lie or trying to read more into it?

"What else do you expect? Think I'd run off with the Stranded, or come here to do their dirty work? What, Gaussica?"

"They're alive? The tribe survived?"

"Yeah," Wish said. "No one was hurt except me. They ran off and left us – don't even know what direction they took."

"They're not my concern. Did they say anything? Do you feel anything?"

An echo of Emi's questions, but these carried more weight. Wish said, simply, "No."

"Interesting." Gaussica drew the word out. "It's . . . But you have the mark now. You communed with the Stranded."

"Sure, big deal, I'm making a habit of this shit."

"You've had experiences with other races?"

"No. I mean. I keep getting thrown in with creatures no one is supposed to see, and even when they appear friendly things go stupidly wrong. I'm just a damn sniper, Gaussica." Wish rolled her eyes with a huge puff of irritation. "And I don't know why I need

A WINTER'S MERCY

225

to justify any of it to you – I've got a platoon to get back to. Where does this leave me? Or us? Tell me *something."*

Gaussica considered this carefully, then looked past her to Emi. He called out, "You felt it, didn't you?"

The mage glared at him, saying nothing, and Wish glowered between the cryptic pair.

Failing there, he frowned at Iggy instead and asked, "What do *you* feel?"

"Got a bloody headache coming on." She shrugged. "And seriously, hanging a bit?"

He looked stunned by the response, like someone trying to figure out complex mechanics. Wish sensed he was doubtful enough that the danger was passing. She said, "Gaussica? Are we done, or do I smell too much like death or what?"

"No," he said, slowly. "There's a definite shift, the balance is so fluid around you, but it's hard to unravel. Even for me. I have to be sure, though. It's why they sent me."

Wish gave him a sharp look. "You were sent to kill that mage."

Gaussica reached into his jacket and Wish tensed, as Ohno straightened up beyond him with a rush of worried murmurs around her. He revealed the black envelope he'd been given when all this started. He held it out and Wish came closer to warily take it. She drew out the mysterious black paper. It took her a moment to decide that it was, indeed, solid black, before she said, "I can't read this."

"It's an order of the Arbitration. They wanted you investigated."

"Shit." Getting the attention of the Arbitration was about as appealing as stepping on broken glass, and usually meant you were in the worst kind of trouble involving illegal magic. It made sense of his concern here, if he'd been tasked with watching out for something like, say, her interacting with a rogue race like the Stranded – but this order had come before anyone could've predicted she'd encounter them. Wish asked, "Did you tell them this would happen? With all your jumping around in time. Damn, Gaussica, if anyone should be investigated it's you – you make no damn sense."

"I have been," Gaussica replied without offence. "And will be.

But no, I had no sense for any of this before I met you."

"Why, then?" Wish said. "I'm not magic – the most I have to do with mages is trying to get Emi to behave."

"Yet you gained the mark," he pointed out. "And Terrifold is not the first mage you've killed. There's also concern over the Mire. What else you might be capable of."

"All I've done is get myself and others hurt, again and again. It's war, that's the point! You can tell them that."

His eyes went to her bandage and his brow creased. "I believe their fears are . . . unfounded, but you have done something much more. You don't see it yet but you will."

"With this? It's a wound, not something magic!" Wish snapped. "Just tell me what *you* see. Here's your burnt flesh" – she pointed harshly at her arm – "so what's it mean? What next? And what the fuck does it matter when I've killed so many people already?"

Gaussica had a worried expression now, almost like a struck dog, and she was surprised to hear how calm she'd kept her voice. No tears, or trembling, pitiful emotion. Just the cold truth.

She admitted it, plainly, out loud, "If you're looking for a monster, I've been one for a long time. And yesterday, I did a lot worse than take this mark. So why don't we get on with it?"

"Because *that* is something different," Gaussica said snappishly, the confusion frustrating him, too. "There's life in that mark – life in the Stranded, and around *you,* that doesn't make sense to me." He glanced at Emi again. "A kind of earth magic, made new through the nevolk?"

"New my arse," Emi replied unhelpfully. "They've been around longer than us."

Gaussica paused, mouth open. "Yes. Longer." To Wish, he said, "I told you it's not about killing. Not numbers or actions, but the way the balance shifts. I cannot say where this will take you. I only know I'm needed. Near you. You are . . ." His eyes narrowed. "You don't feel it but you have strayed and you will stray."

Wish held his gaze. He just wanted to understand, the same as her, and while she wasn't convinced yet that the night with the Stranded wasn't just a vicious trick, a niggle deep down told her maybe there was something more to it. Just as there'd been more to the Mire than even Havik understood. She said, "I'm only trying to survive out here. There's no grand design."

"That you can see," Gaussica said. "You are . . . You *do* matter. I will tell the Arbitration – they have no case here. But I need to see what's next."

"Next? Next I try and forget this whole bloody mission and hope to never see the Stranded again. Then we enjoy Relight, don't we? We've bought that break for the army at a terrible price, after all. Then comes more shooting and dying. Nothing else has changed."

He was silent. Not convinced.

"There's no next for you here, Gaussica. I'm serious. No dark magic or religion in me. You can go – I've got enough problems without having a ghost on my back."

"Not on your back," Gaussica said. "By your side."

Oh shit. She had to take a moment. His shoulders were slumped and his face abashed again. Had she misread all of this? "You as well? Why is everyone so damn quick to follow me into trouble?"

A shy glance.

"Why?" she exclaimed.

"You'll need me," he said.

Wish was speechless for a moment. Damn. She could do without the complication or confusion of this man, jumping sharply between a thing of terror and a terrified thing. And surely there *had* been a risk of his judgement here. She said, "You were standing out here like you might kill me a second ago!"

"I don't understand you, Captain, or this situation, but I am learning. I can help you. And your people. I do understand that it matters."

Wish hesitated. She could insist on him leaving, and he would go, she was as sure of that as she was that the Stranded would've let her walk without this damn brand. But she also understood that he was offering more than regular support. He was someone who could defy Command. He could jump around time itself. And she somehow sensed that idea of helping *her people* was a loaded comment.

She quietly told him, "Okay. We'll see what we can do."

His eyes glinted then, meeting hers, with what appeared to be genuine relief. He wanted to say more but was back to struggling to speak. She nodded to let him off, and at last walked by. He remained motionless, head bowed, as the others followed, Emi glowering and Iggy smiling to say, "Take a day off, mate."

28

A great leader is willing to die alone, but never fights alone.

Winning War, Takata, p. 23

A dam broke with the tension of leaving the Azirian behind, and the crowd flooded in, well-meaning soldiers cheering and clapping as they swarmed in. The Blood Scouts were at the front, the Rawboys expressing disbelieving horror and quips at their injuries, before offering heartfelt congratulations. They were followed by a mob of strangers – the scale of their celebration showing how unlikely they thought Wish's return would be. She saw one soldier crying – a man she didn't know, overwhelmed by her survival. Or maybe just relieved that it meant they could finally confirm the Stranded were gone. This was as much a celebration that her march into the woods had bought their escape, after all. She tried to smile and enjoy the attention, and the relief, underneath her exhaustion.

Graveguard picked up on her pain and yelled at the men to give her space, threatening castration. Equally threatening was Scraper appearing at her side silently warning everyone back with the slits of her eyes. But the crowd only properly parted when Major Bluefern arrived, striding importantly towards her with Crash at his side. He said, "Good to see you're alive, Captain. If you got a fix on their location, we can still bomb the woods."

"They're gone, Major," Wish said, noting his willingness to hit the tribe with a barrage after they'd evidently allowed everyone safe passage out.

"Then I guess you'd better fill me in."

"She needs medical attention, sir," Graveguard said, with only the barest hint of deference, and Scraper shifted defensively at her other side. The major's expression hardened.

"I can last a minute, thanks Grave," Wish said. She had already defied Bluefern going out there, and proved him wrong in showing she could come back safely, more or less, and she sensed her scouts' insubordination might push him too far. "There's not a great deal to report, sir – they insisted I stay, drink and eat. It was an assurance we weren't going to attack them whilst you left, that's all. They kept their word and left us alone. Kept Iggy safe. But we might've drunk a bit much, or had something we weren't used to, and – well, the camp was abandoned this morning. I don't think anyone here will have any more trouble with the Stranded."

"They gave no indication where they were going?"

"No, sir."

"But you're injured. What happened?"

Wish hesitated, finding a simple instinct to protect the tribe. It wasn't that the truth was shameful, that she'd got caught up in a hysteria and let herself get injured when there might've been another way. In fact, giving her mostly true account, she recalled again the nevolk *had* kept their word. They had, in their crazed way, taken her in, and left her with a lasting impression. She didn't want Bluefern at all involved in it, and realised with her growing disquiet for the likes of his command, and this sickening war, she might choose the Stranded and their brand again over more of this. She told him, with another lie that came easily: "I tripped. Caught my arm in a fire. It wasn't their fault. I had such a damn long day yesterday. They tended the wound."

"Indeed, did they? Well, there's more to be learnt from even that, I suspect. What medical supplies do they have? Weapons? How many were they?"

"I'm not sure, sorry, sir. Perhaps if I have some time to rest."

"Ah, so be it – very good. You'll get your rest, see what you can recall. Anything at all that can help with those freaks."

"Absolutely," Wish said, fully intending to avoid talking to him ever again.

"But one more thing to clear up, before you go – these gentlemen were waiting to talk to you."

Wish bristled, and felt her scouts tightening in behind her, as the major stepped aside to let two men approach. Officers Castin and Vash, the CEF officers in their inappropriately clean uniforms. Two inconveniences she had utterly forgotten about. Hadn't she had enough surprise confrontations this morning?

"Captain Wild Wish, so glad you made it," Castin said, almost sounding like he meant it. "And I'm happy we can finally catch up with you."

"This can definitely wait," Graveguard growled, as Ptrangus added, "Fucking police? Thought I smelt something."

Wish threw a betrayed look to Bluefern; his arms were folded and his gaze stern. This was a duty that he did not regret, at least in part a petty respite for her stepping out of line before. She said, "By the Flesh. Let's just get it out of the way."

"Better be worth it," Ohno put in, pressing her bulk that little bit forward.

Vash took a step back but Castin resisted the urge, to his credit. It took a particular sort of policeman to find enough confidence in his authority that he could stand firm before a dozen hardened scouts, amid a crowd of aggravated artillerymen, and an ogre. He said, "Captain, it need not concern you or your men. If you would step aside and allow us –"

"If you're after Quickness," Wish interrupted, "she's dead."

The officers froze, wrong-footed by the gravity of such a statement. But Castin shook his head. "No, Captain. Private White –"

"That's her," Vash said, pointing.

Wish looked behind her. "Iggy? You want *Iggy?* Who I just rescued from the Stranded?"

"Are you fucking kidding?" Dalliance said, shouldering his way forward, but Wish flapped a hand at him to stay back. The movement made her brand flare up, but she fought the reaction down as Castin cleared his throat.

"I appreciate what you've been through," he was saying, but Wish's mind remained on the tingling brand as it throbbed harder. It stirred a panic in here: fear, nerves, should she run? *No, don't run* – she insisted to herself, but had an odd, drifting sense. She turned a frown back over her shoulder as she caught the last of Castin's words: "– AWOL for almost two months."

"Desertion?" Wish exclaimed. "Are you serious?"

There was fear on Iggy's face, where she had shown none before the Stranded, and Wish saw a woman ready to bolt, never mind how many people surrounded them. The confusion of swimming emotions came into relief, as Wish understood they were *her* feelings. She was willing Iggy not to run, and she saw understanding in Iggy's eyes. Her expression resolved.

Wish took a breath, internally calming as Castin was saying, "She destroyed a historic property in western Lome. It would be best discussed in private."

"It's not what it sounds like, boss," Iggy insisted, but Wish didn't care. She broadly remembered Dalliance's account of their meeting, and that Iggy might've done some damage, but she had saved people. The details didn't matter. There was no question of not defending her. She was a Blood Scout, now. *Hers.* And there was nothing anyone could've done, no property that could've been destroyed, that was worse than what they'd all been complicit in at Sober Sound.

Wish assured Iggy again with her eyes, and her thoughts, and scanned the others: Emi eager to strike, Dalliance angry, Latebite and Ptrangus ready to fight for any excuse, Crag and Lugger and Grebe all grim-faced and defiant. Hell, even Bluefern's scores of men whose names she didn't know looked ready to throw these CEF officers out on their arses, invested now in this rag tag team who had tagged along and distracted the nevolk from the company. And further back, far off, she felt the support of something more abstract – a distant rightness, that belonged to the land and would be there if she only called.

Tempting as it was, Wish defied the lust for violence. She shook her head and said, very plainly, "We've all destroyed historic property. She's not going with you."

Castin set his shoulders. "This was not part of a military operation. Private White absconded from her unit with a large amount of explosives which she set off during our efforts to secure Passerlee Manor. The property was rendered inextant."

"Inextant?" Who even used a word like that? "Are you serious? We bombed a town to ashes yesterday, and you want to arrest my soldier for blowing up a *house?*"

"It wasn't even like that, Captain!" Dalliance said. "I was there, and she didn't mean to –"

"Stop," Wish said. "I don't need to hear it. These men are leaving."

"It was not just any house." Castin stiffened. "Passerlee was a cultural icon; its owners have close ties to the Bundilt dynasty. I understand that this may seem exceptional, in the context of where we find ourselves, but there is a difference between the damage done in war and that done outside it."

"Yeah? What exactly is that difference? No" – Wish raised a hand before he could answer – "if you say another word *I* might explode. Request denied, or however I need to say it. Get out of here, right now, or I'll make you. You do not want me to make you."

Both men wore horror on their faces, as a few shocked murmurs came from further back. Yet still Castin flashed a look Bluefern's way and said, "We are the CEF, Captain. Unfortunately, the choice is not yours. You've been under pressure, so I can ignore such a threat, once, but I'm not sure you understand the gravity of this situation."

"I'm not sure you do," Wish said, finding herself again impressed by her own calm. She could bare her teeth like she might bite his throat out, but she didn't need to. There was a platoon watching her back, and she had danced with the Stranded and bloody well did not need to rise to this. "The Blood Scouts were established under special command by General Macwest himself to be the Empire's most elite soldiers. We step outside the lines every damn day of this war, meaning your rules do not apply here. Go near Iggy, or any of my scouts, and I will personally see that General Macwest hears of it. You've already wasted enough of my time; are you seriously going to waste his, too?"

Castin went quiet again, his courage finally failing.

"No?"

The officer was weighing it up, plainly worried but clinging to that tiny bit of righteousness he had left. He deferred at last to Bluefern. The major's expression hadn't moved through this whole exchange, and Wish now itched for him to take the CEF's side. Give her an excuse to prove exactly who was in charge here. They'd done so much wrong out here, it was time for a right. Wherever the Stranded had gone, they had left her with *some* hope, and she was connected to Iggy, at least, through that experience. Bluefern studied her face, considering her carefully. Go on. He wanted to have it out with her. But he studied their expansive audience, too, and she saw the recognition in his eye. He finally said, "Plainly, a mistake has been made and the CEF has no business being here."

A load flew out of Wish's chest as Bluefern's expression now promised he, too, had her back. Castin tried once more, "Major, I must insist –" but Crash immediately hissed: "That girl is a war hero, dammit."

With that, the crowd erupted into agreeing jeers and words of encouragement, and the officers baulked as if struck. Wish continued on into camp, as Castin was cajoled out of her way, before Crash shouted for order. She didn't look back, only sideways to Graveguard, saying, "Getting a little dizzy now."

"I've got a tent set up." As he led her on, others dipped in and out of her awareness with brief appearances at her sides, everyone trying to join her. Ohno lumbered closest, letting her size warn off anyone else, but still they pressed in with familiar pats and congratulations and thanks. She felt them all around her, her tribe. Hard to focus, though – was she about to collapse or had something in the Stranded's mark stirred, after all?

"Boss, I'll explain everything," Iggy was insisting, but Wish told her, "Don't care."

"It really *is* a misunderstanding –" Dallianc started, but she insisted more firmly, "Don't care! Latebite? Where is he? Get us something to roast and a drink for later, will you? Captain's orders. Crag, Lugger, help him. Everyone report for a feast this evening. Where's Macmiddan?"

"Got his own tent, boss," Grebe said, trotting closer. "But won't be up for a while. I've not left his side. He'll survive just fine."

"And you?"

"I'm good, boss. I am."

Wish nodded him off, to be replaced with Ptragnus's sly face. "What about the ghost? Creep's hanging about like the fucking spectre he is. Want us to shoo him off?"

"No. He's coming with us."

"You're joking? What was that out on the road, then? Thought we'd have to plug him for sure."

"In here," Graveguard instructed, holding a tent flap open as Ptrangus fell back with disbelief. Beyond him, Emi was eyeing her suspiciously, though, waiting for her to answer.

"Gaussica believes in the Blood Scouts. He wants to help us," Wish explained, particularly eyeing the mage. "And first point of action, we're gonna get the rest of the platoon back. Start asking around. These guys had their ears to the ground here – find out anything they've heard about women soldiers on the front. Or behind enemy lines." Another thought caught her, uninvited. She hesitated before voicing it, but had to. "And anything you can learn about Havikare and her goblins."

"You want me to contact Command?" Ohno suggested. "They'll have people on it."

"Sure, but we'll not hold our breaths," Wish said. "As soon as we've taken a beat, I want to get on this."

"A beat like over Relight?" Ptrangus suggested.

"No, a beat like this meal Latebite's getting us. I don't know if I could enjoy Relight knowing some of ours are out there in need."

There was a wave of solid agreement, all of them stoked by the fire in her, even if most of them didn't even know the people she wanted to get back.

"Then let's go, go! Boorah!"

They moved off in different directions to do whatever they'd do. Dalliance hesitated before Iggy smiled and told him they'd be fine, and would catch up later. The parting crowd, as usual, left Emi behind, studying Wish. Scheming. Did she realise Wish had sensed something unusual during that confrontation, between her and

Iggy? That the Stranded hadn't left her with nothing. But the mage nodded, put her hands in her pockets and turned to leave.

"Come on," Graveguard said, and Wish entered the tent, to sit on a cot as he muttered about tending her at last. Iggy sat on a cot opposite, just the three of them now – except, of course, Scraper slid into the shadows. Graveguard checked Iggy's wounds, scolding them both for being so reckless, not entirely seriously. He said the wounds were nowhere near as bad as he expected. The Stranded's salve had really helped and he decided to mostly leave their dressings in place. Though he asked just how big an explosion Iggy *had* set off. And what, if any of this, had the Stranded done? To Wish, he said, "Tripped in a fire my arse."

Iggy laughed and told him, "All part of the fun, ain't it?"

But she met Wish's eye, over his shoulder, with a questioning, hopeful look. It asked if they were okay and said she was confused by what might have passed between them. Wish smiled back to say damned if she had any answers, but they were in it together.

"You're a one-woman maelstrom, you know that," Graveguard said, crouching over Wish's arm. He peeled back the bandage and she winced as he tutted distaste. "You'll get us all killed eventually. But damn if you're not going all the way."

As he roughly turned her head to one side, checking her scratches, she replied, "Well as long as *I* survive." But she couldn't keep up the light tone. In this quiet tent, without the crowd, and the tension of facing Gaussica and the CEF having passed, her energy was failing, dragging her mood down with it. She went on, "I lost Quickness. And we did a terrible thing out there. Not for the first time. All those people. It's so . . ."

The medic turned her face forwards him again, looking her deep in the eye as he waited for her to finish.

"There's so much going on in this war, and this world," she said. "And we're not even trying to understand, just killing, and killing. It's too much. I need to stop, but I have to keep going – and you said it, everyone's looking to *me*. What'll it cost us all next time?"

He considered her carefully, then nodded, like this little outburst was exactly what he might've expected. "I can't say for that. It'll be what it is, and the best we can look out for right now is to live another day. But whatever else went on in those woods, I guarantee *everyone* got a little more hope this morning. Seems to me they all saw a leader come back to us. That's worth more than you know."

Wish accepted his words without brushing them off lightly, as he continued his examination. Iggy was smiling at her again, in agreement. She *had* got her back. She would get the others back, too. And she now had a ghost in her platoon, and the mark of the Stranded on her arm. They believed in her. They all did.

It was time, she told herself, to be better.

She would give the Blood Scouts a captain they deserved.

29

GENERAL DIAMOND: Any leader worth their mettle, any leader at all, will tell you the same. We do what must be done. We do what must be done and we do not regret it. We do not move backwards and we do not question Command. JUDGE WATT: Are you suggesting, General, that there was no other way –
GENERAL DIAMOND: I am not suggesting it damn you. No, I will not sit down, I will not be talked to this way, you louse, you brigand, you. How would you like to suppose and suggest? You live in a damn dream world, where any of us could have walked away, at any time. In reality, you scum of the pond – get your hands off me! – in reality we had to fight! Those people had to die!
Transcript from the Hingbarman Trials, 734

After four days of pain and confusion, drifting in and out of consciousness, they came for Pitt. He was stirred from half-sleep by a man clearing his throat, scraping the legs of a chair against the tiles. Pitt struggled for a moment, then hurriedly sat up straight in the bed when he saw the uniform. The scarlet-piped emerald suit of the Purification – a rare garb, as their agents normally walked in anonymous clothing. The man had a round head and a thin, dark moustache, hair hidden under a square cap. He crossed one leg over the other, hands on top.

"They tell me you are well and cogent," he said, in the refined accent of the East Drail Glens. "Is that so?"

Pitt hesitated, wary of even a simple question from the Purification. The man waited with cold eyes, and Pitt croaked, "Yes. I'm recovering." He cleared his throat and reached for a glass of water. The movement sent pain through his shoulder, making him cringe. His guest made no movement to help him.

"Officer Wron Dawn," the man said, and pulled out a lapel demonstratively. "Purification Magic Liaison. We have questions I hope you can help with."

Pitt shook his head to slow him down. This was the first anyone from the army or government had come to him since he'd found himself in this grey-walled room, where the nurses locked the door at night and people screamed at all hours. He had questions of his own. "Where am I?"

Wron Dawn did not move, delaying the answer. "Highscythe Ward. One of the finest medical facilities on the front."

"Am I under arrest?" Pitt asked.

Dawn raised a delicate eyebrow. "Should you be?"

"They've been locking the doors."

"For your own safety, I expect. Who's to say what the enemy might attempt if they knew we had a vulnerable mage in here? Even in our own ranks, you never know who can be trusted."

The firmed up Pitt's resistance. "Am I accused of something?"

"Should you be?" Dawn repeated.

"Just fucking tell me," Pitt snapped. "If I'm to be locked up or executed or not, just tell me. I've had enough. Almost lost my arm, *did* lose my eye –" He pointed at the bandaged side of his head, which throbbed fiercely in agreement. A tear welled in his remaining eye. "Just tell me."

Dawn considered this at length, uncrossed his legs, then crossed the other on top. He picked at something on his trouser leg and Pitt fought not to lose his calm again. The officer said, "We lost the better part of an entire legion, an entire town and, most importantly, one of our strongest mages. You were a key factor in our defences and one of the only survivors. I am inclined to doubt any man would sacrifice so much of his body in subterfuge, but I have seen stranger things. I am hoping you can clarify what happened." Dawn drew a small leather notebook and pencil from his jacket, flicking through to a blank page. "If you're ready?"

Pitt stretched out a pause, trying to regain some sense. "Maybe you could answer a few questions of mine first."

Dawn wet his lips, eyes on the notepad. "Not really my job, but what would you like to know?"

"There was a woman. A civilian. I tried to help her."

"Oh, Ms Axefell. That was on my list, too – did you personally tend to her wounds?"

"What? Why's that on your list? Wait. How is she? Is she . . ."

Dawn let it hang for a painful second, cruelly, before smiling. "She is fine. That is, she is alive and will make a full recovery – as far as the parts she has left are concerned. She lost an arm and a leg, and will have plenty of scarring, including on the face. It could have been a lot worse. She would have died if you hadn't intervened. It was you, I take it, who stopped the bleeding?"

"I did what I could with pipe magic," Pitt muttered, not sure if he should be relieved or horrified. Chiara was alive. But disfigured. Maimed. "Can I see her?"

"That won't be possible. They've taken her somewhere far better equipped than this. You knew who she was, I take it?" Dawn opened the notebook again, pencil ready.

"Is that important?"

"Everything is until I can confirm it isn't."

"I met her in town. That's all."

"But you knew her father was the mayor. You knew the name Rotus Axefell?"

"Yes. You said *was?*"

"They are quite sure they found his remains. His ring, to be precise. So the question I have is if you were acting in the interests of preserving an influential heiress, or if it was the impulse to protect a conquest that drew your attention away from our military assets?"

Pitt bristled at the accusation. Dawn watched him with a smile as thin as his moustache. "You want to pin what happened on me? The Comity came out of nowhere."

"The matter was personal, I see, thank you."

"That's not what I said –"

"It is, Mr Sonland, if not in so many words. Now, I have sworn accounts that you *did* manage a partial shield, even without Dalton

Terrifold. Until you got distracted by Ms Axefell – that's what went wrong?"

"It was more than I could handle, that's what went wrong," Pitt snapped. "I'm a pipeman; you can count the times I've seen combat on one hand. I tried and failed, is that what you need to hear?"

Dawn gave him a moment to calm, unmoved, then wrote something down. "Some would consider a few weeks under Dalton Terrifold worth a lifetime of training, but there you go."

Pitt glowered, not bothering to argue, even if he doubted anyone would back up such a claim. There was no point trying to convince this man that Terrifold was no teacher. "Is that all you need?"

"Oh no. It brings us to the crux. How exactly did Terrifold die?"

"He was shot. Before the bombing started. No one else saw it?"

"In your own words, please. As I said" – Dawn rolled a flippant hand – "varying accounts and all that."

"There was a sniper on the ridge. They shot Dalton and the barrage started right after. We never had a chance."

"Dalton Terrifold could stop a bullet without seeing it coming, did you know that? He was quite famous for it." Dawn's eyebrow raised again, challenging Pitt to make another mistake. Pitt kept quiet, so he went on, "How did a sniper get past his defences?"

"I don't know. Maybe he wasn't as good as everyone thought."

"Or maybe he was distracted, too?" Dawn left it out there. He already knew, Pitt supposed. This was futile. They needed someone to blame, some incompetence to suggest it was a personal error that cost the entire operation, and so many lives, his eye, Chiara's limbs. It wasn't enough that the enemy had outmanoeuvred them. Dawn scribbled again, finding something noteworthy in the silence, then said, "Anything you can recall might help us in the future. We can take advantage of even the greatest tragedy."

"We were arguing," Pitt admitted. "If you must know, Chiara's friendship *helped* me use my magic, while Terrifold's interference got in the way. He disagreed and we were all arguing about it when the sniper shot him. If you want to look at it that way, the argument got him killed and compromised my shield, never mind the damn Stains were more than ready and able to slaughter us all. So are you going to have me taken out and shot or can I go home?"

Dawn was writing quickly, nodding along, and took a second to catch up before looking at Pitt again. "That's it? You stand by that, a sniper shot at you during this argument?"

"What's to stand by? That's what happened."

"Did you see them? How close was the sniper?"

"On the ridge, like I said. No, I didn't see anyone – but their troops came in once the bombing stopped. They didn't hang around. It was after I lost my damn eye. I only heard a voice. A couple of voices maybe, but one in charge . . . she sounded young. That's what I thought. Way too young to be in charge."

"She?" Dawn echoed.

"Yeah, you don't mistake a surprise like that, even if my eyes were full of blood and my ears were ringing. A young woman giving orders. She . . ." Pitt went quiet, recalling the moments before he drifted away, in the despair and pain and fear. He'd been moved. She had called for help. Sent someone to Chiara. Pitt shook his head. "I don't know, it's hazy. But there was a woman soldier."

"And she shot Terrifold?"

"How the hell would I know that?" Pitt spat. "If there's some kind of trick you're trying to catch me on, I'm not seeing it. What else am I supposed to have done?"

Dawn hummed, unbothered by the outburst, and flipped through the pages of his notes. "I believe you. I expect it's true that you couldn't have done much more to protect Sober Sound even with your full focus – but I doubt there's weight in any suggestion that you yourself attacked Terrifold on behalf of the local resistance."

"What?" Pitt exclaimed.

The officer moved on. "A lot of people were confused, angry and upset. They see the Purification and embellish things, hoping to confound us. But you, no, I can accept your account. This isn't the first mention of a woman soldier, nor a sniper, and the two together . . . It's troubling. But also useful to confirm. Is there anything else you think might help, about Dalton Terrifold, the enemy attack?"

"I don't think so," Pitt said warily. "But you're okay with what I've said?"

"It's workable. Of course, the official report will be that you did all in your power to protect the Axefell family. Very heroic of you – it will be appreciated by the Council. You did not lose us half the gun-power on the Palicier frontier, no, you put yourself on the line to protect one of the Empire's darling princesses."

"Princess?"

"Figuratively."

"Can I visit her? Can you find out where she is? I'd really like –"

"Oh, absolutely not," Dawn said brightly. "Quite aside from the fact I'm sure she never wants to see you again, that wouldn't be proper, would it? As you say, you're a pipeman. And I would work hard, if I were you, to avoid any hint that you did have a connection to her, other than the love of a brave subservient."

Pitt felt himself deflating. Indeed, the way she had last spoken made their divide clear enough, so what chance was there now? He could write, to try and mend bridges, and make a connection, but never mind her own resistance, the Purification probably wouldn't allow it. It was over, and the best he could hope for was to put all this behind him. He said, "Do you think . . ." He looked to the window, snow falling outside. "Do you think I'll make it home in time for Relight?"

"Home?" Dawn almost laughed, then fixed his face seriously when he saw Pitt glowering. "Oh, Mr Sonland, has there been some miscommunication? Did one of the doctors suggest you were going home?"

"I've lost an eye. I almost died. I'm ready to go back to piping – if I'm even up to that."

"Well, you'll have a few weeks' rest and you will surely be compensated," Dawn said. "There may even be a medal in this for you, should you play your cards right. But you are a parser trained by Dalton Terrifold at the army's expense. The Empire has plenty more use for you."

"You can't be serious. I'm done –"

"Only when we say so." Dawn punctuated his interruption by standing up, straightening his jacket. "Not to worry, Mr Sonland. You'll find plenty of opportunity to prove that these heroics were no fluke. We may have lost Dalton Terrifold, but we've gained a fine, youthful battle mage in you." Dawn paused, as if to sniff the air, then decided it was good, with a nod. "Something like that, yes? Now get some rest. Sober Sound was quite a misstep, and we'll have our work cut out for us this winter. Who knows, if you're lucky and these stories of your woman sniper pan out to be true, you may even have a chance of joining the task force to deal with that."

Pitt bit down his response, wanting to get up and hit this man, knowing he wouldn't have the strength even if he found the will. He watched the smug officer leave, heard the lock turn, and stared at the door. He held onto his anger. The injustice. That feeling that he had done enough. Didn't belong here. Didn't ever want to hear such explosions and screams again.

He couldn't hold it for long before it turned to tears.

Acknowledgements

Despite being the third book in a series, *A Winter's Mercy* was surprisingly simple to plot (though if Gaussica threw you, rest assured he threw me, too). However, this was still one of the hardest novels I've had to write so far. Certain stories come ready-made, with a path they have to follow, and I knew from the start exactly where this journey would take us. I can't say I especially liked getting there myself, but I did so with an awareness that it's important to have tough war stories, ones that might hurt to read (and certainly do to write), because without them we'd only have those stories that make war look simple, honest and good. It never is and never will be.

My thanks then, here, first and foremost go to you, the reader, for returning to this series and making it through this sometimes difficult story. I trust you enjoy the characters' company, and the world they inhabit, but I appreciate this journey isn't always pleasant.

My thanks too for the writers who've gone before me to explore the reality of war; without their experience, I couldn't have put together such a story myself. I continue to keep in mind *The World At War* by Mark Arnold Forster and *The Unwomanly Face of War* by Svetlana Alexievich, both of which explore the truly diverse impacts of global conflict. In writing this book, my reading was further supplemented by the classic *All Quiet on the Western Front* by Erich Maria Remarque and Kate Adie's *Corsets to Camouflage* (I have a stack of her writing to help me go on!).

Next, another massive thanks to Stefan Koidl, whose tremendous artwork I expect has done more to sell this book than anything I could've done myself. He's wonderfully captured Iggy here, despite my abstract instructions that I fear resembled something from a Monty Python sketch. My only reservation was that he's perhaps produced art too beautiful for such an unpleasant tale!

As always, my special thanks too to my friends, beta readers and fellow writers who've supported me during the production of this book, whether it was with specific feedback or just reminders that I'm not alone in all this: Travis M. Riddle, Jennifer Stebing, Luke Watkins, Adawia Asad, Luke Scull, Damo Larkin and all the team of the Creative Commune, selflessly managed by Phil Parker and Holly Tinsley.

Thanks as well to all my advance readers and reviewers, and all those who've supported me along the way, including Timy and all the Queen's Book Asylum; Mihir, Lukasz and the Fantasy Book Critic crew; Lynn Williams of Lynn's Books; Mark Lawrence and everyone involved in making SPFBO great, and all those involved in SFINCS.

Finally, my deepest thanks remains for all my family and friends for always being there, even when I'm not especially present myself, particularly my siblings Nick, Fran, Alex and Christen, and my father and Sandra. Most of all, though, thanks to my incredible wife, Marta.

Get More from the Rocc

Hey wait, before you leave! It's harder than ever for a book to get noticed out there, so if you enjoyed reading this, please let others know: leave a review, tell your friends, wrestle a passing cyclist to the floor and smear the pages on their face, this sort of thing. Visibility is everything for books these days, and we authors live and die by enthusiastic readers helping spread the word.

The Blood Scouts' journey must go on, and it will as long as people keep sharing their tale.

And if you want to be the first to hear about all my new projects, and you somehow missed this in Book 1, I have a **special offer** just for you. You can return to this world with my prequel novelette, *Oksy, Come Home,* available exclusively, and totally free, by joining my newsletter here:

https://phil-williams.co.uk/hmmd-offer

Also By Phil Williams

THE BLOOD SCOUTS SERIES
HOWEVER MANY MUST DIE
DROWN DEEP
OKSY, COME HOME

ORDSHAW SERIES
The Sunken City Trilogy
UNDER ORDSHAW
BLUE ANGEL
THE VIOLENT FAE

THE CITY SCREAMS

The Ikiri Duology
KEPT FROM CAGES
GIVEN TO DARKNESS

DYER STREET PUNK WITCHES

THE ORDSHAW VIGNETTES VOL. 1

ESTALIA SERIES
WIXON'S DAY
BALFAIR'S CONFINEMENT
AFTAN WHISPERS

FAERGROWE SERIES
A MOST APOCALYPTIC CHRISTMAS